AN INDEPENDENT WOMAN

Recent Titles by Anna Jacobs from Severn House

CHANGE OF SEASON
A FORBIDDEN EMBRACE
MARRYING MISS MARTHA
MISTRESS OF MARYMOOR
REPLENISH THE EARTH
SEASONS OF LOVE
THE WISHING WELL

AN INDEPENDENT WOMAN

Anna Jacobs

This first world edition published in Great Britain 2005 by
SEVERN HOUSE PUBLISHERS LTD of
9–15 High Street, Sutton, Surrey SM1 1DF.
This first world edition published in the USA 2006 by
SEVERN HOUSE PUBLISHERS INC of
595 Madison Avenue, New York, N.Y. 10022.

British Library Cataloguing in Publication Data

Jacobs, Anna
An independent woman
1. Legacies - Fiction
2. Fathers and daughters - Fiction
3. Love stories
I. Title
823.9'14 [F]

ISBN-10 : 0-7278-6283-9 (cased)
0-7278-9152-9 (paper)

Typeset by Palimpsest Book Production Ltd.,
Polmont, Stirlingshire, Scotland.
Printed and bound in Great Britain by
MPG Books Ltd., Bodmin, Cornwall.

I'd like to express my thanks to the staff at Oldham Local Studies and Archives for their prompt and invaluable help in researching what the town centre was like in 1918.

PART ONE

One

November 11th 1918

On the day the Great War ended, Serena Fleming saw her neighbours running outside, heard them calling to one another, dancing and cheering, and couldn't resist going outside to join in the celebrations. It felt as though everyone from the small town of Tinsley was in the streets, crowded together, sharing their happiness, and she loved being part of it all, even if her contribution to the war effort had been only small. There was such a sense of joy, it was as heady as wine. People were smiling, some groups were singing, strangers hugged one another.

Occasional people simply stood there with tears running down their faces, and you guessed that they'd lost loved ones. Well, she had herself, knew that pain, because her brother Frank had been posted missing presumed dead the previous year.

Everyone in England had paid a high price for this victory.

She didn't want to go home again but her mother was ill and couldn't be left alone for long, so in the end she turned back to Cavendish Terrace, where many of the richest people in the town lived, not far from the main street, in a small enclave of privilege. And even these people kept their distance from the Flemings.

When she slipped into the hall, her father called out from his study, 'Where have you been, Serena?'

She realized he'd come home early from his place of business and her heart sank. 'Just out, joining in the celebrations.'

He came into the hall, clad in the usual sombre grey suit that matched his eyes and hair. Not for Ernest Fleming the vulgarity of brighter colours. Not for his womenfolk, either, she thought mutinously.

'Oh?' he asked.

He could put such a wealth of meaning into that word, but she wasn't going to pretend about her feelings, not today. 'It was wonderful to see everyone so happy.'

'Common people. Not us.'

'Well, people of all sorts have worked together to defeat the Germans, so why should they not celebrate together? And everyone was perfectly polite.'

'That is not the point.'

She bit back hot words of protest that it was the other way round. People were more likely to keep their distance from her because her father wasn't liked in the town, indeed, was feared by many, especially the tenants of his slum properties. She couldn't help knowing that, though he rarely spoke of his business dealings. As Ernest Fleming's daughter, she received prompt service in shops and regular invitations to social functions, but no one offered her friendship – no one except Frank and he was gone now. She could feel tears rising at the thought of her brother and turned towards the stairs to conceal them. 'I'll just go and change my clothes.'

She heard her father go back into his study and wondered what had brought him home at this time of day. It had seemed safe to go out because he usually spent the whole day at his office. She'd learned many years ago that outright defiance always brought retribution sooner or later – to her and to anyone who crossed him.

That was also well known in the town.

As she walked slowly up the stairs she vowed that one day soon she would escape from this unhappy house, and most of all from *him.* She didn't care if he was her father. She hated him.

After breakfast the following morning Serena went back up to her bedroom to tidy up, wondering what would become of the Comforts for the Troops group now, and whether she should still attend the following day's meeting.

Suddenly she heard the crash of breaking china and ran along to the bedroom at the other end of the landing. There she found her mother lying on the floor by the bed. In her fall, Grace must have knocked her cup off the bedside table and it had smashed on the floorboards near the window.

Serena knelt down and lifted her mother's head to rest against her. Grace's lips were tinged with blue and her face was grey-white.

'Serena?' It was hardly more than a whisper.

'I'm here, dearest.'

'Are we alone? It's so dark in here, I can't see. Is it – tea time already?'

The room was filled with the weak sunshine of a fine winter's morning, but her mother's eyes had a blind, blurred look to them and Serena guessed what this meant, had been expecting it for a week or two. She had to swallow hard before she could speak calmly. 'Yes, we're quite alone.'

'I need to tell you something, should have told you sooner, didn't dare.'

Serena watched her mother struggle for breath, the pulse in her neck showing faintly against skin crumpled like yellowing tissue paper. 'Tell me what?'

'Ernest is not – your father.'

'*What?*'

Tears trickled down Grace's cheeks. 'Don't think badly of me – please!'

'I never could. *Never*. Don't agitate yourself.' But she couldn't help asking, 'Are you sure?'

'Of course I am! James was your real father – James Lang. I loved him so much, but my parents wouldn't let me marry him.'

She gasped for air before continuing, and for a moment Serena thought the end had come, then the confidences resumed.

'When I found I was with child, James wanted to marry me, so we arranged to run away. But I waited all night and he didn't come. I'd no money – had to go back to my parents – and they forced me to marry Ernest. He wanted my dowry, you see. But he's *not* your father. That's why . . . he hasn't always been kind to you.'

'I'm glad he's not.' The words were out before Serena could stop them. 'What happened to James Lang – my real father?'

'I never found out. His family didn't know, either. I went to see them before I married Ernest – just to be sure. They said he'd run away rather than marry me, but I knew better. James would never have left me, never – not unless he was dead.'

Serena closed her eyes for a moment, so shocked by what she was hearing that the room seemed to be spinning round her. When she opened them she saw a man's shadowy reflection in the mirror and realized *he* was standing outside. How much had he heard? But Grace raised her hand to caress her daughter's face just then, so Serena ignored him and looked back at her mother. The glowing smile in Grace's eyes spoke one last time the love she felt for her daughter, then her head fell back, her hand dropped and the gasping stopped abruptly.

In the silence that seemed to echo round her, Serena bent her head and wept, cradling the still body in her arms. She was glad the suffering had ended – how could she not be? – but she would miss her mother desperately.

He came in then, the man she had always called father, the man she had feared all her life. Even as a child she had sensed he didn't love her, had never understood why. But now that she knew, it was a burden lifted to realize it wasn't her fault, that she wasn't so unlovable after all.

He said in his usual quiet voice, 'Her mind was rambling, going back to her childhood sweetheart, this James person. You *are* my daughter.'

Serena knew it was wiser to nod and act as if she believed him, but she was quite sure her mother hadn't lied to her. Not at such a moment.

'Give her to me. I'll carry her across to the bed.' His voice was as calm as ever, his expression showing no sign of grief.

Serena let him take her mother's body but couldn't help weeping for what she had lost.

'You'd better send for Dr Tolson to sign the death certificate. I'll arrange for the funeral.' He made no attempt to give his wife a final kiss and stared with his usual disapproval at Serena. 'Get yourself some mourning clothes, especially a good silk dress for the funeral. And see if for once you can find something a bit more flattering.'

He turned to leave, stopping at the door to add, 'Make sure the servants put a black crepe bow on the door knocker. We want people to respect our grief.'

Ernest Fleming spent his life giving orders in that chill voice, never doubting they would be obeyed. *Respect our grief*, indeed! He would probably be delighted to be rid of his invalid wife.

She couldn't stop what her mother had told her from repeating in her mind. *He wasn't her father!* Oh, the relief of that!

Why had her mother not told her about her real father before? The answer was obvious. Grace would have been terrified of her daughter betraying what she knew.

Keeping her face expressionless, Serena murmured, 'Yes, Father,' to the departing figure. She had long ago perfected an expression as calm as his and could summon it up at will to keep her feelings hidden. Which was a good thing today, because behind that mask, her thoughts were in turmoil. She straightened her clothes and caught sight of herself in the mirror, grimacing at what she saw.

Ten years before, when she was just growing into womanhood, she'd overheard him discussing with her mother the possibility that their daughter might make a *useful* marriage once she had outgrown the baby-fat stage. The men he'd named as possible husbands were all from families Serena disliked, and some were his own age. Like other girls, she'd dreamed of handsome young men, of love and happiness. Men like those he'd mentioned wouldn't make her happy, she knew that instinctively.

After thinking long and hard, she had decided to make herself so unappealing no one would possibly want her. As her body took on a woman's curves, she experimented to find the most unflattering hairstyles and clothes which made her look plump and shapeless. Her mother did nothing to prevent this, though she clearly realized what her daughter was doing. Serena had worked hard to earn a reputation not only as a plain Jane, but as a bore, taking a perverse pleasure in the fact that she did no credit whatsoever to her father's position in society, something he harped on about endlessly. As though everyone didn't know he owed his position as a property owner to his wife's money!

She gazed down in perverse satisfaction at the fussy dress in mustard and black checked wool. The colour and pattern overwhelmed her pale skin and near-auburn hair, hiding the gentle hint of rose in her cheeks, while the style was old-fashioned, with a skirt far too long for modern taste. When she joined the groups of women rolling bandages, knitting socks and scarves, or doing other war work, it hurt sometimes to see how fresh and pretty the younger women could look. She never had, and now, at almost thirty, she knew she was past her best anyway. She had wept about that in private but she hadn't changed her mind about the need for it.

And as the years passed, the only men who attracted her were ones her father would never allow her to marry, a young officer seen in the street, a cousin of an acquaintance, a man from the poorer side of the family. She could only dream of what she was missing. So far she'd avoided being trapped like her mother in an unhappy marriage, though it had been a close thing a couple of times when her father had set his mind on her marrying someone.

The only person Ernest Fleming had ever truly cared about was his son, and even that in his own way, without any demonstrations of affection. Serena missed her younger brother desperately – no, he was only her *half-brother*. Well, that didn't matter, not at all. Frank hadn't been like his father, either in looks or personality, but had taken after their mother's side of the family, as Serena did herself: slender, not very tall, with the same nearly auburn hair. Brother and sister had been good friends, although there were five years between them. A gentle boy, he'd been harried cruelly at school because he hated fighting, bullied and harangued constantly at home because he didn't do his father credit, either on the sports field or academically. He'd often turned to his older sister for comfort and advice.

With a sigh of regret for yet another young life cut short by the war which had just ended, Serena went to send one of the maids for Dr Tolson. Her mother's death would make little practical difference to the household or its head, because she'd been in charge of housekeeping for the last few years, but it would make a huge difference to her, because now she would no longer feel obliged to stay under this roof. Joy flooded through her at the mere thought.

The escape would have to be managed carefully, though. She was certain Ernest wouldn't want her to live on her own in the same town as himself, because people would talk and wonder why. He set a lot of store on keeping up appearances. And if she wanted to stay free of him, she knew that once she'd got hold of her inheritance from her godmother, she'd need to go as far away as she could. America perhaps, or Australia. You couldn't get much further away than that.

After the funeral, kept simple because of wartime restrictions, their lawyer read Grace's will to them. It was short and contained no surprises. She had left everything she owned to her husband, except for her jewellery, which she had left to her daughter and a small bequest to her maid, Ruby.

When the lawyer had gone, Ernest took out one of his cigars and prepared it carefully for smoking. As he was about to light it, he said casually, without even looking at Serena, 'Let me have your mother's jewels and I'll put them in the bank for safe keeping.'

She took a deep breath, finding that it was one thing to plan rebellion, another to carry it out. 'They're – um – already in the bank, except for her wedding ring and gold locket.'

'Oh? Dewison didn't mention anything about a recent deposit.'

'No. They're in my own bank. Mother told me about her will and gave her jewellery to me a while back because she knew she'd never wear the things again. I wanted to keep them safe.' Which was a lie. She'd wanted to keep them from him. There were a few pieces from her mother's family that she loved and she didn't want him selling them.

He had been bending to light a spill in the fire but straightened up abruptly. His voice grew even quieter but a pulse beat rapidly in his throat, always the first sign of his anger. 'I wasn't aware that you even had a bank account. Why did you not consult me about it?' The spill burnt his fingers and he threw it into the fire, not taking his eyes off her. 'How much do you have in it and where did you get the money?'

She'd practised what to say, but couldn't prevent her voice from wobbling as she answered, 'The money came from birthday and Christmas presents mostly. It seemed foolish to leave it lying around when it could gain a little interest, and you made sure I never lacked for anything, so what would I have spent it on?' She despised herself for the flattery, but hoped it would soften his anger.

'How much do you have in the account?'

'Just over thirty pounds.'

He stared at her, his eyes gleaming like chips of ice in his pale, neat face. 'Which bank?'

'The Yorkshire Penny Bank.'

He made a scornful sound. 'That place is for housemaids and mill workers! You had better move your account to my bank so that I can be sure your money's safe. You can get the jewels out tomorrow and bring them to me at the office.'

He was turning away even as he spoke, so sure was he that she would do as she was told. She didn't reply but watched him go into his study, where he sat most evenings, a habit started once her mother became bedridden. He would sip a glass of brandy as he read the newspaper, never seeming to need company. Serena said nothing, just went back up to her room.

When he came home the following evening, he reminded her about the account and the jewels.

'I f-find the savings bank more convenient for my needs, thank you, Father.'

There was a long silence. He kept his eyes on her face, waiting for her to break, but she didn't.

'On your own head be it, then, but I'm not leaving your mother's jewels there. It's a shabby little place and I don't trust the people who run it.' His voice became steely. 'You will fetch them for me tomorrow.'

'Yes, Father.'

The following morning Serena pretended to come down with influenza, and since the epidemic had already killed many people and had put fear into the hearts of those who were still well, he didn't come near her for the whole week that followed. It was tedious staying in bed, but she had to gain some time.

Even when she left her bed, she played the invalid for a few days, lying on a sofa in her bedroom, complaining of a headache and eating very little. That was easy enough to do because she wasn't hungry, hadn't been since her mother died.

She was not only bored but nervous. Fear skittered down

her spine every time he walked up the stairs in case he came into her room and insisted they go and get the jewels. But as the days passed and he still didn't come near her, she began to hope her ploy would succeed, so that she would gain the time she needed to put her other plans into operation.

The train stopped at Horton's small branch-line station and Marcus Graye got out slowly, signalling for the porter, who was a female. He was forced to let her take his luggage because he was still too weak to carry both bags himself, but it went against the grain to let a woman do that and he couldn't help asking, 'You're sure they're not too heavy for you?'

She gave him a cheeky grin and he couldn't help smiling back.

'Thank you, sir, but I'm quite used to it now. Do you want a cab? Vic Scott's waiting outside. His cab's a bit old but it's clean.' Then, as they turned to leave the station, she caught sight of his right cheek and her smile faded. In a softer voice she added, 'Copped one, did you? We're all grateful to those who fought for us.'

He found it touching that she would come straight out with that remark, but then Lancashire folk had always been known for being forthright. 'It's not serious, just annoying.' The wounds had been deep but not life-threatening as long as they didn't get infected, so he'd had to wait to get them tended, lying on a stretcher in a cold tent, hearing the screams coming from other more seriously wounded men.

He hadn't thought himself vain, but now hated to see his face in the mirror. That side of his face would always be a mess of scars, though they said it'd look better when it healed properly. He'd had to let a beard grow, since he couldn't yet shave the injured cheek, so that added to the strangeness of the face that looked back at him every morning. Two weeks before the war ended, it'd happened. Several men closer to the blast than him had been killed by the same shell, poor devils, so he was fortunate really. But the deep wounds on the right side of his body and his right leg were taking a long time to heal and this journey had proved that he wasn't as well as he'd thought.

But at least he was back in Blighty for good, invalided out

early instead of having to wait months for a discharge, sent home to recover in his own time. He still found it hard to believe that he'd survived the horror of four years of killing, unlike most of his friends. But it had left its mark on him, he knew, as it had on all who'd been out there.

Realizing that he'd been standing lost in thought while the porter waited patiently, he apologized and limped through the station entrance into the circular turning space outside. But there he had to stop again because seeing it suddenly proved that he really was home. It was two years since he'd been back to Horton, and then only to bury his father, but he'd dreamed of it many a time and nearly wept as he woke up to find himself still in the trenches.

The horse cab was driven by another ex-soldier, this one with an artificial leg, from the stiff way he set his foot down. You got to recognize those who'd served. Something in the upright posture, perhaps, or the smart way they were turned out, or just the look in the eyes. They exchanged understanding glances, then the other asked, 'It's Mr Graye, isn't it?'

'Yes. You look familiar. Should I know you? I'm afraid I don't remember you, though.'

'You'd not recognize me now, but we played together as lads during the school holidays. Then I went to work in Tinsley when I was fourteen and didn't come back to Horton all that often. I'm Vic Scott. My brother was one of the gardeners at the Hall, but he was killed in '16.'

Marcus offered his hand. 'You've changed but I do remember you now.'

'We've all changed, haven't we? War does that to you. Mind your greatcoat.' Vic closed the door of the shabby but clean vehicle and swung himself nimbly up on to the driving seat.

The gentle gait of the elderly mare was soothing and Marcus leaned his head back thankfully, closing his eyes as the animal trotted the half-mile or so to his home. He must have dozed off, because he was woken by cool air on his face and Vic's voice.

'We're here, sir.'

'What? Oh, yes. Sorry.' Marcus shook his head to clear it and stepped carefully down, grateful that his companion didn't try to help him, because he preferred to manage on his own.

Vic was frowning at the untended garden and shabby cottage, which had no plume of smoke coming from the chimney. 'Shouldn't someone have opened up the place for you, sir, lit a fire at least?'

Marcus stared at what had once been the gatehouse and was now called the Lodge. His mother had been the younger of the two children born to her generation of the Lonnerden family, who'd been squires of Horton for more than two centuries. She'd been bookish, had married late in life a man despised by the family because of his studious ways and lack of fortune. And then she'd died in childbirth within the year, leaving his father to look after him. Saul Graye had made it very plain that he hadn't wanted the bother of a child in his old age, and would rather have had his wife still, so Marcus had been sent away to boarding school when very young, and had come home only for Christmas, Easter and the summer holidays, to run wild in the grounds of the Hall.

He realized he was getting lost in his thoughts again. 'Sorry, Vic. I'm more tired than I expected. I didn't have time to let the family know I was coming back. They needed more beds at the convalescent home, so turfed a few of us out early. I'll nip across to pay my respects to my cousin and aunt, and ask Cook to give me enough food to last until tomorrow. It's not far to walk to the big house if you cut through the kitchen garden. I can manage that. And perhaps you could come back tomorrow morning and drive me into Tinsley? I shall have to do some shopping and put an advert in the *Tinsley Telegraph* for a daily maid.'

The other man stared at him, pity in his eyes. 'Didn't they tell you?'

'Tell me what?'

'About your cousin being dead.'

'John? Yes. He was killed in '15.'

'Not John, Lawrence. He died last month. Influenza, it was. He never really recovered from being gassed.'

Shock made Marcus reach for the gatepost to steady himself. 'I didn't know. If anyone wrote to tell me, I didn't receive the letter. I've been moving around a bit, though, from France to England, then from hospital to a convalescent home.'

'Well, there's only old Mrs Lonnerden left now. She hasn't

been well for a while, but I heard she had to be sedated when Mr Lawrence died. They're all at sixes and sevens at the big house, from the sounds of it. Cook held things together after your uncle passed away, but she died in the spring and there are only two elderly maids left now.'

'Cook's gone as well? Ah, I'm sorry for that! The place won't seem the same without her. *Why* didn't they let me know?' He'd been very fond of Cook, who'd had a lot of time for a lonely, motherless lad when he was growing up. 'What about Hill? Is he still running the stables? And Parker – is he still in charge of the gardens?'

'Hill's looking after the horses, though there are only a couple of them now, ones that were too old to go to war. Parker died a few months ago as well, so Hill does a bit of gardening when he can, but he's half-crippled with rheumatism.'

'Oh, hell!' Marcus rubbed one hand over his beard then stared down at himself. 'I'm in no fit state to go calling on a lady, but I think I must pay my respects to my aunt and let her know I'm back.' He turned to walk towards the small house, tripped on the uneven paving and lost his balance.

Vic caught his arm and steadied him. 'You look like you need a bit of help.'

Marcus nodded, hating to admit it.

'I could stay. Help you unpack and change, then go with you across to the big house, carry stuff back. Old Dolly here will be happy to be turned loose on that lawn of yours. Only, I'll have to ask for some payment, I'm afraid. I'm still paying off the loan for the cab, you see, and only just scraping through. But I might as well work for you as for anyone else, and I'd only charge you three shillings for an afternoon's work, because that's what I'd normally make.' He sighed. 'It doesn't bring in as much as I'd hoped, driving a cab, not in a small place like Horton.'

'Thanks. I'd be most grateful for your help.' Leaning on Vic's arm, he started off again towards the front door. 'You're very steady on that peg leg of yours.'

'I was lucky. Got used to it quickly, and since I lost it below the knee, I can still bend my leg. How about you? You're favouring your right leg? Will you always limp?'

'No. But I'm still healing and that whole side hurts when I do too much, as I have today.'

'You're one of the lucky ones, though.'

Another person telling him that! Marcus didn't feel lucky, just extremely weary.

And if his two cousins were dead, what would happen to the Hall? It wasn't all that big, a pleasant little manor in a few acres. He could see its outline through the bare-branched trees. He hoped it wouldn't be sold to some war profiteer. But whoever inherited the Hall couldn't touch the Lodge and its half-acre, because that had been his mother's dowry and now belonged to him. Not that he'd be able to stay here for long. He'd have to rent the place out, because he needed to find himself a job, could go back to his old one in Manchester, though he didn't know if he could settle down to working in a bank again.

Time enough to make decisions and plans when he was feeling better.

After a hasty wash, Marcus donned a clean shirt, hoping its crumpled state wasn't too obvious. He limped across to the big house, steadying himself with a walking stick he'd found in the hallstand. Vic walked next to him but didn't offer to help, except to open and close the two gates. It felt comforting not to be on his own. He wasn't looking forward to seeing his aunt again, because his being alive would rub salt in the wound of her loss. She'd cared about nothing in life except her two sons, certainly not her husband, a bluff man of few words, who'd died before the war. It was dreadful that she'd lost both John and Lawrence, dreadful.

He stopped for a moment to stare in shock at the vegetable garden, which hadn't been cleared for the winter, and was a mass of mainly dead vegetation, with a few cabbages and Brussels sprouts standing sentinel in one corner and something green drooping in the middle.

Vic shook his head sadly as they studied the mess. 'I'd heard things were bad here, but hadn't realized it had gone so far downhill. What a waste! And there's me without a garden at all, just a poky little bedroom in Granny Diggle's cottage.'

When Marcus knocked on the back door of the Hall, the

entrance he'd always used, no one answered. He knocked again, waited, then pushed the door open and called, 'Hello!' The place was tidy, but it didn't smell like Cook's kitchen. There was nothing simmering on the stove, no trays of cakes and bread cooling, a memory which he'd summoned up sometimes in the trenches to cheer himself up. 'Perhaps you'd better wait for me here, Vic? I'll go and see if there's anyone around.'

'Right you are, sir.'

Marcus went through into the front part of the house, still using the walking stick, hearing its tapping noise echoing up the stairwell. He heard a faint sound of voices from somewhere above and called, 'Is anyone there?'

There was silence, then footsteps and his aunt's elderly maid appeared at the top of the stairs looking anxious. 'It's me . . . Marcus,' he called.

She clapped one hand to her meagre breast. 'Oh, sir, you did give me a shock. I didn't recognize you with that beard. But I'm glad to see you.'

As he limped slowly up the stairs, she hesitated, looking over her shoulder, then saying in a low voice as he reached the top, 'I'm at my wits' end how to manage here, and that's the truth.'

He paused to rest the leg and it was only then that she seemed to notice his walking stick.

'You're injured, sir.'

'Yes. I've been invalided out. How's my aunt?'

'Didn't you get my letter?'

He looked at her in surprise. '*Your* letter, Ada?'

'Yes, sir. Madam wasn't in a fit state to write, so I did.'

'I've not received any letters for weeks. Yours will have been chasing after me. And I only heard about Lawrence this afternoon. I'm so sorry. My aunt must be very upset.'

'She's taking it badly.'

'I'd better go in and see her.'

She hesitated, still barring his way. 'You'll not – take offence at what she says?'

'Of course not.' Grief took people in many different ways and he reckoned he'd seen them all after four years of war.

The big front bedroom was hot and stuffy, smelling of some sickly perfume, with other less pleasant smells concealed beneath that. The woman in the bed was so shrunken and old-looking that he stopped in shock.

'It's Mr Marcus, come back from the wars,' Ada said.

'Why was *he* spared and not my boys?' Pamela Lonnerden began to sob.

Marcus moved closer to the bed, concerned at his aunt's sallowness and the wild look in her eyes.

She flapped her hands at him. 'Get away from me! I don't want you in here, gloating.'

As he looked questioningly at the maid, his aunt shrieked, '*Get out!*' and began to sob wildly.

'Better leave, sir. Give her time to get used to you being back.'

When they were outside the bedroom, with the noise muted into a thin, despairing sobbing, Ada said, 'I'm sorry, Mr Marcus. She's not in her right mind at the moment, and that's a fact. She won't see the doctor, won't eat or drink properly, won't even wash herself. I've my hands full trying to look after her, I can tell you.'

'That's obvious. I can't leave things like this. Why hasn't the new owner come to take charge?'

'No one knows who that is. I think you'd better go and see the family lawyer about it, sir. Mr Redway will know what to do, if anyone will, and he's a distant cousin, so he's family.'

Marcus made his way slowly down the stairs, finding Vic in the kitchen talking to an older woman who had been a housemaid before the war. Now she seemed to be in charge of preparing the meals, because she was chopping up a single onion and had a very small pile of chopped meat on a plate beside her. They both looked at him expectantly and he could only say, 'My aunt doesn't want to see me.'

'She's not seen anyone but Ada and the lawyer since the funeral,' the woman volunteered. 'Won't even see the doctor, says he can't help what ails her.'

'I'll go into Tinsley to see Mr Redway tomorrow. For now, I wonder – Gladys, isn't it? – if you could let me have something for my tea and breakfast? I've only just arrived and there's nothing to eat at the Lodge.'

Gladys looked dubiously at the food on the table. 'I'm sorry, sir, but we haven't got much to spare, what with the rationing and all. I can let you have some bread and cheese, though, and an egg. Oh, and there are some apples in the attic, if someone will go up and get them.' She looked at Vic, who smiled cheerfully. 'Here, take this bag. You might as well fill it right up. They're only going to waste. The orchard did well this year and we managed to pick quite a lot, but there's no one to eat them, so we could have saved ourselves the trouble, because madam doesn't eat more than a bird. Just follow the back stairs up to the very top, you can't miss the smell of apples.'

When he had left she looked apologetically at Marcus. 'I'm sorry it's such poor pickings, sir, really sorry. But what with the bills not being paid and all, we're lucky they're still letting us have any groceries.'

He looked at her in shock. '*Bills not being paid?*'

She nodded. 'Not for a long time. Your uncle hadn't a head for business, if you'll excuse me saying so, only, everyone knew. And anyway, us servants couldn't help knowing that things were going downhill, because they sold off some of the land. Mr John kept things going for a while, but when he and Mr Lawrence were called up there was no one to take things in hand and then – well, things went from bad to worse. After Mr Lawrence was gassed and invalided out, he kept to his bedroom mostly, except to sit with madam in the evenings sometimes or go out to that club in town that the gentlemen use. There's only me and Ada left indoors now, and Hill outside. It's hard to keep the place going, though we do our best, I promise you.'

'I'm sure you do, Gladys. No one can work miracles.'

The two men walked back to the Lodge in silence, with Vic carrying the food. Marcus couldn't hide the fact that he was exhausted and allowed himself to be persuaded to rest in front of the sitting-room fire while Vic bustled round upstairs, making up a bed and unpacking the suitcase. The larder was completely empty and all the furniture covered in dust, but there was wood in the outhouse still, so he could light fires to chase away the feeling of damp and neglect. There was even enough oil to fill a couple of lamps, and a packet of candles.

As it grew fully dark, Marcus paid Vic, who had more than

earned his modest fee. 'I'm grateful for your help. If you can come here tomorrow, take me into Tinsley then stay with me for the whole day, I'll pay you whatever you think right. It'll be easier than taking the train, because I can leave parcels in your cab as I buy things. I'm not in a fit state to manage on my own yet, I'm afraid. And if you know of anyone who wants a job as cook and general maid . . .'

'I may do, sir. I'll ask her.'

Marcus was sorry to see the other man go, because the darkness was so quiet and still around the house that he felt as if it was pressing in on him. He boiled the egg and ate a solitary supper, after which, though it was only eight o'clock, he made his way painfully up the stairs to the front bedroom, where two earthenware hot-water bottles had made a cosy nest of the creaking old bed.

He'd expected to lie awake, but exhaustion quickly claimed him and he only had time to wonder what the hell had brought the senior branch of the family so low before he fell into a deep sleep.

Two

On the tenth of December Serena turned thirty. She made no attempt to celebrate the day or even to remind Ernest that it was her birthday, because she was still pretending to be unwell. Since her mother's death, he had spent every evening at his club, virtually ignoring her. Today he had once again left word that he would be dining at his club that evening, and there was no sign of the envelope with five guineas in it which he normally gave her in lieu of a present. She could only presume he'd forgotten what day it was, and hoped he had. It would make things easier.

When informed that her master would be out that evening, Cook said disapprovingly, 'You should have reminded him that it's your birthday, Miss Serena. You shouldn't be on your own today.'

'It wasn't worth troubling him. Please don't say anything or it'll put him in a bad mood.'

Cook shuddered and nodded. All the servants dreaded rousing their master's temper, because although he remained icily calm at all times, he could make the most cutting remarks Serena had ever heard, unerringly pinpointing a person's weakness and playing on their fears. And when he was in a bad mood, he'd been known to dismiss maids on the spot for behaving in a manner of which he disapproved. The trouble was, no one knew why he got these sour moods, which seemed to happen out of the blue.

Serena ate a solitary meal that evening, too nervous to feel hungry even though Cook had made a special effort to please her. She pushed the plate aside then, rather than upset Cook, she cut a large piece of the elaborate birthday cake and dropped it into the hottest part of the fire, using the poker to make sure it was totally consumed. It was a pity to waste food when it was in short supply in the whole country, but she wouldn't like to hurt Cook's feelings. When she rang to have the table cleared, she sent the cake back with her compliments and instructions that all the servants were to have a piece. How Cook had got the ingredients for it she had to wonder, but then they always ate better than most folk and she guessed it was because of her father's black-market contacts.

The evening passed pleasantly. She allowed herself one small glass of *his* brandy, on the principle of doing something to mark the occasion, and settled down to read the new novel she'd bought herself as a birthday present from the bookshop near the station. She kept an eye on the clock and went to bed before he was likely to return. Sometimes he didn't come home till the small hours of the morning, but you could never be sure.

As she brushed her hair out in front of the dressing-table mirror, she turned from side to side, thinking how much more flattering it looked loose. Her mother had always said she had beautiful hair, the dark brown showing auburn highlights where the lamp shone on it. But she always pulled it back into a low, very tight knot which sometimes made her head ache, and frizzed the short hair at the front into an unflattering fringe using pipe cleaners. Tonight she wouldn't do that, she decided, because very soon now she hoped not to be here for him to notice the change.

Tucking the ends of her hair into her dressing gown, she tried to see what it would look like bobbed. One rather dashing member of their Comforts for the Troops group had had a bob and it had been much admired. It must be so much easier to manage shorter hair.

So now, Serena thought as she climbed into bed, she had turned thirty and was legally mistress of her inheritance. But first she'd have to prise it out of *him* and that would be difficult, she was sure. He liked to control everything in the house, especially money.

And he was going to be furious when she left home, absolutely furious, not because he would miss her but because it would reflect badly on him if she left for any reason other than marriage. He might also come to realize then that he'd lost a very efficient housekeeper, which she knew she was. She had taken over that job from her mother years ago and had done it well, but she'd never received a word of thanks or praise from him, only blame or cold silences if something didn't please him. She only hoped he wouldn't take his anger out on the servants after she'd left.

The next day, Vic arrived at the Lodge at nine o'clock prompt to pick up Marcus and take him into Tinsley to see his aunt's lawyer.

'You look a bit better today, Captain,' he said cheerfully.

'Against all the odds, I slept really well, thank you. We'll go and see the lawyer first, I think, then do some shopping. He's a distant relative but I only met him once, when my father died, so can't really remember him: Justin Redway of Bridge Lane.'

'Whatever you say, sir. I'm at your service. Oh, and – ' Vic hesitated – 'I may have found someone to help you out in the house. Well, it's the girl I'm going to marry, actually. She's been working in the munitions factory over the other side of Tinsley, but they're laying off workers, so she needs to find something else. She used to work as a maid at the Hall, though.

We're saving up to get married, but we can't do that till I'm earning enough, and even then we have to find a house to rent. There's a shortage of houses round here, because no new ones were built during the war.'

'What's your young lady called?'

'Pearl Diggle, sir. She lives just down the road from you, with her parents, in that row of seven cottages on the outskirts of the village. You'll want to meet her first, of course, and her mother wants to meet you.' He grinned. 'Bit of a tartar, Mrs Diggle, thinks a lot of her girl. She terrifies the life out of me. I'm lodging with Pearl's grandmother and she's just the same.'

'You don't look the terrified sort.'

'Ah, well, I get on all right with most folk. But I have to watch my step with the Diggles, I can tell you.'

'When is your young woman free? Can we go round to see her on the way back?'

'She'll not be home from work till after seven, sir. I'll bring her round to the Lodge later, if that's all right. Oh, and she's a canary. Thought I'd better tell you in advance so you aren't surprised at how she looks.'

'I honour the women who've put up with yellow skin for the sake of the war effort. Where would we soldiers have been without them making our shells?'

'It's her hair that still surprises me, more than her face even,' Vic said with another of his grins. 'Ginger it is at the front now, which isn't flattering. Her hair's dark brown usually, lovely colour. But the ginger will grow out, they say, once she's not handling the TNT, and her skin will go back to its normal colour too. She used to have lovely rosy cheeks.'

The elderly mare clopped the two miles into Tinsley and Vic dropped Marcus off at the lower end of Bridge Lane. 'I'll be over there by the river, sir, when you've finished. There's a horse trough and it's quite sheltered. This old girl won't mind a bit of a rest. She's past working really, but there weren't any other horses available when I was setting up. All the good ones got sent off to war, poor things.'

Marcus made his way slowly up the narrow street and soon found Justin Redway's rooms. There was an elderly clerk in the front room who became very attentive once he found out who this unexpected customer was, fussing over Marcus, offering him a cup of tea and apologizing that he'd have to wait until Mr Redway had finished with his first client.

Accepting the offer of tea, Marcus went across to a hard, upright chair by the window and sank down on it with a sigh of relief. He was stupidly weak still and probably ought to be resting, only there seemed to be too many problems to sort out and no one but him to do it.

Twenty minutes later he was shown in to see Redway, whom he recognized vaguely– a sprightly gentleman with silver hair, probably in his mid-sixties.

Justin gestured to a chair. 'I suppose you've come about the will.'

'Well, my aunt's maid suggested I see you, because someone has to sort things and I seem to be the only one left.'

'Yes. She wrote to you about Lawrence dying, I believe?'

'So she says, but the letter never reached me, I'm afraid. I came home yesterday to find my aunt in bed and the Hall very run down. My aunt went into hysterics at the mere sight of me, and when I spoke to Gladys, who now seems to be acting as cook, she said the tradesmen hadn't been paid for a while. Obviously there are financial problems, so I wondered if there was anything I could do to help.'

'Hmm. So you're not aware of how things have been left?'

Marcus shook his head.

'Well, the fact is your cousin Lawrence left everything to you, with the proviso that you provide a home for your aunt and look after her until she dies.'

'*Me?* But – Lawrence and I didn't get on. He was older than me and used to bully me unmercifully when I was little. I thought he'd have left everything to one of the relatives he does like.'

'There aren't many others left now, well not close ones, anyway, and most of them are elderly and – disapproving.'

'Of what?'

'His gambling. Lawrence realized he wouldn't make old bones after being gassed, so he made a will. He said—' Justin broke off and shrugged. 'Well, that's not relevant now.'

'You may as well tell me everything.'

The other gave him a wry smile. 'Well, Lawrence said it'd

serve you right if he died before his mother and you were lumbered with her as well as a pile of debts. She was upset about his gambling, tried to get him to stop.'

Marcus drew a deep breath. This was getting worse by the minute. 'Oh. Did he gamble locally?'

'Oh, yes. He could always find himself a game.'

'Who with?'

Justin hesitated. 'It's only hearsay.'

'Tell me.'

'Fellow called Fleming, another called Hammerton. They're the two ringleaders. They use the private rooms at the Gentlemen's Club for it, I gather. The war didn't stop them. The Government couldn't ration gambling, after all. Your aunt even confronted Fleming in the street once, haranguing him, though what good she thought that would do, I don't know. He's not a man to antagonize.'

'I don't remember much about him.'

'Shrewd fellow, made a lot of money in the war.'

'But you don't sound as if you like him.'

Justin shrugged. 'I don't have much to do with him, except when I try to get a bit of justice for his tenants.' He waited a moment, then added, 'So there you are, proud owner of the Hall.'

'I'm not sure I even want the place. Perhaps there's someone else it could go to? I was thinking of selling the Lodge and going out to Australia, actually, because I fancied living in a sunnier climate.'

Justin grimaced. 'I'm afraid you can't legally turn down the bequest. The Hall is yours whether you want it or not, and if you don't look after things, what will happen to your aunt? She needs caring for, hasn't been well lately, I'm afraid. She's had a hard time of it over the past decade. Your uncle mismanaged things and they had to sell off most of the land. If your cousin had lived much longer, there'd have been nothing left for you to inherit, but if you're careful, you may be able to turn things round. There's still the home farm and a few cottages bringing in rents, plus one or two investments.'

'Hell and damnation!' Marcus couldn't bear to sit a minute longer and went across to stare out of the window, grateful when Justin left him in peace for a few moments. He felt helpless as well as angry, because you couldn't abandon an elderly relative to her fate or walk away from the family inheritance, and Lawrence had damned well known it. After taking a minute or two longer to calm down, he turned round and limped back to his chair. 'You'd better give me all the details.'

'I don't know everything yet. But I'll tell you what I've found out so far . . .'

When he left the lawyer's rooms, Marcus carried a box crammed with papers and his head was spinning with figures. He'd authorized Redway to obtain statements of bills unpaid from the various tradesmen and until he knew the full total, he couldn't do much.

As he walked slowly down the lane to the river, he felt as if he'd had a heavy burden placed on his shoulders, not an inheritance.

Vic looked up as he limped across to the cab, gave him one of those shrewd, intelligent looks that seemed to be so much a part of the man. 'Bad news, sir?'

Marcus nodded and stood clutching the box. He couldn't think of this man as an inferior, not after playing with him as a lad. And certainly not after fighting with chaps like him, seeing their bravery, listening to their hopes and fears, holding their hands when they were dying. 'Not good news. Well, *I* don't think so, anyway. I've been left the Hall, together with the responsibility of providing for my aunt, but there are debts, so things aren't going to be easy. I may even have to sell up to pay off the creditors. I'm coming back to see Mr Redway after I've thought things over, and we'll do some initial planning then.'

His companion gave him a twisted smile. 'I wouldn't mind your problems, nonetheless. You'll have a fine house to live in, so you've at least got somewhere to bring a bride.'

'I've no intention of marrying until I've cleared up the mess at the Hall. I haven't had much chance to meet eligible young women in the past year or two, and anyway, this will probably put many of them off.' Marcus indicated his scarred cheek.

'Shouldn't think so. Decent women don't care about things like that.'

'What do they care about? Money? I shan't be rich, either.' He smiled and turned up his face to the winter sun for a moment. 'Ah, you're right. I'm lucky really. It's just – I was going to sell up and go out to Australia, so I'm feeling a bit disappointed.'

'Too hot for me out there, I reckon, from what I've heard. Besides – ' Vic looked across the river towards the blue-green outlines of the moors in the distance – 'this is home.'

'Where did you serve?'

'Mostly in France.'

'Rank?'

Vic hesitated, then said, 'Sergeant. They were going to send me to officer school last year, but this happened and I got discharged instead.' He gestured towards his leg.

'You must have done well.'

The other shrugged. 'I did my duty, we all did. What choice did we have?'

'They didn't promote just anyone. My cousin Lawrence remained a lieutenant for years, right until he was invalided out. And look, I'd prefer it if you stopped calling me sir from now on. After what we've both been through, such distinctions seem stupid to me. We were always Vic and Marcus when we were lads, let's keep it that way.'

'Are you sure?'

'Yes.' At the other's nod of agreement, he added, 'I've a proposition to make you, Vic, and a job offer of sorts. It'd bring in more than driving a cab and there'd be living quarters with it.'

'I'm very interested in that, sir – I mean, Marcus.'

'Good. Let's find some tea rooms and get something to eat and drink. I'm ravenous this morning.'

They left the horse and cab in the charge of an old man, whose eyes brightened at the offer of a shilling for minding them, and went up to Yorkshire Road and Tinsley's only tea room.

Marcus leaned back in his chair. 'I'm ravenous. Haven't been so hungry for weeks, actually.'

'Well, they'll only be small scones,' Vic warned him. 'Rationing, you know. There's a fixed size to what this place can serve with morning tea, one and a half ounces of bread or cake, not both. I found out when I got back that they feed the troops much better than they do the civilians.'

'Then how the hell do I get a decent meal?'

'We'll go and register you with the grocer and butcher – they did give you a ration book when you left the convalescent home, didn't they?'

'Yes.'

'Then we'll buy some food and take it back to Pearl's mother. Mrs Diggle will cook it for you and make it spin out. It's not a meatless day today – Wednesdays and Fridays, those are, outside London – so you may be able to get something at the butcher's.'

A surly waitress brought their food and slopped away again in shoes that seemed too loose. They were the only customers at the moment, so could talk freely.

'About this offer of yours . . .' Vic prompted.

'I'm not sure of the details yet, but I'm definitely going to need help. You can tell me what you'd consider a suitable wage – I have some money of my own saved, so you needn't be afraid I won't be able to pay you – and I can offer you and Pearl accommodation at the Hall. God knows, there are enough rooms there gathering dust. It's one thing I have plenty of – space. If I move into the Hall, I can rent out the Lodge and that'll bring in something. If Pearl could help out as well, that'd be perfect, and I'd pay her the going wage, of course.'

'What would I be doing exactly?'

Marcus spread his hands wide in an admission of uncertainty. 'Anything and everything. And so will I, once I've recovered. Part of the time you could ply your trade with the cab. There'd be some physical work, even digging in the garden if necessary, though not as much of that at this time of year. Then you could drive me around, who knows what else? It won't be like the old days of being in service, I promise you, we'd be working as a team. I couldn't treat a fellow soldier as an inferior, or a woman who's worked in munitions either.'

Vic's face creased into a grin and he held out his hand. 'I accept your offer.' As the two men solemnly shook hands, he added, 'Sounds more interesting than driving a cab, which means a lot of hanging around, and, to be frank, I get bored. It was all I could think of to do, though, because Pearl won't move away from Horton. Fond of her family, she is. And well, I'd do anything to keep her.'

'Which reminds me, there's plenty of room in the stables for your horse and the cab too, if you've bought it.'

'Good. I won't have to pay for stabling then. If there's a vehicle in the stables for getting around in, I could maybe sell the cab.' His expression grew thoughtful. 'Or I'll even let someone else pay me to use it. There won't be a lot of petrol available for a while yet, so we can't get a motor car, which would be the best form of transport.' When Marcus said nothing, Vic looked sideways, wondering if he'd taken too much on himself. But his companion was smiling at him.

'I can see I picked the right man to work with me. Any ideas you get, trot them out, Vic lad. Any profits they lead to, we'll share. Nothing like a team for getting things done.'

For the first time since his return, Marcus experienced a feeling of hope and a sense that he wasn't alone, that he could make a decent future for himself. 'Right then, let's go and buy some food and on the way back we can visit your young woman's mother.'

They both stood up and, without another word being needed, turned and left the tea room, Marcus paying. He stood for a minute in Yorkshire Road, looking along it at the shops, the small, square, three-storey Town Hall, with the major bank next to it, and beyond them the comfortable villas of the better-off folk. He was glad this place hadn't changed too much.

The day after her birthday Serena put on her new black mourning clothes, pulling the felt hat down to an unflattering angle and fastening the belt loosely around her waist instead of fashionably above it. Since she had deliberately had the skirt made too long, the outfit was unflattering, even worse with the full-skirted topcoat she'd chosen, which was very bulky and came down to six inches above the skirt. She nodded approval of her reflection and went down to tell Cook she was going shopping. In reality she intended to look for a lawyer of her own.

It was only now that she'd turned thirty that her godmother's will allowed her to have full control over her inheritance, and she was very nervous about what she was doing, in case word got back to her father. No, she had to stop calling him that –

he wasn't her father and she was glad of that! Fleming, that's what she'd call him, though not to his face.

In such a small Lancashire town, there weren't many lawyers to choose from. She didn't want to use the family lawyer, so intended to consult a man whose premises were just off the main street. She'd met him socially, and he'd seemed quite friendly.

He greeted her with a smile. 'What can I do for you, Miss Fleming?'

'I need a lawyer.'

He blinked at her in surprise. 'But surely you already have a family lawyer – Pearson?'

'I need my own lawyer to help me deal with my inheritance.'

'Does your father know you're here?'

'No. This has nothing to do with him.'

'Then it ought to. I suggest you go home and ask *him* to help you with your inheritance. It's most unsuitable for you to be going to strangers about this when your own father is a respected businessman in this town.'

'But—'

'And anyway, I'm rather busy at present, can't take on any new clients. Let me show you out.'

'I can find my own way.' But she stopped him opening the door, looking at him very sternly. 'I expect everything I've said to you today to be treated in the strictest confidence, as is my legal right. And if it isn't, I shall take steps—'

He turned red and puffed out his plump cheeks. 'Believe me, I've no intention of revealing your foolishness to anyone, Miss Fleming, let alone upsetting your father by revealing your disloyalty to him.'

She knew what that meant. He didn't want to get on the wrong side of Ernest Fleming. She'd hoped a man of his status wouldn't be afraid of her father, but he clearly was. What had Fleming done to inspire such fear?

She went into the tea room and ordered a pot, sitting thoughtfully over it as she considered her problem. She wasn't going to give in, but she did need a lawyer to help her. Surely there was someone in Tinsley who wasn't afraid of Fleming? Yes, she'd heard her father mention one scornfully from time to time. What was his name? Oh, it was on the tip of her tongue. Why could she not remember it? And how was she to find him without revealing what she was doing?

When she left the tea room, she turned into a side street that she rarely used. It led down to the river and she thought she'd have a stroll along the water, because it was quite a fine day for the time of year. She couldn't bear to go home yet, especially since she'd failed to do what she'd come out for.

She'd passed the sign before it occurred to her that this might be a place to start seeking help. She turned and went back to stare at a huge piece of yellowing card which covered most of the shop window, saying in large purple letters: UWSPC. Bows of mauve and green ribbon, somewhat faded, adorned each corner.

She glanced up and down the street before entering, because it could be disastrous for her plans if anyone who knew her father saw her getting involved with the Women's Social and Political Union. They would certainly tell him about that, and the mere idea of votes for women was heresy, as far as he was concerned, one of the few things which made him show outright anger.

Her heart was thumping with nervousness as she stood just inside the doorway, but the three women sitting chatting around a low table covered in papers looked nothing like the unnatural harridans her father insisted *those women* were.

The oldest of them had greying hair, a lined face and a vividly alive expression. She stood up and came towards the newcomer with a friendly smile. 'First visit to our den of iniquity, is it?'

Serena tried to summon up an answering smile but was too worried. 'Yes. I – um – need some information and was hoping someone here might be able to help me.' She hesitated, glancing across to the other two, not wanting to reveal her business in so public a place.

The woman studied her, head on one side, then said quietly, 'Come upstairs, my dear. We can talk privately there.'

Serena followed her up some narrow, twisting stairs, whose bare wood echoed and creaked under their feet. The front room at the top was small and furnished as an office, with a big sofa at one end.

When they were sitting down on this, her companion said, 'I'm Evadne Blair.'

'Serena Fleming.'

The other woman looked surprised for a moment, clearly recognizing the name, but didn't comment. 'It's obvious you don't want to waste time with small talk, Miss Fleming, so tell me immediately what your problem is. If you need help and I can give it, it'll be my pleasure. If we women can't support one another, it's a sad state of affairs.'

When Serena had finished explaining, Evadne gave her another of those warm, conspiratorial smiles. 'It isn't easy to rebel with a father like yours, is it?'

'No. No, it isn't.'

'I do know a lawyer who might help you, but he's not a polite sort of man.'

'I don't care if he's the rudest man on earth as long as he can help me take back control of my inheritance from my father. Without it, there's no way I can be independent.'

Evadne stood up. 'I have a cousin who's a lawyer, Justin Redway.'

'That's the name I've been trying to remember. I've heard my father mention him once or twice.'

The other woman chuckled. 'He won't have been saying anything complimentary then. Look, there's no time like the present. Why don't I take you round to meet him?'

'Thank you.' Serena followed her outside, greatly relieved.

Redway's rooms proved to be much shabbier than those of the other lawyer Serena had visited, being merely the ground floor of a large terraced house in the next narrow thoroughfare, which was called Bridge Lane. Judging by the row of brass signs outside, it was used as a place of business by several other people as well, but the ground floor was separate and seemed to be occupied wholly by Mr Redway. The clerk occupying the room nearest the street was elderly, his clothes shabby, his expression shrewd. He led them through to the rearmost office, which looked out on to a small back garden.

Evadne walked forward, hand extended. 'Well, Cousin Justin, I've brought Miss Fleming to see you. She needs some legal help.'

Redway looked at her in surprise. 'Fleming?'

Evadne nodded. 'Let her explain. She's trying to rebel.'

'I'm very much in favour of rebellion,' he said with a smile, gesturing to a chair.

Serena liked him at once. His clothes might be shabby and his shirt collar crumpled above a carelessly knotted tie, but, like his cousin's, his face had the glow of good health and confidence, and also kindness. Once again she explained her situation.

'I have to warn you that your father hates even the sight of me.'

'May I ask why?'

'Because he's a bad landlord, doesn't do repairs if he can help it. I've acted on behalf of his tenants from time to time.'

She didn't know what to say to that. All she knew of her father's business interests was what she'd heard at dinner parties or overheard at home, because he didn't believe in discussing such things with the female members of his family.

'I have to ask if you're sure you want to go through with this, Miss Fleming? It won't be easy for you. Your father has a reputation for being hard on those who cross him.'

'I believe it's my only chance of happiness, though I hope to leave home before he finds out what I'm doing.'

'How can you refuse a plea like that, Justin?' Evadne said lightly.

'I can't. Tell me about your inheritance, Miss Fleming. Of what does it consist?'

She could feel her cheeks growing warm and was embarrassed to admit, 'I'm not exactly sure. An annuity and a few other bits and pieces. That's what my father always called them, but when I asked for details he said I'd no need to know and wouldn't understand financial matters anyway.' Her cheeks grew even hotter. 'At the time it would have done no good to press for an explanation. He'd have grown angry and taken it out on my mother, who was an invalid. Anyway, I could do nothing about the inheritance until I was thirty, so it would have been pointless to insist.'

He looked at her black clothing. 'And now your mother's dead.'

It wasn't a question. Well, everyone in town must know

that Ernest Fleming's wife had died. It had been a very ostentatious funeral.

'Have you actually turned thirty?'

'Yesterday. He forgot it was my birthday, but when he remembers I'm sure he'll want me to sign papers that allow him to continue handling things, so I feel I have to get away quickly.'

Justin's grin was that of a street urchin about to steal an apple. 'Well, if you're sure you have the courage to go through with this, I'll take great pleasure in helping you escape, Miss Fleming.'

Serena sagged back in her chair in relief. She liked Mr Redway and felt better not to have to face her father without support. 'Thank you so much. I've been making plans and now I must find somewhere else to live. I suppose I can book into a hotel, but I need somewhere to send my trunks and boxes and there's no one I can trust. Can you suggest anywhere? I'm sure my father will make it difficult for me to retrieve any of my possessions from home once I leave, so I thought I'd send them away before he finds out what I'm doing. I'll say I'm disposing of my mother's things but send mine away instead.'

'You can send them here, if you like. They can sit in the middle room, which only contains a few layers of dust, because I never did find myself a partner.'

'Are you sure?'

'Of course I am.'

Serena should have felt happy as she made her way home, because she'd solved two of her immediate problems, but she was too filled with apprehension. What if someone had seen her today going into Justin Redway's rooms? What if things went wrong before she got away?

What would her father do when she left? Something dreadful, she was sure.

She wasn't used to acting on her own, might make mistakes – no, *would* make mistakes. But she mustn't let the fear of that stop her. Her whole life's happiness was at stake here.

When his new client had left, Justin cocked one eyebrow at Evadne. 'Poor downtrodden thing. She must have had a hell of a life with *him.* Think she'll hold firm?'

'We can but give her the chance. Thanks for agreeing to help her, Justin.'

'You know how I love to tweak that fellow's tail.'

'Yes. And one day he'll pay you back for it.'

'He'll have to catch me first.'

'Well, it's a good sign that she's planning carefully ahead, finding a lawyer, getting her clothes out of the house, don't you think?'

He grimaced. 'If the rest of her clothes are as unflattering as that hideous tent of a garment she was wearing today, she'd be better throwing them away and buying new ones.'

'Maybe I can help her with that later.'

'My dear cousin, you can't help the whole world.'

She shrugged. 'I can try to help the female half of it, though.'

The next morning Serena's father said over breakfast. 'You should have reminded me about your birthday.'

'You seemed busy. And you know I don't care for a fuss being made.'

'I'm always busy, but the money your aunt left you comes into your own hands when you're thirty. It's only a modest legacy but you'll still need me to manage it for you. I'll have the necessary papers drawn up by my lawyer. You can come to my office the day after tomorrow to sign them.'

She said nothing, merely inclining her head. As she poured his second cup of tea, she said casually, 'If it's all right with you, Father, I'll send mother's clothes to a charity for governesses who've fallen on hard times. I've found some old trunks and boxes that we don't use. There's nothing of hers you want to keep, is there?'

'What? Oh yes, do see to that for me. Excellent idea. You're too plump to wear any of her things, that's for sure.' He looked at her with disfavour.

She lowered her eyes and forced herself to eat, though the food tasted like cardboard. She was living in a permanent state of apprehension and would until she got away from Tinsley, as far away as she could manage, somewhere he wouldn't be able to find her.

* * *

In her bedroom later that morning, Serena looked at the trunks and boxes which she and her mother's maid, now working as a housemaid, had carried down from the attic after her father had gone to work. She had told Ruby these were for her mother's clothes, which had also been brought into her room, to the maid's surprise.

'Do you think we'll need all these boxes, miss?'

'I was thinking of getting rid of some of my own old clothes at the same time. Would you like something of my mother's to remember her by? You're near enough her size.'

Ruby gaped at her, then stared at the clothes longingly. 'Are you sure, miss?'

'Yes, of course. You can choose what you want, but you'll have to take them away today, because my father wants me to send the rest to a charity at once.'

Ruby chose two of the simpler gowns. 'You're sure the master doesn't mind me having them, miss? I don't want to upset him.'

They both knew that Ernest would definitely not approve of a maid wearing his dead wife's clothes.

'What he doesn't know won't upset him,' Serena said lightly. 'Maybe Cook will give you an hour off to take these things home. Tell her I said it's all right. You might like to alter them a little, though – the trimming, the frills and so on – just to make sure no one recognizes them.' She knew Ruby was shrewd enough to understand what she was getting at.

'Yes, miss. And thank you.'

Serena watched the maid bundle up her new possessions, glad to have made someone happy. Well, Ruby had been a tower of strength during her mother's long years of illness and deserved some reward for that. 'I'll ring when I need you. I find this upsetting and would rather be on my own as I do it.'

She locked her bedroom door and went quickly through her mother's clothes, setting aside a few garments which might perhaps suit her if they were altered, then hanging the rest in her wardrobe. As she packed her own clothes in the trunks, she grimaced at how dull a collection they were. Only her underclothing was pretty, a small vanity. Well, these clothes would have to do until she had time and money to buy new ones or could alter some of them. She also packed her favourite books, trinkets and a few mementoes.

When the carrier arrived late that afternoon, Serena dealt with him herself. He wasn't the man her father normally used but someone she had seen in the street and had stopped to book his services. She doubted any of the servants would even remember his name, because it wasn't written on the side of his cart. After paying him, she stood watching at the front door, heedless of the cold, as he drove off along Cavendish Terrace then turned down the hill to leave the boxes in Mr Redway's rooms. It was silly, really, but she kept thinking something would happen to stop her getting her things away.

She looked up at the grey sky and took a deep breath of fresh air before she closed the door. It tasted of freedom, unlike the house, which was always stuffy, because *he* didn't like draughts.

She didn't sleep at all well that night.

Could she do it? Did she dare? Would he find out and stop her?

Mrs Diggle greeted Vic warmly, found a wizened apple for the old horse and tutted in dismay to think of poor Mr Graye being hungry. 'And you wounded for your country too,' she said indignantly as she installed the two men to one side of her kitchen fire. 'Well, we'll soon have something for you to eat. Good job it's baking day, though it's not what I'd like to set before you, given the restrictions on using flour.'

'I can't take your food rations!' Marcus protested, having seen for himself today how little was allocated to each person.

She drew herself up, seeming suddenly much larger and far more intimidating. 'I hope you're not refusing my hospitality, Mr Graye!'

He found himself disinclined to argue with her and saw Vic hiding a smile.

When they left, they were both full of meat and potato pie, followed by scones which had even had a small dab of butter on them. Marcus had left some of his provisions behind and been promised a pan of stew, which would be delivered to the Lodge before tea time by Mrs Diggle's youngest.

Vic grinned at him. 'Told you what she was like. You find

yourself doing what she says whether you intended to or not. She's a good-hearted soul, even if she is bossy, always the first to help out in times of trouble.'

'And she's a superb cook. How did she get food to spare when they're so short at the Hall?'

'There's a lot of swapping goes on round here. People grow things or breed animals, and don't see why they shouldn't have a small share for their trouble. There's no profiteering, though. They don't *sell* the extra stuff. I don't blame them, either. They've worked damned hard during the war years, women and old men mucking in with the outside work.'

The inside of the Lodge looked even more shabby and run-down after Mrs Diggle's cosy little house.

'I think I need a rest,' Marcus confessed as he limped across to sink into a chair. 'I'll sit and read through these papers the lawyer gave me, then maybe we'll go across to the Hall later and do an inspection. I need to have a picture in my mind of what the whole place is like, not my youthful memories but an adult's view.'

'While you're resting, I'll nip across to the stables and have a word with Hill, then see if there's anything left to salvage in the vegetable garden. I've been itching to search through it ever since yesterday. It's amazing what you can find that's still edible if a garden's been planted properly, even at this time of year. And I'm sure I saw some late apples still hanging on some of the trees in the orchard. Even if they're wizened they can be used for cooking. If they're not needed at the Hall, maybe we could offer them to Mrs Diggle? She'll organize for them to be picked and put to good use, I'm sure. I'll be back in about an hour.'

When Vic returned, Marcus was asleep and the fire had died down. He set some small pieces of wood on it quietly, but inevitably woke the other man. 'Sorry. But there's a cold wind blowing outside and you'll need to keep a good fire burning, because this place still feels damp.'

Marcus yawned and stretched. 'How are the gardens?'

'There are cabbages and a few leeks, and though the slugs have got to them, you can always cut the bad bits out. Hill says they did manage to dig up most of the potatoes and earth them, so there should be enough potatoes to last you through the winter, and there are even some strings of onions. He plaited them in the evenings and they're hanging in the barn, which is nice and dry. Next year, we can plant the garden properly and provide most of our own vegetables.'

'Next year,' Marcus said wonderingly. 'Isn't it wonderful to be able to say "next year" with confidence?'

They both stood for a moment contemplating that miracle, because for a few years they'd not even been able to say 'tomorrow' with certainty.

Marcus pushed himself upright, willing himself to find the energy to move. 'Right then. Let's go and inspect the Hall, find out exactly what I've inherited.'

'Are you sure you want me to come with you?'

'Yes. I may need your help and it's – well, good to have company when one is raising old ghosts.'

Gladys was working in the kitchen and smiled when Marcus explained what he was doing there. 'I'm glad *you* inherited the old place, sir. It's not good to bring in a stranger.'

The men walked round the ground floor, finding three sitting rooms, a small dining room which the family used to take their meals, and a formal one with heavy mahogany furniture and a massive table with extra leaves stored underneath it.

'How many people could you seat at this table?' Vic wondered.

'More than I shall ever invite round here,' Marcus muttered, not liking the sombre darkness of the wood-panelled walls, which seemed to soak up all the available light.

Beyond the kitchen and pantries were the housekeeper's bedroom and sitting room, currently unoccupied.

'These might suit you and Pearl,' Marcus suggested.

Vic's face brightened, because the rooms were spacious and already furnished. 'I'll bring her to look round, if that's all right.'

'Of course it's all right.'

Upstairs, one of the two wings had four large bedrooms, in one of which his aunt Pamela was still keeping to her bed, and the other had six smaller rooms, two of which had been used as a schoolroom and nursery. There was a bathroom in each wing, with antiquated fittings and rusty stains on the baths.

'Don't they use these any more?' Vic whispered, trying to turn a tap and finding it difficult. When he did succeed, water gushed out, wetting his arm. 'It's very old-fashioned.'

'I think my aunt made my uncle install the bathrooms. They were probably the very latest thing then. But they don't look to have been used much lately.'

On the second floor were the servants' quarters on one side, even smaller rooms than the west wing, with no bathroom here. Piles of discarded furniture and other detritus from former generations of Lonnerdens filled the big open space over the other wing of the house. Between the two areas was a place with slatted shelves where fruit was stored, apples mainly. The smell reminded Marcus of the harvest home services held in the small church when he was a lad.

A narrow staircase led up to the roof and he forced himself up it, even though his leg and side were aching fiercely now. Somehow it seemed important to take proper possession of his inheritance. In the upper attic they found two rooms, some shabby travelling trunks and a tallboy missing one foot and standing on a brick. A door led outside to a short railed walkway which gave access to the roof and also provided sweeping views of the meadows and farmland, with the moors in the distance.

The two men stood there, side by side.

'Home,' Marcus said softly.

It didn't need any other words to express their feelings. Any soldier who'd fought in the trenches knew the intense longing to be home. And now they were back here for good.

After a while Vic pointed. 'There are some tiles missing and cracked.'

Marcus nodded. 'We'll get a tiler in to check it all out.' He turned. 'I think I've had enough looking round for now.'

'Don't you want to look over the cellars?'

'Why bother? Gladys said they were nearly empty. My uncle and cousin apparently drank the wine cellar dry.' He started going carefully down the narrow stairs. 'I'd better see the village doctor tomorrow. I'm going to need these dressings changing.'

'Old Dr Hindhurst died. We don't have a doctor in the village any more. You'll have to go into Tinsley. Dr Marsh came out of retirement when his son went to war, or there's Dr Tolson.'

Marcus sighed. 'I don't like Tolson, so let's try Marsh. Perhaps you can take me there tomorrow morning?'

'I also need to vote, sir. First time I've been entitled and I'm not going to miss doing it.'

'I shan't be able to, because I wasn't in time to register here. Never mind. Next time.'

Three

On the following day, Serena woke feeling very excited. Today, the fourteenth of December, a General Election was being held, and it was the first at which women would be entitled to vote – not all women, however, only those over thirty, but she qualified for that, just, and had made the appropriate arrangements to be registered.

For the past few years she had read everything she could about female suffrage in the newspapers and had followed developments avidly earlier in the year as the Representation of the People Bill was debated in Parliament. She'd also listened in silence, with eyes lowered, to her father's tirades against Lloyd George and, it sometimes seemed to her, against every other political party as well. His fury that women were to have a say in the government of their country was no less fierce for being expressed in a calm, steady voice. The words he used to describe women's capacity to reason were scathing and it didn't seem to occur to him how insulting that was to his daughter and wife.

Serena was looking forward to exercising her rights as a citizen and voting for the first time. It was terrifying to go directly against *his* orders, but to vote would be a symbol, somehow, of the new life she hoped to build for herself, so she intended to do it, whatever the cost.

As she joined Fleming for breakfast, he shook open his newspaper and greeted her with his usual grunt. But he was soon stabbing at the page. 'These fools who write for newspapers are treating the fact that women are voting for the first time today as if it's something to be approved of. Well, no female in my family will ever do such an unwomanly thing.'

She didn't need to reply, since he took her compliance for granted, but simply continued eating. For the first time in weeks she found herself with an appetite and enjoyed the fine ham and crusty new bread, perhaps because it was spiced with the sauce of rebellion.

When Fleming had left for his place of business, Serena put on her outdoor things and made her way to the nearest polling station. She had to do this straight away before she lost courage. If she could vote, she felt she could do anything. After standing patiently in line, she listened to a cursory explanation from the election officer of what to do, before marking her ballot paper. She watched in delight as it slipped through the slot afterwards, and had to be nudged to move on. Such a small thing to do, making a mark on a piece of paper, but such a huge step for the women who were at last allowed to do it.

As she left the polling station, she held her head high, feeling herself the equal of anyone in the country, a *new woman* as some called themselves. However, the exhilaration died down abruptly when she encountered Mr Hammerton right outside.

He tipped his hat then looked at the door she'd come through. 'Miss Fleming! Surely you've not been voting?'

She could feel her face getting hot and knew her blush had betrayed her.

His smile was full of malice. 'Well, well. And your father assured me that you had no desire to vote.'

'Did he?' She moved on quickly, wishing she hadn't met him, because he was as close a friend as Fleming had, as well as a business colleague.

Sure enough, Fleming came home in a towering rage, his eyes glinting like shards of ice. 'Hammerton tells me you were at the polling station!' he snapped as he strode into the parlour.

She looked up. 'Yes.'

'I thought I forbade you to vote.'

She could only look at him, feeling as if her voice was hiding somewhere deep inside her, afraid to come out.

'*What were you doing there?*'

She had never heard him shout like this. Her heart began to thump nervously and she sounded breathless when she at last found the courage to reply. 'Voting.'

He slapped her face hard. 'How dare you disobey me? You know I don't believe in votes for women and I expressly forbade you to join in that circus.'

She jumped to her feet, letting her embroidery fall to the floor. He had never raised a hand to her before, not even when she was a child. 'It's my legal right to do so and I decided to exercise that privilege.' For a moment they stood glaring at one another and she wondered if he was going to hit her again.

When he didn't move, she picked up her embroidery and put it in the bag, then walked towards the door without a word.

He put his arm across the doorway, not touching her but spearing her with a chill gaze. '*My* daughter does not vote. If you ever disobey me again, I'll turn you out of the house with only the clothes you stand up in and see how you manage to live then. That I swear.'

Then he took a deep breath and turned away, moving towards the dining room as if this encounter had not even happened. After a moment pride made her decide not to hide upstairs in her room, so she set her embroidery on the hall-stand and took her usual place opposite him at the table. She'd always wondered what would happen if he let his anger loose and now she'd found out. Her cheek was sore but she wasn't going to rub it and give him the satisfaction of knowing he'd hurt her.

He ate his dinner in complete silence.

With his chill gaze resting on her from time to time, Serena found it hard to eat, but forced as much as she could down, for appearances' sake.

When he had finished his usual hearty meal, he said, 'Don't forget to bring your mother's jewels with you when you come to my office tomorrow morning. And don't even think of disobeying me about that. I've decided to make allowances for today's violation of my rules, because of your mother's recent death and your bout of influenza, but I shan't do so again.'

She bowed her head and let him take that for assent if he wanted to, but she couldn't understand why he was so emphatic that she hand over the jewellery into his keeping. The pieces weren't particularly valuable, though some of them had belonged to her grandmother and were quite pretty.

As soon as she could, she escaped to her bedroom, locking the door and standing with her back against it. She began to shake and stumbled across to sit on the edge of the bed, rubbing her cheek, which was still sore. It was a while before the shaking stopped and she could pull herself together. Getting up, she wrung out a cloth in cold water and held it to her cheek, sighing with relief at its cool comfort. When she looked at her cheek in the dressing-table mirror, she could still see the faint imprint of his fingers.

Could she really get her own way against *him*? Was it worth the risk of even trying? He could be ruthless, she had seen that time and time again, a maid dismissed on the spot, her mother reduced to tears over a trifle and abjectly begging his forgiveness; once, a competitor deliberately driven to bankruptcy, though she had only found that out by accident. And she'd heard rumours of other things too, rumours she hadn't believed true but now wondered about. He had looked so different this evening, so vicious.

Perhaps she should have got married years ago, escaping in the only way *he* would have tolerated? But her mother had always told her only to marry for love, and with the example of an unhappy marriage before her every single day, Serena had agreed wholeheartedly with this dictum. Her only escape from this restricted life had been in her mind and imagination. She had devoured novels where the intrepid heroines defied fate to find true love, and sometimes escaped into daydreams about the sort of man she'd like to marry if she could, the sort of life she'd like to lead . . .

Only she wasn't an intrepid heroine, was still hesitating about acting independently.

Had she just stayed here for her mother's sake or because she was too cowardly to go out into the world on her own? She was about to find out.

Suddenly she remembered her excitement at voting, the happiness in other women's faces at the polling centre, the way they had smiled and nodded to one another, and she felt her lips curl into a half-smile, her spine stiffen. For all his icy rage, there was nothing *he* could do about her voting now. And somehow, because she'd succeeded in voting, she felt she could find the courage to do the rest. Besides, if things went as she'd planned, she would be out of his house tomorrow. And later, out of the town, somewhere far away.

What would he do when he found out?

She shivered suddenly. What could he do but disown her, never speak to her again? She was counting on that, especially since she wasn't really his daughter. He could hardly drag her back here by force, after all.

'I shall expect you at my rooms at ten sharp,' Ernest reminded her before he left the breakfast table the following morning.

He stared at her, not moving until she said, 'Yes, Father.' She stayed where she was as he nodded, walked into the hall to don his coat and settled his hat squarely on his head. As the front door closed behind him, she slipped into the front parlour and peeped out of the window. It might be foolish, but today she needed to be certain he really had left for work. His office was so close he could walk home at any time, but he rarely did. He liked showing off his wealth by using the car. She watched the chauffeur hold open the rear door of the black cabriolet and sighed with relief as he vanished from sight beneath its hood. Even in summer he rarely drove with the hood down, because once someone had thrown mud at him.

When the car had vanished round the corner of Cavendish Terrace, she pressed her hand against her breast, because her heart was pounding furiously. Then she whirled round and ran up the stairs to finish packing the last few items into her shopping basket. As she donned her outdoor clothes, she looked round her bedroom for the last time and felt unexpectedly sad. She had slept here since she was a small child – been quietly happy here on her own, wept here too sometimes. In fact, she couldn't remember ever sleeping anywhere else since she'd turned ten, because her mother's health had prevented them from taking holidays, and anyway, her father disliked having his routines changed.

She walked slowly along to her mother's bedroom for a final farewell, but the furniture was covered in dust sheets and the familiar loving presence seemed to have vanished completely.

Taking a deep breath, she walked down the stairs, left her basket near the front door and went to let Cook know she was leaving.

'What time will you be back, miss?'

'I don't know. Probably not till the afternoon. Don't worry too much about dinner. Something light will do for me, and Father will no doubt be eating at his club again.'

She left the house, forcing herself to walk at a decorous pace along the street and up to Yorkshire Road, resisting the urge to run as fast as she could. As she'd planned, she went first to the grocer's they patronized.

The owner came across to serve her himself.

'Could you let me have my ration book, please?'

'Is there some problem with our service, Miss Fleming?'

'No. I'm going away for a few weeks, so will need to take my ration book. I don't think the rationing will stop for a while yet, do you, even though the war is over?'

'Sadly, no.'

He handed over the book but looked at her strangely as she walked out of the shop, and she knew that was because she had never gone away before.

Arriving at her father's rooms just before ten, she waited round the corner in a spot where she couldn't be seen from his window, glancing anxiously up and down the street. Where was Mr Redway? What if he didn't come? Feeling faint, she pressed her hand to her mouth. She couldn't face this on her own, just – couldn't!

Then Justin turned the corner, striding out briskly, the ends of his scarf flying in the wind behind him, his elongated face rosy with good health and cheerfulness.

'Are you feeling all right, Miss Fleming?'

'Very nervous, I'm afraid.'

'I won't let him eat you. Come on. Let's get it over with.'

He led the way inside. After a moment's hesitation she

followed, her knees feeling stiff with fear, her stomach queasy.

The elderly clerk stared in puzzlement at her companion, whom he clearly recognized. 'If you'd come this way, Miss Fleming? Your father and Mr Pearson are waiting for you. I'll be with you in a moment, sir.'

Serena set down the basket and took a deep breath. 'Mr Redway is with me.'

The clerk gave her a shocked look but said nothing, simply opening the door into the large, comfortable office and announcing, 'Your daughter is here, sir.' He stood back to let them go in.

Ernest was standing at one side of a blazing fire and Mr Pearson, their family lawyer, was at the other, chatting and smiling. They broke off to stare in shock at the man who followed her in.

Her father ignored her. 'What are *you* doing here, Redway?'

Serena summoned up the last few shreds of her courage. 'Mr Redway is here as my lawyer, Father.'

'What do you mean by that?' Ernest demanded at once. 'Have you run mad, Serena? *Pearson* is our family lawyer and you need no other.'

'I felt it better to – to have my own representation today.' She was annoyed that her voice had wobbled and betrayed her nervousness, and the annoyance stiffened her spine a little.

'You don't need representation. *I* am here to take care of your interests.' He scowled at the man behind her. 'I'm afraid your services are not needed, sir. I'll bid you good day. I regret that my daughter has wasted your time.'

'As I'm acting for Miss Fleming, only she can dismiss me,' Justin turned sideways to see if the poor woman would pass the first test, if her determination would hold firm.

'I wish you to stay, Mr Redway,' she said, her voice hardly more than a whisper. 'Please.'

He nodded and turned to face the two older men. 'It seems my client prefers me to remain with her.'

Ernest's voice cut harshly across the room. 'Serena, think what you're doing! You've been behaving very foolishly lately. Don't make matters worse.'

'I prefer my lawyer to stay.'

His face turned first red then white, his lips opening then snapping shut, pressed into a thin line as if he was forcing back angry words. The familiar sick feeling settled in her stomach and her hand went up involuntarily to her cheek. She knew that there was still a slight redness there and guessed by Mr Redway's shocked expression that he understood why.

Mr Pearson said hastily, 'Let us all be seated, then, and attend to the business at hand.' Since Ernest didn't move, he went to pull forward a chair for Serena and after a moment's hesitation gestured to another, some distance away, for the other visitor.

Justin smiled and picked up that chair. 'I think it best if my client and I sit together in case we need to confer about something.' He placed it close to hers and sat down, seeing how tightly clasped her hands were, the fine leather of her gloves creasing and straining under the pressure. He felt a sudden urge to lay his hand across hers in a gesture of comfort. You couldn't help feeling sorry for her.

Mr Pearson took charge. 'As you already know, Miss Fleming, the trust that controls your godmother's legacy ended on your thirtieth birthday, and in accordance with your father's instructions, I've drawn up some papers which will allow him to continue managing the money and properties for you and—'

Justin was pleased when she interrupted of her own accord, though her voice still sounded scratchy and hesitant.

'I'm afraid you've been misinformed, Mr Pearson. I don't – don't wish my – um, father to continue managing my money. I prefer to handle things myself from now on.'

Justin smiled at Mr Pearson and pulled some documents from his inside pocket. 'Handing things over is quite a simple matter, so I've already drawn up the necessary papers for your client to sign.'

Fleming's voice cracked out as sharply as a whip. 'Serena, have you run mad? I forbid this!'

For the first time since she'd sat down, Serena looked at him directly. 'You can't forbid it. I'm thirty years old, not thirteen.'

His tone was scathing. 'You no more know how to handle money than the kitchen cat does.'

Colour flared in her cheeks. 'I've been managing the housekeeping for years, ever since Mother fell ill, and have never overspent or made mistakes in my accounts.'

'Housekeeping! What's that to do with business affairs?' His eyes narrowed and he looked from her to Justin. 'Who's been filling your head with these strange ideas? First you vote, *against my wishes*, then you come here and say you intend to manage your own finances.' He glared at her lawyer. 'Have you been taking advantage of her ignorance, sir?'

Serena answered for herself. 'No one's been putting ideas into my head. I only met Mr Redway for the first time yesterday but I decided quite a while ago that I wished to handle my own money; only, I knew I could do nothing about that until I turned thirty, so I waited.'

When she forgot to be nervous, Justin decided, her voice was quite pleasant, low for a woman, but with a musical tone to it. Fleming leaned forward, ignoring the two men and speaking to his daughter as if she were a halfwit, which annoyed Justin.

'You should think very carefully about what you're doing, Serena. If you persist in disobeying me, I shall carry out my threat to disown you and cast you out of my life and home. And how will you manage then?'

She took a deep breath. 'I've already moved out of home.'

Justin expected Fleming to explode with rage, but he didn't. His hands quivered once on his chair arms then stilled. His face went dull red before losing every last vestige of colour, so that he looked like a marble statue, and a very forbidding statue, too. It must have been hard for a child to grow up in the charge of this man. No wonder she seemed so cowed.

'I'll give you one last chance to come to your senses.' Ernest stood up and pulled out his gold pocket watch, flicking the lid open. 'In fact, I shall give you precisely two minutes to change your mind, Serena.'

He had made such threats when she was a child and somehow she had never dared challenge him. Now, the scornful tone, the way he was treating her, only reinforced her determination to escape, and she sat very straight-backed as she told him in a voice which didn't quaver, 'I shan't change my mind. I'm definitely not coming back to live with you and I wish to control my own money from now on.'

'Then you are no longer my daughter and I wash my hands of you.' With a sense of drama which would have done credit to any actor, Fleming strode out of the room, not slamming the door behind him, but closing it gently, with a sharp little snicking sound. His footsteps thudded down the corridor and the front door of the building closed.

Then there was silence.

Mr Pearson stared at the door, mouth half open, then glanced at Serena. 'Is it wise to burn your bridges like this, Miss Fleming?'

'I don't know whether it's wise or not, Mr Pearson, but it's what I want. He isn't an easy man to live with and, if it weren't for my mother, I'd have left home years ago. He made *her* life a misery.' After a short pause, she added, 'Mine too.'

'He can be a very – difficult man to cross.'

'I shan't be staying in Tinsley for long, not once I've got my money.'

She looked as if one puff of wind would blow her away, she only came up to his shoulder and her face had betrayed how afraid she was, but it seemed to Justin that this act of defiance was one of the bravest things he'd ever seen in his life. 'My client and I had better discuss the inheritance in more detail with *you,* then, Pearson,' he said. 'And if you can't supply the answers we need, presumably you can find out from your client. If not, we'll apply to a magistrate for an order to hand over all documentation. We gather that there is an annual income of five hundred pounds. Is that all?'

'There is also some property involved.' Pearson went across to Ernest's desk and shuffled through the folder of papers. 'The details don't seem to be here, but I can check them for you when I next speak to Mr Fleming.' He frowned at the door, clearly at a loss as to how to deal with the situation. 'If I remember rightly, it was just a few workers' cottages.'

'*I own some houses?*'

Mr Pearson looked at her in surprise. 'You didn't know that?'

She shook her head. 'My father would never discuss business matters with a woman. I signed some papers when I turned twenty-one, and have seen nothing since.'

'We shall need a complete list of the property involved as soon as possible,' Justin made a note in a little black book he carried everywhere.

Pearson shot him a dirty glance then turned back to the desk, picking up a piece of paper and reading it quickly. 'When she inherited, there were seven cottages in the village of Horton. I can only presume that your father has been managing them for you, collecting rents and so on, though there are no records of those transactions here.' He frowned. 'You'll have to apply to him for current details and, of course, I presume there will be money in the bank from the years of rent payments. It should be quite a substantial sum, since it'll have been accruing interest for the past fifteen years, ever since your godmother died.'

Serena felt instantly better. It was easier to act independently when you had a comfortable sum of money behind you. She knew some women went out and earned their livings, but she hadn't been trained to do anything except manage a gentleman's household.

Mr Pearson was reading another piece of paper. 'Yes, I remember now. The end cottage is slightly larger than the others and your godmother left her former maid the use of it rent-free for as long as she lived, in recognition of her services. Your father wasn't happy about the woman occupying the house, which would have commanded a higher rent than the others, but I had to advise him that there was nothing he could do about it.' He looked at Serena again and shook his head. 'This is so *unnecessary*, Miss Fleming. Your father is a respected businessman in this town. Who better to handle your affairs?'

'I'm not acting rashly. I've been considering this for several years.'

Justin cleared his throat to gain Pearson's attention. 'It's very inconvenient that Mr Fleming walked out in the middle of our discussion. Can you find out how matters stand and get back to me later this morning? My client needs somewhere to live, and if she owns some property, that might be ideal.'

Pearson's lips curled scornfully. 'A worker's cottage? My dear fellow, it would be most *un*suitable for a Fleming. But I *will* get back to you as soon as possible. You're still in Bridge Lane? Very well, I'll send word there by one o'clock.'

They walked out, Justin picking up Serena's basket, which she would have forgotten in her agitation.

'We'll go to my office, I think, Miss Fleming. You can wait there.'

'I still need to find somewhere to sleep tonight.'

He grinned. 'My cousin Evadne won't be able to resist offering you shelter when I explain what's happened. Your father isn't liked by many people and has been particularly rude to her and her friends more than once.'

'He has?'

'Oh, yes.'

'I can't imagine him being rude to a stranger. He's normally so quietly spoken. Why was he like that with her?'

'It seems he disapproves very strongly of women voting. He not only threw things at Evadne when she was marching along the street to gain attention for the cause, but he encouraged others to do the same.'

'Oh.'

'My cousin considered her suffering worthwhile in the struggle for women to obtain the vote, but *he* made it more a vendetta, even had them thrown out of their former premises and tried to fine them for damage to the property. Fortunately, the men who moved their possessions were able to testify that all had been in order when they vacated the premises. He was clumsy with that, which surprised me, let his anger rule his common sense, I suppose. Ah, here we are.'

Justin opened the door to his rooms and led her inside. 'I'm afraid you'll have to sit in the middle room, because I have another client coming to see me soon, but I'll make sure my clerk provides you with refreshments and a copy of the *Tinsley Telegraph* to read. Oh, and the usual conveniences are out at the back.'

'Thank you. You're very kind.'

But she couldn't settle and time seemed to pass very slowly when she checked it on the little gold fob watch pinned to her lapel.

It wasn't until two o'clock in the afternoon that they heard from Mr Pearson, by which time Serena had decided to take a room in a hotel for the night, not wanting to inconvenience Miss Blair.

Justin suddenly appeared in the doorway, waving a piece of paper. 'This has come from Pearson. It doesn't contain nearly as much information as I'd expected, but it appears your father sold six of the cottages some time ago and invested the money for you. There is only one left, the one in which the maid lived until her recent death. Apparently your father is negotiating to sell it at the moment and recommends that we let the sale go through. He says he hasn't got the key, has given it to the person who's buying it, but he'll get one to us within a day or two if we need it.'

'How can he have sold the houses without consulting me?'

'You must have signed something.'

'Indeed I didn't! Believe me, I'd have remembered.'

Justin frowned at her, then pulled out his notebook and scribbled a reminder. 'I'll look into that as well, then. What about this final cottage?'

'I don't want to sell it. If it's at all suitable, I could go and live there until this is sorted out, couldn't I?'

He raised one eyebrow. 'It's only a cottage.'

'And I'm only one person. How many rooms do I need?' She smiled. 'I think I should like to live on my own for a while, very quietly, with nothing but my own needs to think about – just a daily maid to help out, perhaps.'

'Very well, then.' Justin gave her one of his mischievous looks. 'Let's go and have a look at it now. If the door is locked, there's bound to be a key on the lintel or under the doormat. There always is.'

Excitement began to curl through her. 'I'd love to do that!'

They went out and took a horse cab, whose driver agreed to stay with them for the rest of the afternoon.

'It's situated in the village of Horton, just outside town,' Justin said. 'Number seven, Lodge Lane. I've passed that row of cottages several times, but can't remember one being bigger than the others.'

Number seven was at the end of the row of seven dwellings, a two-storey place, its windows dull and its garden untended. The garden went round the side and rear as well as the front.

'Well built,' Justin said, 'and has an extra room at the rear, I see. But like the others, it needs a coat of paint and some maintenance work.'

As they walked down the path, a woman came out of the next cottage and hurried across to them. Justin raised his bowler hat, murmuring to Serena, 'Always useful to get on good terms with the neighbours. Good day to you, ma'am.'

'If you've come to see the old lady, she died two months ago.'

'Yes, we know. This is Miss Fleming, the owner.'

'I'm Mrs Diggle.' She frowned at Serena. 'They said the house had been sold to Mr Hammerton.'

'No. He may have wanted to buy it, but Miss Fleming doesn't wish to sell.'

Serena held out her hand. 'How do you do. I'm very pleased to meet you, Mrs Diggle.'

The woman looked down at her hand, which was covered in flour. 'Better not shake hands, miss. I'll only dirty your gloves.'

'Do you happen to know where the spare key is kept?' Justin asked.

She looked at him, suspicious again. 'Don't you have a door key?'

'Mr Hammerton has taken it, apparently. I'm Miss Fleming's lawyer and my client wished to see the property, so I came with her.' He fished in his pocket and pulled out a card, handing it to Mrs Diggle with a flourish.

She read it carefully before nodding, as if to say he'd passed a test. 'Well, there's a spare key on the lintel above the back door. The same one opens both the front and the back doors. I used to pop in and help the old lady out towards the end, but she didn't like to leave the front door open when she was lying in bed upstairs, so I always went in the back way and so did the district nurse.'

'You sound to have been a good neighbour.'

'It's a poor sort of person who can't help their fellow human beings.' She took a step backwards. 'Well, I'll leave you to look round, then. It's strange though, I was sure they said it had already been sold and I don't usually make mistakes. Anyway, if you need to know anything, just knock on my door.' She nodded and went back inside the house next door.

Justin watched her go with a frown. 'I'll look into the question of whether or not it's been sold, Miss Fleming. I doubt he can have legally sold it without your permission and signature.'

'He sold the other cottages. And I never signed anything then.'

'That's on my list for investigation as well, believe me.'

They walked round the back and found the key exactly where Mrs Diggle had said. Justin handed it to Serena with a flourish. 'You should do the honours.'

She turned the key in the lock and opened the door. The narrow passage revealed a coal store and a cupboard for household equipment, then led into a large scullery, where a slopstone sat under a dripping tap, and a boiler for washing clothes occupied one corner, with black marks from countless fires beneath it. From there they went into the kitchen.

'It seems still to be furnished,' Justin remarked, as they stood looking round. 'I wonder if the furniture belongs to you now?'

'That would be very convenient.'

A scrubbed wooden table took pride of place, and there were three pans hanging up, dull brasses on the wall beside the kitchen stove and dusty crockery on the dresser. It was cold inside and yet there was a cosy feel to it, as if someone had been happy here.

Serena walked through into the next room, which had an air of having been long unused, though it was furnished as a dining room. There was no corridor. It led directly into the front room, a parlour which had the main door in one corner, opening straight into a small porch. Old-fashioned furniture and ornaments filled the room so that there was only a narrow path through to the door.

When Justin joined her, he said, 'I was investigating the pantry. There are plenty of dry goods there, still in a usable state, I should think.'

'I like this house.'

He turned slowly round, examining the front room. 'Yes, so do I. Let's check upstairs.'

Upstairs proved to have three bedrooms, the front one

clearly having been used by the old lady. The bed was no longer made up but was covered by a very pretty patchwork quilt. The other two bedrooms were smaller, had ornaments sitting neatly on starched, crocheted mats on the dusty surfaces, and again, beds covered by patchwork quilts. But they felt long unused.

When they went down to the kitchen, Serena looked at him. 'I don't need to stay in a hotel when I have a whole house of my own here.'

He frowned. 'I don't think you should move in until I've sorted out the legal situation.'

She shook her head, feeling stubborn for some reason. 'There's coal and wood, so I can light a fire. I'll have to go back for my holdall and basket, and I can buy some food at the same time, then I'll spend tonight here.'

Justin tried to persuade her to wait until the next day, but she wouldn't change her mind, so he helped her to retrieve her things from his rooms and buy food, then drove back with her to Horton, just to be sure she got settled in safely. He didn't know why, but he felt uneasy about her doing this.

Serena waved goodbye to him then turned to go back into the cottage, only to find that Mrs Diggle had come out to see her.

'Excuse my asking, miss, but will you be staying here now? Only, we keep an eye on the place and we need to know.'

'Yes. And thank you for keeping an eye on things. I'm grateful. Perhaps tomorrow I can come and ask your help about where to buy my food, and so on?'

Mrs Diggle beamed at her. 'I'd be honoured to help you, miss, and if you don't think it forward of me, I'll send our Charlie across with a piece of my apple pie for your tea. I've just been baking.'

'That'd be wonderful.'

While they were talking, a cab had driven along the lane and stopped beside them. Serena looked at it, half expecting Justin to pop out again with further news. Instead, a much younger gentleman opened the door and came across to join them.

'I'm sorry to interrupt, ladies, but I wondered if you'd be interested in some apples, Mrs Diggle? Only there are more than we need at the Hall and some are still hanging on the trees.'

'I'd be delighted, sir. We don't want good food going to waste. Don't leave yet, miss!'

Serena turned round.

'This is your nearest neighbour up the lane, Mr Graye, who lives at the Lodge just now, but is moving into the Hall. Mr Graye, this is Miss Fleming, who's just moved into the cottage next to us, which she owns.'

He had been smiling, but the smile faded at the sound of her name and he inclined his head only very slightly, not moving forward to shake her hand.

Nodding in return, she went inside, weary now and too tired to puzzle over why a complete stranger would look at her so coldly.

When the door had closed behind her new neighbour, Mrs Diggle looked at Marcus and said quietly, 'Mr Redway brought her here – and he asked me to keep an eye on her, to let him know if there was any trouble.'

'You know whose daughter she is?'

She nodded. 'Yes. But I speak as I find, and let alone she came with Mr Redway, she spoke to me as civil as you like.'

'Hmm.'

'Mr Fleming owned this row of houses, all except the end cottage,' Mrs Diggle went on. 'Luckily my Harold keeps our place in good order, because *he* wouldn't spend a farthing on repairs.'

'I wonder why she's come to live here when she has a comfortable home with her father?'

Mrs Diggle shrugged. 'She'll no doubt tell me when she knows me better. People do. Would you want to live with *him*?'

'Definitely not. But then, he isn't my father.'

Four

Marcus frowned as he got out of the cab at the Lodge. 'What do you make of that – Fleming's daughter moving into a workman's cottage?' he asked Vic.

'I don't know. She doesn't look like a rich man's daughter though, does she?'

'No, anything but. Which makes it all the stranger. I don't like the man. I've met him once or twice and he's a cold fish. And it was apparently he who encouraged my cousin to gamble – and won most of the money Lawrence lost.'

'Fleming's tenants aren't fond of him, either. Pearl's parents have to do all the upkeep themselves if they want to keep their cottage watertight.'

'Well, I suppose it's no business of ours what Miss Fleming does.' Marcus looked down at his leg and frowned. 'I have to go back into town tomorrow so that the doctor can tell the district nurse how he wants her to dress my injuries. Things were more convenient when we had a doctor in the village. I'm sorry you have to keep driving me to and from Tinsley like this, Vic. I'd hoped to provide more interesting work for you.'

'As long as I'm earning money, I don't mind.' He grinned. 'At least you're more interesting to talk to than my usual passengers.'

Marcus chuckled. He enjoyed Vic's company too and felt as if they'd resumed their boyhood friendship. 'I'm looking forward to meeting your young lady tonight. After you've introduced us, I'll leave you to take her across and show her round the Hall, if you don't mind, then you can bring her back to the Lodge to discuss things – if she wishes to work for me, that is. I won't move across to the Hall until I've found some extra help. Those two elderly maids have enough on their plate looking after my aunt and I'm deeply grateful that they've been so loyal. Now, I need to sit with my leg up for a while. Though it *is* getting better, thank goodness, which is why the doctor intends to hand me over to the district nurse.'

'I'll just tie up Dolly then come and make you a cup of tea.'

'Make *us* a cup of tea.'

Vic nodded, appreciating the subtleties of that attitude, though he intended to tread carefully until he knew the other better. They weren't lads any more, after all, and the glow of wartime comradeship might wear off after a while. However friendly his manner, Marcus was from carriage folk and Vic was only a carter's son.

As he got things ready in the kitchen, he hoped Pearl would like the job that was being offered. It'd make a good start for them to move into the Hall. He reckoned Marcus would have been a good officer, you could usually tell from the way they spoke about their men. Vic was sorry he hadn't had a chance to try being an officer himself. Though if he had, he'd probably not have lasted the war. There had been a high loss rate among junior officers.

Some time later, when he heard the gate click, he went outside to see Pearl hurrying down the path. At the sight of him she ran forward to fling herself into his arms, then, as he began kissing her hungrily, she pulled away and looked round guiltily.

'What are you thinking of, Vic Scott, kissing me like that in broad daylight? We don't want Mr Graye catching us cuddling, do we?'

'He wouldn't mind. He's – different. More like one of us than gentry.'

She looked at him in surprise.

'I hope you take to him, because I think we'll do well working for him.'

'I'm not sure about the job, I will admit. I'm not going to wear silly caps and bow and scrape to the upper servants again.'

He grinned. 'There aren't any upper servants left now, and I can't imagine Marcus expecting anyone to bow and scrape to him. He's told me to call him by his first name, as I did when we were lads.'

'Well, we'll see.' She straightened her clothes and put up her hand to feel her front hair self-consciously. 'I don't feel comfortable about him seeing me like this the first time we meet.'

'No one who served during the war would be anything but grateful to women like you, who risked their own lives to keep us supplied with ammunition and shells.'

She linked her arm in his. 'Don't you believe it. I've had unkind comments about my appearance from men in uniform, complete strangers who passed me in the street.'

'If I'd been there, I'd have punched them in the face.'

'Oh, I gave as good as I got, I promise you, love. Well then, lead me to him!'

Marcus was in the sitting room, lost in thought, and it took him a moment or two to realize someone had spoken. 'What? Oh, sorry.' He pushed himself to his feet at the sight of a woman.

'This is Pearl.'

Marcus moved forward, hand outstretched. 'Pleased to meet you, Miss Diggle. I gather you and Vic are engaged to be married.'

'Yes, sir.'

'I hope you'll be very happy together. Do sit down.'

She sat on the edge of a chair. 'About the job . . .'

'I need help in the Hall. Let alone my leg isn't healed properly yet, I don't know how to cook or anything and the two maids up there have their hands full looking after my aunt and trying to keep the main rooms in order.'

Pearl looked at him with a dubious expression on her face.

'Is something wrong, Miss Diggle?'

'I worked at the Hall before the war, sir. Things were very – strict. I don't think I'd want to go back to that sort of life.'

Vic looked at her in dismay. Trust Pearl to come out with it just like that.

Marcus smiled. 'I remember only too well how things were. I got into trouble with my aunt sometimes when we went to tea there for being overfamiliar with the servants. But it's *my* house now and I shan't treat the people who work for me like that. In fact, come to think of it, you'd probably be the one in charge of the housekeeping side, because Ada looks after my aunt, and Gladys is quite elderly herself and is not the sort to take charge of anything.'

Pearl gaped at him. '*I'd be in charge?*'

'Yes, but there won't be many servants. I've been left a pile of debts and I'll need to watch the money very carefully. As I've said to Vic, I need people working there who won't mind turning their hands to whatever needs doing, whether it's turning out the bedrooms, cooking a meal or doing the shopping.'

Pearl sat straighter in her chair. 'Well now, that sounds *much* more interesting to me, Mr Graye. I've lost the habit of bowing and scraping to rich folk, I've got to admit.'

'Good. I never did want anyone bowing and scraping to me. Oh, and there are two rooms off the kitchen that you and Vic could live in. Go and see what you think of them, then come back and let me know your decision.'

Vic and Pearl walked slowly across to the big house, his arm round her shoulders, her arm round his waist. They didn't say much, were just happy to be together.

'Your Mr Graye looks tired,' she said as they approached the house.

'He's still recovering from his injuries.'

'Pity about his face. He'd be good-looking otherwise.'

'There are a lot of tired men in England just now, worn out by the war, and a lot whose bodies have been damaged.' His glance lingered for a moment on his leg. 'I reckon I'm not alone in wondering how to fit into civilian life.'

She gave his arm a quick squeeze. 'You know I don't care about your leg, but I can't see you staying a servant for ever.'

'I don't intend to. But I don't feel I have to be servile with Marcus, and I always did like him.' He knocked on the back door and heard footsteps coming towards it.

Gladys peered round the edge of it, as if nervous of who might be lurking there. 'Oh, it's you, Mr Scott. Come in. I'm just having a rest.'

He introduced her to Pearl.

She looked at the younger woman in relief. 'I'll be that glad to have some help. I can't keep up with things, and that's a fact. What has Mr Graye taken you on as – housemaid?'

'More like housekeeper cum housemaid, I think, if *you* don't want to run things.' As the other woman shuddered visibly, Pearl smiled. 'I'll do anything I need to, but I'll tell you straight out, I'm *not* wearing a silly cap and uniform.'

Gladys looked at her anxiously. 'Madam won't like that.'

'Isn't it Mr Graye who's in charge now?'

'I keep forgetting. And *she* won't admit that he owns the house. You'll find her – um – a bit difficult.'

Pearl grinned. 'Then she'll find me difficult too.'

Vic nudged her and gave Gladys one of his best smiles. 'We'll all be mucking in together, I reckon. I'll be doing anything from driving Mr Graye around to polishing the silver or digging the garden. I don't think things will ever go back to what they were before the war.'

Gladys sighed. 'You're right, I suppose. But you knew where you stood then, at least. I don't know how to deal with people now, or what I'm supposed to be doing here half the time. It's very unsettling.'

'We'll soon work out a routine for ourselves,' Pearl said.

Gladys cheered up marginally. 'A routine. Yes. That'll make things easier. So will another pair of hands. You don't . . . cook, do you?'

'Yes, actually. Just plain stuff, but I enjoy doing it. My mam's the cook, really. Everything she does tastes good. Now, Mr Graye says we can look at the rooms off the kitchen and live in them if it suits. Will that be all right with you, Gladys? You don't use them, do you?'

'Dear me, no. I'd be afraid to be on my own down here at night. They're through that door over there. Light another lamp and have a good look round.' She went to fling open a door leading to a small storeroom and gestured to a shelf of lamps, then went back to sit by the fire.

Vic lit the lamp and the two of them went through a small vestibule next to the store room and opened the heavy panelled door at the other end of it, to find themselves in a very large room. He held up the lamp and they turned round slowly, studying the place in silence.

'I never expected anything so big,' she said. 'And it's still got furniture, so we won't have to buy any. Let's look at the bedroom, then.'

This was equally large, and furnished with a very old-fashioned double bed. They stood together at the foot of it, then Vic turned her in his arms and kissed her. She put her arms round his neck and returned his embrace enthusiastically.

'We can get married now,' he said in a low, husky voice. 'How soon can you leave the munition works?'

'As soon as you like. They've told us to find other jobs quickly, said they'd let most of us go with only a day's notice. They're expecting the men who used to work there to come back to their old jobs.' She stepped back, shaking her head when he would have stolen another kiss. 'No, Vic. Not till we're married. It only gets me all het up when you kiss me like that.'

'Me, too,' he said softly, his eyes full of love.

She smiled, then took a deep breath and resumed her normal crisp tone. 'Now, when we come back tomorrow to look round the rest of the house, I'll make a list of what there is here and we'll see what else we shall need.'

'And if your parents are still up when I walk you home, I'll tell them it's time to have the banns called.'

Her hand went up to touch the ginger hair at the front. 'I'd wanted this to grow out before we got married.'

'It doesn't matter to me. You're not going to make me wait, are you?'

'No. But it'll show in the photographs. It'll look as if I'm going grey.'

'It's a badge of pride, as far as I'm concerned, that hair. Let's go and tell Marcus we're happy with the rooms.'

The following morning Serena woke with a start as someone crashed open the front door below her bedroom and men started calling to one another downstairs. She blinked in shock in the grey light of an early winter morning, then pulled on her dressing gown and picked up a candlestick to defend herself with, before rushing down to confront the intruders, who were about to carry in some empty tea chests.

'What on earth do you think you're doing?' she demanded.

They gaped at her for a moment then put down the tea

chest. One said, 'What are you doing here, miss? We've orders to clear out this house. They said no one was living here.'

She pulled the dressing gown tightly around her, only too conscious of her bare feet and dishevelled hair, which she'd been too tired to plait last night. 'Well as you can see, *I* am living here, and since I'm the owner . . .'

He looked at her scornfully. 'Don't give me that. Mr Fleming owns this cottage, only he's just sold it. And now that the old lady's dead, he needs her stuff clearing out.'

'Indeed he isn't the owner! I am. Kindly take those tea chests out with you as you leave.'

They exchanged glances. 'Can't do that,' the one who seemed to be the leader said. 'We've strict orders from Mr Hudd to have the place cleared by nine o'clock. You'll have to see him about this, so if you'll just get dressed and take yourself off, leave us to do our job, we'll say nothing about finding you here.'

'I'll do no such thing.'

His expression grew ugly and the way he looked her up and down made her shiver and take an involuntary step backwards.

'If you don't get dressed and leave, we'll put you and your things outside ourselves, and we won't be gentle about it.'

'But this is *my* house.'

'It can't be.'

'My name is Serena Fleming and my father definitely doesn't own the house, I do.' The look that had frightened her for a moment vanished abruptly from the man's face and he stared at her as if uncertain whether or not to believe her. 'Take your things and leave. I'll let my father know I sent you away, if that's what you're afraid of.'

'Even if you *are* his daughter – and I'm not so sure I believe you about that, because why would you be living here when he has a big fine house in town – you'll have to take this up with him. Mr Hudd doesn't like it if we don't obey his orders. So, if you'll please leave us to get on with our job . . .'

'I'm not going anywhere.' She backed into the house again.

'I did warn you.' He grabbed her and dumped her outside the door, banging her elbow against the door frame as she began to struggle and scream for help.

Mrs Diggle, carefully keeping out of sight of the men, nudged her youngest and bent to whisper in his ear. He set off running into the village and as she turned back to see what would happen next, her neighbours came running out of the nearby cottages and a man who'd been strolling along the lane came hurrying to join them. It was his voice which cut through the babble of exclamations and questions like a knife.

'What's going on here?'

Something about the tone of it, the sense of confident authority, made them all turn towards him. He looked at the woman standing on the path, barefoot, her hair flowing down over her shoulders, her eyes flashing with anger, and it took him a moment or two to realize who she was, so different did she look. 'Miss Fleming, can you tell me what's going on here?'

He frowned as she came to the end of her explanation and turned to the two men. 'I think you've made a mistake. And this *is* Miss Fleming.'

'Even so, Mr Hudd gave us strict orders. Clear it by nine,' he said, 'so that the new owner can take over. And we're already late.'

'There *isn't* a new owner!' Serena exclaimed. 'How many times do I have to tell you that?'

'I'm sorry, sir, but we have to do as we're told.'

Marcus went to stand beside Serena, pushing open the front door behind her. 'If you'd like to go inside, Miss Fleming . . .'

One of the men grabbed him, trying to drag him away from the door, and the other took hold of Serena's arm. As Marcus punched the man on the jaw, Serena gasped in outrage and slapped her attacker's face for him good and hard. With a growl of anger, he clouted her round the ears and drew back his hand to give her another wallop, but some of the men in the circle of people around them rushed forward to stand between him and her. Others came to stand next to Marcus as his assailant struggled to his feet and glared at him.

A voice from the distance boomed, 'Stop that at once!' and Constable Yedhill, a burly man in his sixties, came pushing his way through the crowd, panting with the effort of running from the police station a few hundred yards away in the village centre. The people who lived in the other cottages seized the moment to slip back and stand at their doors, trying to look as if they'd been there all the time. They didn't want to get on the wrong side of Fleming's men. The others, from further down the road, bunched together to watch.

'What's going on here?' the constable demanded.

One of the men pointed. 'This woman is stopping us doing our work.'

She glared at them. 'They're trying to take away my furniture. This is *my* house, Constable, and I don't know why they think they have the right to steal my things.'

Marcus watched with amazement as Serena's eyes flashed and her cheeks grew rosy with indignation. She looked like a younger sister of the prim spinster of yesterday – and a very much more attractive younger sister at that.

The constable looked from one to the other. 'Do you have any proof of ownership, miss?'

'Yes, of course I do. But my lawyer has it, Mr Redway of Bridge Lane in Tinsley.'

'I know the gentleman.' The constable scowled at the two men. 'Until I find out who's the owner, I'm ordering you to stop at once.'

'But the new owner is coming to take possession at nine o'clock,' the taller man said.

Marcus decided to intervene. 'Perhaps the best thing to do, Constable, would be to send someone for Mr Redway immediately.'

The constable nodded to him. 'Exactly what I was going to say, sir. Only, who's to go? I shall be needed to keep an eye on things here.'

'We could send Vic Scott.'

'You'll pay the cab fare, sir?'

'No need. He's working for me now. I'll go and tell him.' He nodded to Serena and walked off towards the Lodge.

She looked down and realized she was still in her dressing gown, pulling the front more tightly around her. 'Constable, will you be staying here?'

'Yes, miss.' He gave the two men a look that said he mistrusted them.

'Then I'll go inside and get dressed.'

'Certainly, miss. You'll be quite safe with me here.' As she closed the door, he went to stand in front of it, arms folded, watching the two men, who seemed uncertain what to do. He looked around to find that most of the villagers had slipped away to get about their daily business, though the women from the cottages were all standing outside their front doors still, watching with great interest.

The carriers went to lean against their cart, muttering to one another as they lit up cigarettes. Peace settled for a short time until Vic drove up in his cab.

Marcus got out and Vic drove off. 'I thought it'd be best if I came back, Constable, just in case you needed help.'

'Very thoughtful of you, sir. I appreciate that, though they haven't given me any trouble so far.'

Serena popped her head out of the door. 'Would you two gentlemen like a cup of tea?'

'That'd be very welcome, miss,' the constable said enthusiastically.

'Would you like to come inside to drink it?'

'Better stay out here and keep an eye on these two, I think.'

'I'll come inside, if I may,' Marcus said. 'I'd appreciate the chance to sit down. My leg isn't fully healed yet.' He followed her inside, surprised once again by her appearance. The dowdy woman was back, in clothes, in hairstyle and in guarded expression. If he hadn't seen the transformation for himself, he'd not have believed it possible. But he had seen it and, by hell, she was an attractive woman when she let herself go. His body had woken up for the first time in months at the sight of her flushed, indignant face, soft female curves and that mass of shining, wavy hair. He'd welcomed the revival of feeling in his lower body because he'd been rather worried about that aspect of his life.

Inside the front room she indicated a comfortable chair. 'I'll just go and make some tea.'

'I'll join you in the kitchen if I may. I'm better on a more upright chair at the moment.'

She suddenly noticed the bruise on his chin and then glanced down at his knuckles, which were grazed. The tight expression vanished and she hurried over to him.

'You're hurt!' She picked up his hand to examine it.

He felt a warmth run up his arm and she must have felt

something too, because she slowly raised her eyes to his with a puzzled look, which made him realize she wasn't used to interacting with men. Was the dowdiness used as armour to keep them away? If so, why? 'It's nothing,' he said when the silence had gone on for too long.

She let go of his hand. 'You must let me bathe that for you. We don't want it getting infected. I'll just start the tea brewing first.'

He sat down and leaned back, enjoying watching her. She had a neat way of moving, her hands sure on the teapot and kettle, though she hesitated for a moment when searching for cups.

'I'm still finding my way around,' she confessed, as if she knew what he was thinking.

'What brought you here? It's not the sort of place I'd expect to find Fleming's daughter.'

'Oh. Well. Now that I've turned thirty my inheritance has come into my own hands. Or it should have.' Her expression turned angry and her cheeks became slightly rosier. 'My father's been managing things for me and it seems he's sold the other cottages without telling me, and was about to sell this one, too. Only, I never signed anything, so how can he do that?'

'Redway will know the ins and outs of it all, I'm sure.'

'I hope so, because I've nowhere else to live and not much money.' She blushed. 'I – um – left my father's house the day after my birthday, you see. I don't – get on with him. I'm supposed to have inherited an income as well as some cottages, but I need somewhere to live temporarily. If I can't stay here, I don't know what I'll do. But I'm *not* going back to live with *him* again, not now that my mother is dead.' She hesitated and added, 'I could tell yesterday that you don't like him – not many people do, actually – and that you didn't want anything to do with me because of him. Well, I don't like him either. I just – want to go and live somewhere quiet and peaceful, make a few friends, get a dog, perhaps. I like dogs.'

He was touched by the picture she painted and by the way her voice softened as she confided these modest dreams. 'I'm sorry. I shouldn't have judged you by him.'

'Can I ask what he's done to upset you?'

'The main thing is that he encouraged my cousin Lawrence to gamble and get into debt. Who knows what else he's done, however? He has a reputation in the town for being a – difficult man.'

'Yes. Difficult to live with, too. He's always frightened me.' She poured some hot water into a bowl and brought it across to bathe Marcus's hand. She also dabbed at his forehead, an activity which brought her very close to him. He could feel her soft breath against his skin and her hands were gentle as she cleaned. He was sorry when she stopped.

'There, I think they're all right now.'

'Thank you.'

She went to pour away the dirty water. 'How do you take your tea?'

'White, no sugar.'

She nodded and began filling his cup. She seemed to be regretting her confidences, because she sat and sipped from her cup as if it was the only thing in the world she cared about, avoiding his eyes and making no attempt to speak.

He was sorry about that, because he'd enjoyed talking to her.

He was sorry for her, as well. But it wasn't his business to interfere once he'd helped get today's problems sorted out, so he too sipped his tea and let the silence flow around them. He enjoyed that. There weren't many people who could sit quietly, and not try to fill every minute with meaningless chattering.

At nine o'clock there was the sound of a carriage pulling up outside the cottage. Marcus and Serena exchanged glances and stood up. Without a word they went to the front door and saw a very shiny new motor car standing on the road outside the cottage. The chauffeur got out and opened the rear door, then a gentleman descended from it.

Marcus didn't recognize him. He was dressed like a gentleman, but his nose had been broken at some stage and he looked more like a pugilist wearing a richer man's clothes. He stared from them to the two men and their empty cart and frowned, then beckoned imperiously to Marcus, who folded his arms and stayed where he was. He wasn't at anyone's beck and call. 'Who the hell is that?' he muttered.

'Cyril Hammerton, a colleague of my father's,' she said in a low voice. 'We've had him to dinner several times. He's got a son about my age and I think he and my father hoped at one time to make a match between the two of us, but I made sure Gregory Hammerton, who's as bad as his father, didn't take to me.'

Marcus glanced sideways in surprise. 'How the hell did you do that?'

For a moment her eyes danced with mischief and the other Serena was back again, the real Serena, he was sure. 'I can be very silly and boring when I want,' she said with a smile. 'And I have a most irritating laugh.'

After a moment's hesitation, Hammerton came across to them. 'Miss Fleming.' He looked questioningly from her to the man standing beside her.

'Mr Hammerton, may I introduce Captain Graye, owner of the Hall.'

He smiled and stuck out his hand.

Reluctantly, Marcus shook it.

'I came to take possession of the cottage,' Hammerton said to Serena. 'Thought I'd find your father here ready to hand it over.'

'I'm afraid there's been some mistake. *I* am the owner of the cottage and I've no intention of selling it.'

Hammerton frowned at her. 'But you signed the contract. And I've paid over the money.'

'I didn't sign anything! Nor have I received a penny.'

'I'm afraid I have to contradict you there. I've seen your signature before and I'd recognize it anywhere. It was on the previous contract for the other cottages, which I also bought recently.'

'That wasn't my signature either. I had no idea my father was selling them and would have prevented the sale if I'd known.'

He scowled at her, but before he could say anything, there was the sound of another motor vehicle approaching and he turned round. 'Ah, here's your father now. He'll be able to sort things out, I'm sure.' He marched forward to greet his friend.

Marcus turned to Serena and saw how white she'd gone. The knuckles of her clasped hands were bloodless with pressure and her eyes shadowed by what could only be fear. 'He can't hurt you,' he whispered.

She looked at him, a pitying look as if he was talking nonsense. 'Oh, but he can. He hurts as well with words and the threats behind them as other men do with deeds.'

We'll see about that, Marcus thought as he turned back to watch Hammerton and Fleming conferring, looking in their direction from time to time. Then Fleming said something and walked across to his daughter with a disapproving expression on his face. 'What are you doing here, Serena?'

'Living in my cottage.'

'It isn't your cottage any longer. You signed the contract to sell, remember.'

He was talking to her as if she was a fool, Marcus thought as he watched them, and she was shrinking into herself, her face more like a death mask now than that of a living woman.

Her voice wobbled as she replied, 'I didn't sign any contract and you know it.'

'My dear girl, you're getting very forgetful lately, not at all yourself. Your mother's death has upset you. Come home and we'll discuss this later.'

'I'm *never* coming back to live with you!'

Fleming flushed and for a moment anger sparked in his eyes, then it was quickly veiled and his face became calm again. 'Don't be foolish. You've nothing to live on.'

'I've my inheritance! An annuity of five hundred pounds a year, isn't it? I'm not greedy. That'll be plenty for me to live on. And the income must have been accumulating.'

He sighed and looked at her pityingly, though to Marcus he looked more like a bad actor than a sincere man now.

'I'm afraid the money saved for you has been lost. An investment that went wrong. I feel dreadfully guilty about that but I'll make it up to you. And the investment company is in difficulties. But you'll never want for anything as long as you're living with me.'

There was a hidden threat behind those words, Marcus decided.

Serena stared at her father in horror. '*What?* You *can't* have lost the money from all those years! And why should an annuity fail? It's not stocks and shares, after all.'

At that moment Vic's cab came round the corner, its shabbiness in great contrast to the two motor vehicles. Redway got out of it, followed by another gentleman whom Marcus vaguely recognized but couldn't put a name to. They came across to join him and Miss Fleming.

'We'd better go and discuss this inside,' Marcus suggested.

'You're not going inside my house again without my permission,' Hammerton declared at once.

'It's not your house. I've never signed a contract for sale,' Serena repeated.

'I can prove that you have,' her father said at once, with one of his cool, confident smiles. 'I have the contract in my office. No one can doubt that it's your signature.'

She looked at him in dismay. 'Then you've forged it, because I signed nothing.'

Fleming looked at the stranger, still smiling. 'I'm delighted to see you, my dear Marley. Perhaps as magistrate *you* can persuade my daughter to be sensible.'

The stranger nodded a greeting but didn't move forward to take Fleming's outstretched hand. He took his time, looking from one person to the other, studying their faces before he spoke. 'Since there seems to be a dispute about who owns this property, I shall have to close the cottage to everyone until I've reviewed the evidence, I'm afraid.'

Serena gasped. 'But I'll have nowhere to live!'

Justin murmured, 'I'm sure my cousin Evadne will take you in.'

'Or you could come home with me.' Fleming turned to the magistrate. 'The recent death of her mother has upset her and she's behaving rather irrationally, I'm afraid.'

'I'm not behaving at all irrationally!' she said at once. 'I'm merely trying to claim my inheritance.'

Ignoring her, he looked pleadingly at the magistrate.

Marley turned to her, his polite tone in great contrast to that of her father. 'I'm afraid I really must close the cottage for the time being, Miss Fleming.'

'Then I'll need to retrieve my clothes and some food I'd bought.'

'She's not stealing any of the contents,' Fleming said at once. 'I've sold them to these men here, who specialize in disposing of deceased estates. Be reasonable, Serena! You can't possibly want the old furniture your aunt's maid left you.'

She looked at him. 'I wasn't aware she'd left me anything, had assumed the furniture must have belonged to my godmother. Why did I not hear about her maid's will?'

'You *are* getting forgetful. I showed it to you weeks ago.'

'No, you didn't! And you've given me no money for any of these sales.'

For a moment his anger showed through, then he glanced at the others. 'It's waiting for you in my bank account. Since you ran away immediately after your birthday, I haven't been able to discuss it with you.'

'Well, now you can discuss it with me,' Justin said calmly. 'In fact, since I'm her lawyer, I'll be happy to receive it on my client's behalf.'

Serena nodded. 'Thank you.'

'Go and get your things now, Miss Fleming,' Marley said with a puzzled glance in her father's direction. 'I'll have to check exactly what you're taking, though, I'm afraid.'

'I could go in and help her,' Marcus said. 'I'd be able to bear witness then as to exactly what she's packed.'

Justin looked from him to Serena and smiled. 'Thank you, my dear fellow. I'll be better employed keeping an eye on these two, in case they make any other slanderous charges against my client.'

Fleming glared at him and breathed deeply. He didn't speak but there was a lowering look behind his calm expression and a rigidity to his body which said he wasn't really as calm as he appeared.

Serena led the way inside, stopping for a moment to pull out her handkerchief and wipe her eyes. She then blew her nose and straightened her shoulders. 'I'll just go up and pack my things.'

'I think it might be best if I came with you, Miss Fleming.'

She hesitated then nodded, but when they got to the bedroom she blushed to see her underclothing scattered across the bed where she had pulled things out of her holdall when she dressed in a hurry this morning.

'It must have been hard for you growing up with a father like that,' Marcus said.

'That man is *not* my father.' Then she clapped one hand across her mouth and stared at him in consternation. 'I didn't mean to tell anyone that.'

'I'll keep it to myself, though I can't help wondering what makes you say it.'

For some reason, she felt comfortable confiding in him. 'My mother told me on her deathbed and I believed her. My real father is a man called James Lang, but her parents wouldn't let her marry him. He disappeared on the very day my mother and he had planned to run away together, so they made her marry Fleming to stop the scandal – she was already expecting me, you see. She apparently had a very large dowry.'

As she spoke she looked towards the front of the house, from where her so-called father's voice could be heard. 'I believed her. I'd always wondered why I couldn't love him – and why he was so cold towards me. It was an enormous relief to me to find that I'm not related to him, I promise you. But though he overheard her telling me, he's made it plain to me since that he still considers himself my father, I suppose because of the scandal it'd cause if people found out that he wasn't. I haven't told anyone else about this because I don't want to blacken my mother's name, and also because, if I spoke out, who knows what *he* would do?'

'You can be assured that I'll keep the information to myself. I'm honoured that you trust me.'

She began packing her things into the holdall, stopping once to say, 'And how *dare* he imply my wits are addled! As if I'd not remember signing a contract to sell the house.'

'You haven't received any money from the sale?'

'I've not even received any from my annuity for the past fifteen years, let alone . . .' Her voice trailed away and her mouth fell open in surprise as she suddenly realized something. 'That's why he wants to continue the fiction that I'm his daughter. He must have been taking my money. But why? He's a successful businessman. Why does he need my money as well?'

'He could have debts.'

'Debts?'

'From his gambling.'

She stared at him. '*Gambling?*'

'Yes. It's known in the town that certain gentlemen like to have a flutter at that club they all belong to. But it's not as well known that considerable sums of money are won and lost. My cousin Lawrence was one of those who lost. If he'd gone on playing much longer, I'd have had nothing to inherit except the care of my aunt.'

She went to fetch the rest of her clothes from a drawer, shaking her head as she tried to take in this new information. It would explain so much. Fleming's bad moods for no reason that anyone could work out. His meanness with money lately.

When she'd closed the holdall, she turned to her companion again. 'I don't know what I'm going to *do.* I've not got much money of my own, but if I go back to my former home, *he* will make my life a living hell.' She dashed away a tear with the back of one hand.

Marcus hesitated, wondering if he was being a fool, then decided he had every right to be a fool if he wanted. 'If you need somewhere to live, you can come to the Hall. There are plenty of spare bedrooms there.'

She gaped at him. 'I couldn't do that! I don't know you. And it wouldn't be – well, proper.'

'Vic's fiancée, the daughter of your neighbour Mrs Diggle, is coming to live there and could no doubt come earlier, to keep you company, if that'll make you feel safer. There are also two elderly maids and my widowed aunt at the Hall, and I'm still living at the Lodge.'

Serena looked at him, doubt warring with hope in her eyes.

'I mean it. It'll be no trouble to me and you can keep an eye on your property from there.'

'You believe me, then?'

'Oh, yes.'

'And you don't think I'm losing my wits?'

'I'm sure you're not. Just as I'm sure your so-called father is not the successful businessman he likes to appear, but a reckless gambler.'

'Thank you. I'll take you up on your offer, then.' As Serena finished packing her things, her thoughts were in turmoil. She couldn't understand why this near stranger had offered to help her, so in the end she closed the bag with a snap and asked him. 'Why?'

'Why am I helping you? Mainly because I'd help anyone who ran foul of that man, and because I believe you. There's also something else, something I've never told anyone.' For some reason he didn't mind sharing his thoughts and feelings with her. 'When I realized I'd survived the carnage of the war, I vowed to put my life to good use and to help as many people as I could. It may sound quixotic and foolish, but that's important to me after seeing so much death and destruction, so many who didn't make it, some of them no more than lads.'

'It doesn't sound silly to me. Some people would say *I'm* the foolish one, running away from a comfortable home. Only, it was more like a prison to me, a place where I had to guard every word, think carefully about every action.' Suddenly she felt hopeful again. 'Thank you, Mr Graye. I accept your offer of accommodation, but I would be grateful if Miss Diggle could come and live at the Hall too.'

'I'll arrange it. Let's go down and face them, then.'

At the foot of the stairs she paused. 'I have some food in the kitchen. I can't let it go to waste, not in times like these. Just a minute.'

She came back shortly with a shopping bag full of lumpy shapes. 'I'm ready.' But she didn't move and her face was full of apprehension as she looked at the door.

He smiled down at her. 'You'll not be alone.'

Her answering smile faded quickly, but she began moving towards the front door.

Five

When Fleming and Hammerton had driven away, Justin looked at Marcus. 'Can I get your fellow to give Marley and myself a ride back into Tinsley?'

'Of course. Vic . . . ?'

Vic looked at Marcus and said in a low voice, 'You're looking tired. Shouldn't I take you back to the Lodge first? These gentlemen won't mind, I'm sure.'

'No. I'll walk there slowly with Miss Fleming. Give us a chance to talk. You could pick her bags up on the way back, though. We'll leave them with Mrs Diggle.'

'If you're sure.'

'I am.'

Justin went over to Serena. 'Can you come to see me this afternoon? I don't think we should waste any time deciding what to do.'

'Yes, of course.' Then she turned to Marcus with a smile and he offered her his arm.

In the cab on the way back to town, Marley looked at his old friend. 'On the face of it, right is on Fleming's side.'

'On the face of it . . . but I *believe* her.'

'I do too, though I'd deny saying that. How did you come to be representing Fleming's daughter anyway?'

'Evadne brought her to see me and I couldn't resist the irony of it.'

'Bring her to my rooms this afternoon and I'll take a statement, ask her a few questions. We'll also get some samples of her signature for comparison.'

'I don't suppose you'd give me an order to search Fleming's records and accounts this very afternoon?'

'Not without good reason. After I've questioned Miss Fleming, perhaps, if I think it's warranted. He's a tricky customer and is on good terms with my fellow magistrate.'

'No one knows better than I do how tricky he is. Just keep an open mind, eh? I find Miss Fleming extremely rational, by the way. Why does he keep harping on that?'

'To discredit what she says, I suppose. Don't worry. I'll keep a very open mind.' He grinned. 'Though I never did like the man. For all his parade of wealth, he's not a gentleman.'

Left alone with Miss Fleming, Marcus looked down at her luggage. 'I'll just ask Mrs Diggle if we can leave these with her for Vic to bring up to the Hall, and also if Pearl can move in with you tonight.'

'You're being very kind.'

He picked up her two bags, but she took the basket off him and they went across together to the next cottage.

Afterwards they walked slowly along the road towards the Lodge and she could see that he was in some discomfort. Her eyes kept going to the great carved sweeps of the moors that sat watch over the village. There was dirty-looking snow in patches on the highest parts and the slopes below were wearing their dull winter colours. It must be pretty out here in summer, she thought, and closed her eyes for a moment to beg whatever fate was hovering over her to let her keep her little house, even if she lost most of her money. Above all, she needed to stay away from Ernest Fleming so that she could feel secure. Why he was trying to coerce her to go back to him, she couldn't think. Surely he didn't care that much about what people thought and said?

Or did he just need her money?

The Lodge was only about three hundred yards from the row of cottages but by the time it came into sight Marcus was looking pale so she stopped as if to look at it in order to give him a rest. 'This is your home, isn't it, the one where you grew up?'

'Yes. But it's only a house . . . not a home.'

She didn't answer but could understand that feeling all too well. 'You're looking tired. I think you should rest for a while.' It was then she noticed it: blood seeping through the grey cloth of his trousers on the right side. 'You're bleeding! Why didn't you tell me you'd been hurt?'

He looked down and grimaced. 'I didn't think it was enough to worry about. It was a deep wound and it's taking a while to heal fully.'

'I've done some first aid. Let me have a look at it.' She took his arm and he leaned on her as they walked up the path to the front door of the Lodge.

Inside, she took charge in no uncertain manner, ordering him to take his trousers off and lie down on the sofa. He hesitated because he wasn't exactly used to undressing in front of young women who weren't nurses, then that side of his body throbbed again and he felt the sticky ooze of blood, so knew he had no choice but to let her tend it. He heard her run upstairs and then she came back with a blanket to cover him.

He could tell she was trying not to show her embarrassment, but she had probably never seen a man clad only in his underwear before. Fortunately for their mutual modesty, he was wearing knee-length under-drawers of wool, not full-length pants like older men wore, so he wouldn't need to take those off to expose the wound, which was just above the knee.

She rolled up the bottom edge of his drawers with fingers that trembled a little, then checked his injuries. 'This must have been bad.'

'It was certainly deep. It's a lot better than it was.' He enjoyed watching her. She was holding her head on one side like a neat little sparrow, and she had a delightful air of earnestness that he found very attractive.

'Is it just the one place that's bleeding?'

'What? Oh, yes. Well, I think so. The others are—'

'You have other wounds? Show me.'

'I don't think they're bleeding, though they did get knocked a bit.'

She pulled the blanket off him before he could say anything else and repeated, 'Show me!'

He took off his jacket and began to unbutton his shirt. 'I'm sure these are all right. See. There's no blood on my vest.'

'It'd be sensible to check them properly.'

'Oh, very well!' He tugged up his vest and exposed the other wounds in his right side. The dressings were unmarked by blood, but that side was a mess still, not fully healed yet, with pink scars everywhere and a few scabs flaking away. Her fingers danced over his flesh, tender, light as butterflies. When she raised her eyes to his face, he waited for the look of revulsion or pity, but it didn't come. Instead she seemed thoughtful as she studied his scarred cheek.

'Your wounds seem to be healing well, and luckily for you, this time you were hit on the forehead not the cheek. I think you must have bumped the wound on your leg against something when you were struggling with that man who wanted to take my furniture away.'

'His boot.'

'He kicked you?'

Marcus nodded. It should have been embarrassing to lie here half-clad in front of a near stranger, but instead it felt comforting to have Serena tending him. Her eyes, he discovered, were beautiful, light, clear blue with a dark ring defining the border of the iris.

'But this latest injury won't have done the big wound on your leg any good. I'm so sorry you got hurt defending me.'

'I'm not. It was worth it.'

This time her glance was startled, as if she doubted her own ears, then she flushed slightly and rushed into speech. 'I think I should bathe it and put on a new dressing. It's time that is the healer in such cases, I was taught, time and scrupulous cleanliness.'

'Yes, you're right. I have some clean dressings in my drawer upstairs. Are you sure you know how to change one?'

'I did a first-aid course in '16, though I never got to use my skills, except for a short time practising in the local infirmary, because I had to look after my mother.'

'What was wrong with her?'

The words were out before she could stop them. 'Severe arthritis plus years of being married to Ernest Fleming. She was very low in spirits for the last year or two, and if I hadn't been there – well, I don't know what would have happened. Towards the end she worried a lot about what would become of me after her death.'

'With reason, it seems.'

'Yes.' It was as much a sigh as a word. 'I'll just fetch those dressings.'

He watched as she dealt with his wound, working as deftly as she seemed to do everything else. He had a desperate urge to tug the pins out of that hard little knot of hair she wore, because it had looked so pretty spilling over her shoulders this morning and it was a shame to hide it. But, of course, he didn't. 'You're good at that.'

'I wanted to volunteer for the VADs. I had it all planned, was going to apply through the Red Cross to drive ambulances in France, but *he* wouldn't let me learn to drive a motor car and he said he needed me at home to look after my mother, threatened to make her suffer for it if I left.'

'He threatened you with that?'

'Not in so many words, but that was what he meant. You heard him today, telling me that the only way I'd have any of my money would be to go back and live with him. What I don't understand is how he can legally keep it from me.' She was silent for a moment or two, then finished her tale. 'So anyway, in the end I stayed in Tinsley. All I could do to help was roll bandages and knit comforts for the troops. I felt ashamed of doing so little for the war effort.'

'You did what you could. And the scarves and comforts which women knitted and sent out were much appreciated by the men. It got very cold at times in winter. And more importantly, they showed that somebody cared. Some of them had little notes inside.'

'I used to write notes.'

'That was particularly appreciated. There were some men who never received letters from home.'

'You're being kind to me again, saying that.'

'I'm telling you the absolute truth.'

She smiled at him as she picked up the bowl. 'Then I thank you for saying it. Now, would you like me to bring you down some clean trousers so that you can get dressed again, or do you need to lie quietly for a while?'

'I'd like to get dressed.' He smiled at her. 'I feel rather at a disadvantage like this. And I'm feeling a lot more comfortable now, thanks to you. I have some other trousers in the wardrobe if you wouldn't mind fetching them for me.'

When she went upstairs, it felt curiously intimate to be going through his things, and before Serena took anything out she spent a moment looking at the neat way he had hung his clothes, all the shirts together – two jackets, some trousers, and his uniform – all arranged by length when hung up. The civilian clothes dated from before the war, judging by the styles. She found some brown trousers and took them down to him. 'Will these do? They'll match your tweed jacket nicely, so I brought it as well.'

'They'll do fine. Thank you.'

She edged towards the door, looking embarrassed now. 'I'll just go and tidy up the kitchen.'

* * *

He was dressed before she came back, so he went to stand in the kitchen doorway. Before he could say anything she turned and jumped in shock at the sight of him, putting one hand to her breast.

'Sorry. I'm enjoying watching you.'

She stared at him as if he'd spoken in a foreign language.

'You work very neatly. I noticed that at your cottage. It's – attractive.'

Colour flooded her cheeks and he felt guilty for embarrassing her, but she was smiling as well as blushing, so he smiled back. When he realized they'd been standing there for a while without saying anything, he forced himself to break the silence. 'I'm ready to take you across to the Hall now and help you choose a bedroom. This afternoon I'll come into Tinsley with you, if that's all right. I'm supposed to see the doctor and the district nurse, who's going to come regularly to change my dressings, and you need to consult Mr Redway.'

'Yes. Though I could change your dressings for you.'

He watched her look down for a moment, frowning and biting the corner of her mouth, and had a sudden inexplicable urge to kiss those soft pink lips, an urge that startled him. It took him a moment to realize she had spoken and was waiting for an answer. 'Sorry. What did you say?'

'I could do that from now on, if you like. Change the dressings, I mean. If I'm living at the Hall, it'd be more convenient than the district nurse cycling out there, surely?'

'You wouldn't mind?'

'No. It'd be good to put my skills to use, even if the war *is* over now.' Her father would have a fit if he knew about this, and even her mother would have said it was unseemly for a single woman to see a man's body, but Serena didn't care. It would be good to be able to help Marcus in return for her accommodation, and he must have had a beautiful body before his injuries, like those of Greek statues she'd studied in books, well muscled but lean.

She stopped to stare as they went through the kitchen garden. 'How pretty the Hall is!'

'Haven't you been out this way before?'

'No. We didn't go out of town much.'

'Not even for holidays?'

'He didn't like going on holiday, or so he said, but that didn't stop him going off alone for weekends in London.' She gave a short, scornful laugh. 'Those were our holidays, the times he was away. Everything felt so much more comfortable. Even the servants seemed more at ease.'

It occurred to him that her situation had been far worse than his, because he'd only had to face indifference, not hostility and bullying, and that made him wonder what her real father had been like, why he had left so suddenly. Had James Lang run away – or had he been forcibly removed? They would never know now.

Marcus opened the kitchen door, explained briefly to Gladys what was happening, and took Serena upstairs to choose a bedroom. As they reached the top of the stairs, Ada came out of the corridor leading to his aunt's room, so he explained once again what he was doing. 'Do you think my aunt would like to meet Miss Fleming?'

Ada put her head on one side, screwing up her mouth as she tried to work this out, then shaking her head. 'It'd be better if I told her about it, and then if she wants to meet Miss Fleming, she can ask. Pearl Diggle's coming to stay here as well, you say?'

He nodded. 'Yes. We don't want people getting the wrong impression about Miss Fleming.'

The elderly maid nodded approval. 'I'll get on with my work then, sir, and leave you to it. Mrs Lonnerden wants something to eat today, which I take to be a good sign. And I'll give the bedroom you choose a good going-over later, miss.'

'Thank you.' Serena chose a room at the front of the house, one looking out over a very neglected formal garden. 'This must have been beautiful when you had the staff to look after things.'

'I lived in the Lodge and rarely came here. I didn't get on with my cousins, you see, and after I went to boarding school, I didn't always come home for the holidays. Not if my father was going away himself.'

'You must have been very lonely,' she said softly. 'Oh, sorry! I shouldn't make such personal remarks.'

'I don't mind. And yes, I was lonely. You probably were

too.' He watched her nod. 'But there are worse things than loneliness.'

She shuddered slightly. 'Yes indeed.'

But she didn't tell him any more about her life and he didn't press the point. He'd find out, he was sure. Fate seemed to have pushed them together and he liked being with her. But he wished she'd take down that damned bun and wear nicer clothes. When she'd been defying the two men, she'd seemed quite slender. With her clothes on she seemed – lumpy.

It was all very intriguing. He didn't know when a woman had last interested him so much.

That afternoon Vic drove them into Tinsley, dropping Serena and Marcus off at the end of Bridge Lane and going to wait for them in his usual place.

She walked slowly up the hill towards her lawyer's rooms, enjoying the feeling of freedom and being outside, with no need to go back *there* spoiling her pleasure. She turned before she went inside, to see Marcus still watching her from the bottom end of the narrow street, so waved again. He waved back and smiled. It made him look very attractive, that smile did. She felt warmed by it as she went inside.

Justin must have been waiting for her, because he came out of his room even before the clerk had time to let him know she was there. At the sight of his worried expression, her heart began to thump. 'What is it? I can tell something's wrong.'

'We've got an appointment to see Marley, so I'll explain on the way.'

As they were striding briskly up Bridge Lane towards the main street, he said abruptly, 'Marley has the contracts you're supposed to have signed. He wants to take a few samples of your signature, then he'll show them to us.'

'Oh.'

'You're sure you didn't sign anything at all?'

'Certain. My father wouldn't even discuss my inheritance with me, let alone show me any papers. I gave up trying. He could make things . . . uncomfortable if you displeased him.'

'Yes, I'm sure he could.'

They were shown in straight away to see Mr Marley. He studied Serena quite openly. 'How are you feeling now?'

'Very annoyed.'

'No headaches or dizziness?'

She looked at him in puzzlement. 'No, of course not. Why do you ask that?'

'Your father claims you haven't been well since your mother died.'

'Oh. I pretended to have influenza, but I wasn't actually ill. I just wanted to avoid seeing him until after my birthday, because he kept insisting I give him my mother's jewellery to look after. She left it to me, you see. So I took the line of least resistance, I'm afraid.'

'Did anyone else know you were only pretending to be ill?'

'One of the maids, Ruby. But she'll lose her job if we involve her, so I don't want to do that.'

'We may have to. Your father's claiming you need looking after, that you're . . . not yourself.'

'Looking after?'

'In a mental hospital.'

She gasped in shock as this sank in, and it was followed by a shiver of fear. But she felt indignant, too, and that helped her to answer steadily, 'I'm more myself than I have been for years.'

There was silence, then Mr Marley pushed a piece of paper towards her. 'Could you give me several copies of your signature, please? One underneath the other would be best, on alternate lines.'

She took the pen he was offering, an elegant, gold-plated fountain pen, and began to sign her name. When she'd finished she pushed the paper towards him without a word.

He looked at it and blew out a little puff of air, as if disappointed, then turned another piece of paper over and pushed it towards her and Justin. The contract. They studied it in silence, but there was only one conclusion to be drawn.

'It looks exactly like my signature,' she said. 'Only, I know I didn't sign this.'

'It's been witnessed, too. By his clerk, Hudd.'

'Hudd isn't his clerk, he's his right-hand man. He'll do anything for Fleming.' She bit her lip, determined not to break down in front of them, but she felt like weeping. Fleming had been so clever, must have practised her signature to get it so close.

'We're not conceding that the signature is hers,' Justin said, 'but in case we can't prove that, what about the money, both from the sale of this last cottage and from the others, as well as the income from the annuity for the past fifteen years? Can you get that for her?'

Serena looked at the magistrate. 'He told me he'd invested the money from the sale of the other cottages – which I also didn't agree to sell – and presumably the income from the annuity over the years. I've received nothing. He said the investment had turned out to be a bad one and he'd lost all my money.'

Marley frowned. 'He said that? When?'

'This morning. Captain Graye was there. He can confirm it.'

The magistrate looked at Justin. 'I can definitely give you an order to view his account books and records, then. You'll want to make sure of this for yourself.'

'Thank you, Gerald. Can you do it now? I'll serve it on him first thing tomorrow morning.'

'Right. If you'll wait a moment or two, I'll have it drawn up.' He rang a hand bell and gave some quiet orders to his clerk, than looked back at Serena. 'I'm sorry, Miss Fleming. I'm afraid there's nothing else I can do for the moment to help you. Are you all right for money and somewhere to stay? Good, good . . . Now, I have another piece of business I need to discuss with Mr Redway. I wonder if you'd mind sitting in my waiting room for a few minutes?'

She went outside to sit in an armchair stuffed with horsehair, which might be hard-wearing but was prickly to sit on. Her thoughts were just as prickly.

Justin came out to join her ten minutes later. 'Sorry to keep you waiting. Will you come back to my rooms for a few moments? There are a few bits and pieces we need to sort out, and I need your signature on a couple of letters giving me complete authority to act on your behalf. My clerk can witness them.'

'All right.' She felt strange and distant, so upset about the way things were turning out that she could have lain down and wept. She was quite sure her so-called father had stolen the money from the row of cottages, not to mention the annuity money, and didn't know what she was going to do if she had no income. But after years of long practice at holding in her feelings she didn't give way, just concentrated on walking beside Mr Redway, setting one foot in front of the other until the turmoil of fury and disappointment inside her had settled down a little.

At Justin's rooms he quickly wrote two letters of authorization and she read them through carefully before signing them in front of his clerk. Then he asked for more sample signatures, in case he needed them, so she wrote another column of them on a clean piece of paper. Again, this was witnessed by the clerk.

After agreeing to do nothing until she heard from him, she took her leave.

He came to the door. 'I'll escort you back to join Vic and Marcus.'

'No need. Vic is waiting with the cab at the bottom of the street, and it's only a short stroll.'

Justin escorted her to the door, went inside again and couldn't resist peering out of the window just to make sure she was all right. She'd looked so pale, her whole body stiff with disappointment, but she hadn't complained once. You had to admire her fortitude. As he watched, he saw a man who'd been lounging in a doorway across the road move out of it and follow her. There could be no doubt of what he was doing because his eyes were fixed on her with a kind of gloating look, and anyway she was the only other person in that part of the street.

Suddenly feeling more than worried, Justin rushed out of the door, by which time she'd turned the corner at the bottom of the street and the man had speeded up to run round it after her.

Just as Serena rounded the corner at the bottom of Bridge Lane, a large motor car pulled up and Fleming jumped out. Without a word he grabbed her arm and tried to drag her into the back of the vehicle. The chauffeur sat looking straight ahead, as if nothing untoward was happening. Serena began to struggle and call for help, scratching and kicking.

A passer-by hesitated and Ernest yelled, 'She's my daughter and she's lost her senses. Stay away. She's dangerous.'

The man walked on, shaking his head, even though Serena yelled, 'It's not true! *Help me*!' She bit the hand Ernest tried to put across her mouth so hard that he yelped.

Then someone yanked her head back by the hair, growling, 'Shut up, you stupid bitch!' and she saw out of the corner of her eye that Hudd had joined them. He and Fleming tried to shove her into the car, but she managed to slow them down by bracing her feet against the running board and screamed again.

Suddenly Justin appeared beside them, yelling, 'Let her go!' Hudd muttered a curse and shoved him back so hard he fell over, but by then Vic had reached them and he squared up to the bigger man.

The latter grinned. 'I can deal with these two, Mr Fleming. You get your poor deranged daughter home again.'

Then Marcus appeared, thrusting past Hudd to drag Serena from her father's grasp. 'What the hell's going on?' He pushed her behind him and braced himself, raising his clenched fists as if expecting a fight.

'I'm trying to rescue my daughter,' Ernest said, his voice as cold and chill as ever, 'before she does herself harm. And *you,* Graye, are interfering in something that doesn't concern you.'

Justin was on his feet by now and went to stand beside Marcus, straightening and dusting off his clothing. 'You were trying to kidnap her. We intend to make a complaint to the police about that.'

'You'll leave well alone if you know what's good for you, Redway!' Ernest's gaze went to Serena. 'Look at her! She acted like a wildcat just then, as my two men will bear witness. That's not reasonable behaviour.'

'Only because of what you were doing,' she said.

Justin made a sign to her to be quiet and said in a more normal tone of voice, 'Miss Fleming is my client and she's of age, not a child under your control. What you were doing was illegal – *sir.*'

'She's clearly lost her senses, and since she's *my* daughter, it's only right that I look after her – as the court will agree. After all, there is no one else to do it. And since I'm taking her to see our doctor, you can hardly call it kidnapping.'

Realizing she'd been cowering against Marcus's chest,

Serena pulled herself together, sucking in a shuddery breath then straightening her shoulders. 'I would never have believed that even you would treat me like that,' she told Ernest, her voice steady and her tone as icy as his. 'You know perfectly well there's nothing wrong with me. Shame on you!' She turned to the three men who had saved her and said, 'Thank you for your help, gentlemen.'

'You should sue him for assault,' Justin pointed out.

'I just want him to leave me alone!' Her voice wobbled in spite of her efforts to stay calm.

'We'll take out a magistrate's order to make sure he does,' Justin promised. He looked at Vic. 'You saw what they were trying to do. Will you testify to that?'

'I'd be delighted to.'

The look Fleming gave him said he'd regret that.

Vic looked back at the older man and said pointedly, 'I didn't fight for the freedom of our country during the war to stand by and let things like this happen in England itself. No threats will stop me testifying.'

Fleming brushed his hands down the front of his coat. 'I don't know what you're talking about. I haven't threatened you in any way. I'm simply a father, that's all, doing the best I can for my daughter.' He smiled then, a cruel curve of thin lips that made Serena's blood run cold. 'And as her closest living relative, I have certain rights in that respect once I've proved my point . . . which I shall do very soon. This matter is only postponed and you know it, Redway. Serena, you've already made a big mistake in leaving the security of your home, don't compound it.' He got into the car, gestured to Hudd to join him, and they drove off.

Serena let out a long, shuddering breath and Marcus turned to her, offering his arm. 'I think we'd better get you home, Miss Fleming. Vic, will you fetch the cab?'

'Yes, of course.'

Justin looked from one to the other. 'He *has* got certain rights as your father, or would have if you were proven to be of unsound mind.'

'But I'm not!'

'Doctors have been bought before. And he's very friendly with Tolson.'

She felt as if the earth were shaking beneath her feet. 'What am I going to do then?' she whispered. 'I have no other close relatives and very little money to hand. If he can have me locked away, he'll be able to take everything I own.'

'Why should he want your money so badly?' Marcus asked. 'Have you any idea, Serena?'

'No. He always seems to have plenty of his own. Unless it's what you told me before, the gambling.'

Justin looked from one to the other. 'It's well known that a lot of money has changed hands at the club in the past year or two. There were some members who wanted that looked into, then suddenly they stopped agitating. I wonder . . .'

'He'll have threatened them,' Serena said in a flat voice. 'I've overheard him boasting that he always gets what he wants. He doesn't do it in an outright way, but he makes sure people are afraid for something or someone they value.'

'What if he's been losing heavily?' Marcus asked. 'You told me you had an annuity that brings in five hundred pounds a year. He could sell that or use the income from it. It all depends on how desperate he is. And if he *is* desperate, you're in real danger.'

Justin was looking from Marcus to Serena, but they didn't seem to be aware of him, were staring at each other as if they were alone. He smiled and then had to clear his throat to gain their attention. 'There's one sure way to make sure he can never get his hands on her.'

'What?' Serena asked eagerly. 'Whatever it is, I'll do it.'

'If you were married, your husband would be your next of kin, not Fleming.'

'Oh.' Her eager expression faded and she looked down at herself with a scornful laugh. 'Who'd marry me? I've worked all my life to be plain and unattractive, not to mention boring.'

Justin looked at Marcus and raised one eyebrow.

Marcus stared back, his mouth falling open in shock as he realized what the other man was hinting. Then he looked at Serena, remembering how she had nestled so comfortably against him, how attractive she looked with her hair loose, how his body reacted to her. He too smiled, then nodded at the other man as if accepting his challenge.

'It'd need to be done quickly,' Justin warned.

Serena looked from one man to the other, puzzled by their expressions.

Marcus took a deep breath. 'In that case, perhaps you would consider marrying me, Serena? That should keep you safe.'

She gasped in shock and had to clutch him to keep her balance. '*Marry you?*'

'Yes.'

'But – we hardly know one another. We only met yesterday. And besides . . .' He was a kind person and she liked him, but all her worries about a loveless marriage came rushing back at her. She looked desperately from one man to the other, trying to explain. 'I always swore I'd only ever marry for love. My mother was so unhappy. Though I'm grateful for your offer, Mr Graye, of course I am.'

'Well, I don't blame you for refusing me. I'm not much of a catch now.' His hand went up in a gesture that took in his scarred face.

Her voice softened. 'It's got nothing to do with your face. What does that matter? Those scars were gained in defence of your country, they can be worn with pride.'

'They'd matter to some women.'

She felt torn both ways, wanting to reassure him and yet afraid she'd be tempted into accepting him. 'Not to me.'

Justin said, 'I don't think you have much choice but to find someone to marry, my dear.'

Fear warred with temptation and won. 'Could I – take a few days to think about it?'

'I doubt you have that long, Serena.' Justin looked from one to the other. 'You've just seen the lengths your father will go to and—'

So she told him. 'He *isn't* my father!'

Justin gaped at her. 'What do you mean by that?'

She explained.

'Good heavens! But can you prove it?'

She thought for a moment then shook her head. 'No. I know my mother wouldn't lie to me, though, not when she was dying.'

'Then that information is no help in your present dilemma, though it must be a great comfort to you, knowing what he's like.'

'Yes.' She turned to look at the man beside her. 'You must think I'm being very foolish, Marcus.'

'No, I don't. It's a big step. But I really would like to marry you.'

'You would? Why?'

His solemn expression softened into a smile, 'Because you make me feel like a man again, which I haven't for months. Because you're pretty – or you could be. Because . . . I'm lonely.'

'Oh.'

She didn't know what to say, couldn't think straight, because she had suddenly realized that she rather liked the idea of marrying him. Any woman would. He was attractive, even with the scars and beard. And he was kind, too. That was so important.

'I won't conceal from you that your annuity would make a big difference to me, but if it'll make you feel any better, I'd agree to postpone consummating our marriage until we knew one another better and *you* felt the time was right.'

She could feel herself blushing and was grateful when neither man spoke for a moment or two, as she tried desperately to think about Marcus's offer. She thought he would make a decent husband, but how did you know for sure? And if she didn't have to go straight into his bed, could first get used to her new self and life, to being with him . . . Suddenly the woman who had voted, who had planned an escape from Ernest Fleming's clutches, who had been hiding behind a mask for so many years, urged her to take a chance, perhaps the only real chance she'd get, of staying free of Ernest Fleming. The words were out before Serena had even realized she was going to say them. 'Thank you, Marcus, and – and I will marry you under those conditions, if you'll agree to be patient with me.'

Justin stepped forward and gave them each a big hug. 'Excellent. This might sound silly, but I feel you two will suit one another. Now, we need to arrange for a wedding. By special licence, I think. Don't want to give Fleming a chance to get up to more of his nasty tricks, do we? We'll get the licence tomorrow, Marcus.'

'Yes.' He turned to Serena. 'Here comes Vic. Let's go home now.'

Home, she thought, and it seemed as if the day was much brighter suddenly. Whatever happened about her inheritance, she would have a home again. And a husband to share it with.

She sat next to him in the cab as it pulled away, staring down at her tightly clasped hands, feeling shy now.

'You're sure about it?' he asked. 'I don't want you to feel forced into doing something you'll regret.'

She looked up then, and it was the way his eyes crinkled at the corners with the faint hint of a smile, the innate kindness and warmth of the man that clinched the matter for her, because Fleming was so cold. 'Yes, I'm sure.'

'Then allow me to do something I've been itching to do since early this morning.' He reached out to her shapeless felt hat, which was jammed down nearly to her eyes, removed it carefully and pulled the pins out of her bun, one by one.

She couldn't move, could only sit there feeling tingles run through her when he touched her, feeling breathless, feeling . . . wonderfully alive in a way she had never experienced before. A man's touch, she thought. I never realized what it can do to you.

He fluffed out her hair over her shoulders, leaned back and studied her, head on one side, smiling slightly. 'There. That's much better. Will you promise me one thing?'

She nodded.

'That you'll never wear your hair like that again.'

'That's an easy thing to promise. I've hated wearing it like this. It was just – wiser. Or he'd have married me off to someone of his choosing.'

'And your clothes? They were deliberately selected to make you look plain and lumpy, weren't they?'

'Yes.'

'We'll have to get you some new ones as soon as possible. These do the job only too well. If I hadn't seen you this morning, I'd not have realized what you can look like.'

He reached for her hand and she let him take it, feeling a little shy. His skin was warm, his grip was strong and her hand felt so *right* in his.

'I think we'll do well together, Serena,' he said quietly, raising her hand to his lips and pressing a kiss against it.

She closed her eyes for a moment as heat flooded through

her body. But she wasn't going to be passive about their marriage, she decided, so opened her eyes again and said firmly, 'It won't be my fault if we don't get on well. I'm not . . . quarrelsome.'

'You're brave and honest and pretty. Good qualities in a wife, I think.'

They sat quietly for the rest of the journey, but when they arrived at the Hall he grew thoughtful. 'I think we should bring in reinforcements, Serena. I intend to keep you very safe until we're married.' He was sorry to see all the pretty colour drain from her face.

'You think he'll – try something else, then?'

'I think he's desperate, my dear. I'll come and sleep at the Hall tonight and ask Vic to do the same.'

'People will talk if you're sleeping there before we marry. You know what they're like in small towns. And there are one or two ladies in Tinsley who can be quite vicious about such things.'

'It's your safety I'm thinking of. To hell with the gossips.'

'Fleming will hardly break into your house to kidnap me! He's more likely to hammer on the front door with a doctor by his side and demand to see me, surely? In which case, I can run out of the back.'

'I suppose so. And there are the two maids and Mrs Lonnerden living there. Look, I'm only a couple of hundred yards away at the end of the drive. I'd hear if there were trouble. In fact, they'd have to pass my house. Maybe if you were to share the bedroom with Pearl . . . ?'

'Yes, I'll do that, I promise.'

'All right, then. And in two days' time at most, we shall be married.'

Her heart started to beat faster at the thought. Married! It was such a momentous step to take, marrying someone whom she'd only just met. But it was a wonderful chance to have what other women had, what she'd been secretly longing for – a home of her own, a husband and children. Surely that wasn't too much to ask?

Six

Vic took Pearl and her things to the Hall after work and she insisted on sitting with him on the driving seat of the cab, even though that was a bit of a squash. As Dolly clopped along at her own pace, he explained in detail what had been happening.

She stared at him in the moonlight, her eyes sparkling with excitement. 'You're afraid her father will try to kidnap her and lock her away? It sounds like one of the stories I read.'

'Well, I heard Fleming myself. He as good as admitted that was what he'd intended to do when he tried to abduct her, though of course he pretended it was because she was mentally confused. If we hadn't been there, he'd have succeeded, too.'

Pearl was silent for a moment or two. 'What's he like, your Mr Graye?'

'Marcus. He says we should call him Marcus.'

'Funny sort of employer, using first names.'

'Funny sort of world, now.' He glanced down at his artificial leg with a bitter twist of the lips. 'Anyway, you've already met him.'

'Only once. You've spent a few days with him, so I wondered what he's really like, underneath it all?'

'Kind. Sad sometimes. Still coming to terms with what he looks like now. I catch him staring at his face in mirrors and fingering that cheek. He's not afraid to stand up to people, though, and fight too, if necessary, even though his injuries aren't fully healed. I respect that, respect him. I liked him when we were lads. He was quiet, but straight as a die.'

'What made him ask Miss Fleming to marry him, do you think?'

'Who knows? It's partly the money, I suppose. She gets five hundred pounds a year, inherited from her godmother.'

'That's a horrid reason for being married. I'd say no if I were her.'

'Not if the alternative was to be stuck in an asylum, you wouldn't.'

She was silent for a moment. 'It's like something you read about in *Pearson's Magazine*.'

He grinned at her and began to rein the horse in. 'You and your adventure stories.'

'I like reading them, especially stories about poor girls standing up to evil men and winning. Hang on, I'll jump down and open the gates.'

She'd jumped off the high cab seat before he could stop her, which gave him an anxious moment, but she'd always been nimble and better than most lads at climbing trees. She opened the gate and he told Dolly to walk on, then watched as Pearl rode the gate shut before fastening it carefully. When he was sure she was all right, he got down more carefully. He'd never again be able to leap around as she did, and that knowledge hurt sometimes, though he didn't let it get him down. 'I'll take you up to the house, then come back and unharness poor old Dolly.'

'I'll do that for you, Vic lad.' Hill came forward out of the shadows, hobbling because he was twisted with rheumatism. He hung his lantern on a wall hook and came across to the cab.

'Thanks.' Vic gave his horse an affectionate slap and lifted down Pearl's bag. Hill knew more about horses than anyone he'd ever met and, if the old man worked more slowly now, he still did things properly and Dolly was very fond of him.

Inside the house they found Serena in the kitchen, stirring something in a pan and peering into it with a dubious expression.

Vic stared in surprise at her hair, which was tied loosely back with a black ribbon and made her look very different; then he realized he was staring and tried not to. 'Good evening, Miss Fleming. Here's my Pearl come to stay with you.'

'Good. Um – you don't know anything about cooking, do you, Pearl? Gladys has a sick headache and she's gone to lie down. She looked dreadful, poor thing. And Ada's busy with old Mrs Lonnerden. This stew was half-cooked, so I said I'd keep an eye on it, but it doesn't look very appetizing. I've only ever watched people cook before so I'm not quite sure what to do to improve it.'

Pearl's eyes lit up. She came forward to stand next to Serena and inspected the bubbling mixture. 'She didn't brown the onions and meat first, just boiled everything up. Here, you keep stirring so it doesn't catch, and let me have a look what they've got in the pantry. I love cooking.' She picked up one of the two lamps that had been lit, because they hadn't got gas lighting out here, leaving half of the huge kitchen in shadow, and went across to explore the pantry. But to her surprise the shelves were mainly bare, only those near the door containing anything. 'Aha!' She pounced on something and came out waving it triumphantly. 'Penny cubes. Don't know what we'd do without them now.'

Vic smiled reminiscently at the sight of the bright red and white tin. 'They were wonderful during the war, made a real treat to drink if you could get hold of some boiling water.'

'Did they send things like this out to the troops then?' Serena asked in surprise.

'Oh, yes. We all looked forward to receiving those little red and white tins with our rations. I even knew one chap whose life was saved by his Oxo tin.'

'Go on!' Pearl scoffed. 'You're having us on.'

'No, really. He had it in his breast pocket and it deflected a piece of shrapnel that'd have gone straight into his heart, the doctor said. My friend carried that tin with him everywhere after that, said it was his lucky piece.'

'Well, I never! And did he survive the war?'

'I don't know. I copped mine soon after and was shipped back to Blighty.'

He sat astride a chair exchanging banter with Pearl and politer remarks with Serena until Marcus came to join them, followed by Ada wanting food for her mistress.

'We'll save yours,' Pearl called as the maid carried out a beautifully set tray containing only a small bowl of stew and a thin slice of bread.

The four of them sat down to eat in the warm glow of the lamps and the fire. The food was a definite improvement on the pallid mess Pearl had found, and the men augmented their portions with chunks of rather solid bread.

'Was this baked by Gladys too?' Pearl asked with a grimace as she hacked through the heavy loaf to give Vic another slice.

Marcus looked up, spoon poised near his mouth. 'She doesn't pretend to be a trained cook, she's just doing her best.'

'I could take over the cooking if you like,' Pearl volunteered.

'That'd be wonderful. Someone had better go up and see how Gladys is as soon as we've finished eating.'

Ada came in as he was speaking, carrying the tray with an empty bowl on it. 'I looked in on her and she's all right, sir. She'll sleep for a few hours and then she'll be better tomorrow. She has these bad heads regularly, poor thing.' She took the tray into the scullery. 'That's the first time madam has eaten all her supper. I told her Miss Diggle cooked it and she wants to meet her and Miss Fleming tomorrow. She's not happy at having people she doesn't know living in her house, but the stew helped. She used to enjoy her food until Cook died.'

'It's *my* house now, Ada,' Marcus corrected quietly.

'I know that, sir, but you'll never change her.'

Pearl got up and served the maid a bowl of stew. Ada sat down, looking uneasy in such company.

'Eat up,' said Marcus. 'You've earned it. And no one has time to set a table for me and Miss Fleming in another room, so you'll have to put up with our company.'

'Yes, sir.'

After the meal, they went in search of a suitable bedroom and both Pearl and Serena agreed on one at the front of the house.

After he'd helped carry the women's luggage up, Vic hesitated and looked at his fiancée. 'Are you sure you two will be all right?'

'Of course we will,' Pearl scoffed. 'No one's going to break in and kidnap us, are they? I know the difference between real life and stories, my lad. But if it makes you feel any better, I promise we'll lock our bedroom door.' She turned to see Marcus speaking quietly to Serena and whispered, 'I think he really likes her. It's not just her money he wants.'

He followed her gaze and smiled. 'I think you may be right.'

But as he and Marcus got ready to leave the house, he felt uneasy. 'I don't like leaving them here on their own, Marcus.'

'No. I don't either. But I'm trying to avoid gossip by sleeping at the Lodge. You know what people are like. Serena's got enough trouble on her plate without falling foul of those old biddies in town.' He went across to a rack of keys and took the spare one for the back door, locking the latter carefully behind them and slipping the key into his pocket.

When they got to the Lodge, Vic hesitated. 'If it's all right with you, I'll stay here tonight, just in case. I don't know why but I feel – well, worried.'

'So do I.' Marcus stared towards the darkened mass of the big house. 'For two pins I'd go back there again.'

'That might frighten them now.' Vic shrugged. 'Ah, he won't come after them during the night, not if he's got a doctor ready to swear Serena's lost her wits. And we can run across in a couple of minutes if they need us. I'll sleep down here on the sofa.'

'We'll both sleep down here,' Marcus corrected, and brought across a footstool, setting it in front of the big armchair. 'I'll just fetch some blankets.'

'I'll go. You need to rest that leg. And I'll keep first watch, eh?'

In the middle of the night Serena woke with a start. She was a light sleeper and was sure she'd heard a door bang somewhere. She listened intently, her heart beating fast, and it seemed to her that she could hear faint noises from inside the house. If the door banging hadn't woken her, she'd have thought nothing of the noises – and indeed this would probably turn out to be a false alarm. But thinking of Fleming's ruthlessness, she decided it was better to be safe than sorry and nudged Pearl awake, whispering, 'I may be worrying about nothing, but I'm sure I heard someone moving around downstairs.'

Pearl sucked in her breath. 'If we hear anything else we'll get up and dress. No one's catching me in this old flannel nightdress. Why my Mum packed this one, I don't know.'

They went to listen at the door. A stair creaked, then another.

'There *is* someone,' Pearl gasped. Without speaking, they

flung on their clothes anyhow, then she went to look out of the window, muttering in annoyance as the moon went behind the clouds. 'I reckon I could climb down that drainpipe and fetch Vic.'

Serena went to stand next to her and, as the moon emerged from the clouds, she could see the nearby drainpipe clearly. It looked very thin and the ground seemed a long way below them.

Suddenly a woman's voice cried out and cut off abruptly from a room in the other wing.

'That's Mrs Lonnerden!' Serena said.

'They're checking all the rooms.' Pearl tied the laces of her shoes and flung the window wide open. She slung her legs over the sill then swung sideways to the drainpipe with an ease Serena envied. It didn't seem to take her a minute to climb down to the ground, from where she beckoned vigorously.

Serena gulped then, as footsteps came towards the bedroom, no doubt drawn there by the noise of the window opening, she too climbed out. The drainpipe moved to and fro under her weight, as if one of the wall attachments was loose, and she couldn't hold back a moan of fear. She heard someone yell 'Come out of there!' and bang on their bedroom door as she inched her way down. Sweat started on her brow and terror shivered through her each time she had to let go with one hand to move lower. Once her foot slipped and when later the same foot jarred on something, it took her a minute to realize she'd reached the ground.

'You're down,' Pearl whispered. 'Now let's get to the Lodge.'

The two of them began to creep along the path. Behind them came the sound of voices calling out as the intruders discovered the open window. Lights came on in various parts of the house.

'It doesn't matter about noise now,' Serena said. 'Run!'

They set off, running along the path that led to the Lodge and the main road. The moon abruptly went behind the clouds and they had to slow down a little.

Suddenly Serena bumped into someone and let out a yell of sheer terror.

‘What is it?’ Pearl cried from behind her.

‘Shh! It’s only me and Vic.’

‘Marcus.’ Serena sagged against him for a minute, then realized this was dangerous. ‘They’re coming after us and we don’t know how many there are. We have to get away quickly.’

‘Damnation. And all I can do is limp. Why don’t the rest of you run ahead into the village?’

‘Why don’t we make for the Diggles’ house, then I’ll run on to fetch Constable Yedhill?’ Vic suggested.

But when they came to the garden of the Lodge, Marcus stopped. ‘There’s a motor car out on the road and someone inside it.’

Vic peered through the darkness. ‘You’re right. Look, you three go and hide in the shrubbery and I’ll run through the fields for help.’

‘No, I’ll do it. You know I’m a faster runner than you.’ Pearl was off before Vic could stop her.

‘Go after her,’ Marcus said. ‘I know somewhere for us two to hide.’ He guided Serena to a side path. ‘Shh. Walk quietly and trust me.’

She did as he said, unable to believe that this was happening, that it wasn’t a nightmare. She didn’t ask where they were going, moving after him as quietly as she could through the dark gardens, glad when the fitful clouds allowed some moonlight to filter through and show where they were going.

Marcus led her round to the back of the vegetable garden, stopping once with the softest of shushing sounds.

They stood in the darker shadow of a shed while a man went striding past them, clearly checking out the rear gardens. Serena couldn’t believe he hadn’t seen or heard them, couldn’t work out either how Marcus had known someone was coming. When he tugged her forward again, she went willingly because she trusted him absolutely.

They came to a huge tree at one side of the orchard and he led her round the back of it. ‘Stand still.’ He bent close to whisper in her ear. ‘We need to climb up a rope ladder. There’s an old platform up there that I built when I was a lad. They’ll not know about it. When I let the ladder down I’ll go up first to check it’s safe. It’ll not have been used for years. Keep hold of the bottom of the ladder. When I shake it, follow me up. Watch how I climb it. There's a trick to rope ladders.'

Her eyes were well enough accustomed to the dark to see that he went up the ladder from what she thought of as the side, putting his legs on either side of the end rope, not treating it like a normal ladder. She felt very vulnerable as the dark mass of him moved upwards away from her.

Suddenly the rope ladder shook in her hands. For a moment or two she froze, terrified at the thought of climbing up into the darkness. What if she fell? What if one of their pursuers caught her halfway up?

The ladder shook again and she drew a deep breath. Kilting her skirts up, she set her feet on the ladder as he had. But she found it hard going and could only climb slowly, fumbling for each new rung, clutching the rope tightly in hands that were sweating with fear.

Then she bumped into something and Marcus grasped her hands, half lifting her upwards on to a small platform.

'Stand perfectly still.' He began to haul up the ladder and when he had the bottom end he took the time to roll it up and push the roll into a crevice. Then he turned and put his arms round her. 'That's my brave girl.'

She leaned against him, not trying to hide her trembling, needing to have him hold her. When he planted a kiss on her forehead, she looked up with a gasp and he kissed her lips quickly.

His voice was low. 'No time for that now, pleasant though it is. We'd be better lying down. In summer the leaves hide the platform. In winter, it can be seen among the branches.'

So they lay down and once again she found herself in his arms. It felt so right to nestle against him, so wonderfully right. She shivered, because she wasn't wearing a coat and it was a cold night. 'I should have given you my coat,' he muttered and pulled her even more tightly against him.

Rain began falling and he cursed under his breath, but fortunately it turned out to be a light shower only. Men were still quartering the gardens, hunting for them, and lights were showing now in both the Lodge and the Hall. But Serena didn't care. Marcus's arms were round her and in their warm strength she felt that nothing could touch her.

Then a voice bellowed, 'Hoy! Who's there? This is the police. Show yourselves.'

'Constable Yedhill,' he whispered. 'Vic and Pearl must have got through safely.'

The heavy footsteps moved towards the house and the constable yelled, 'Stop, you! You're under arrest.'

Marcus chuckled. 'Those villains will be terrified.'

There was the sound of a motor starting up, feet pounding down the drive, then doors slammed and a vehicle drove off.

'I suppose we can go back down again now,' he whispered against her ear.

From near the house Vic called, 'Marcus! Where are you? It's safe to come out now.'

Serena pressed against him, not wanting to leave his arms.

'We have to go now,' he said. 'Come on, love. Stand up.'

She did so reluctantly and, as lanterns began to move through the gardens, Marcus said, 'I'll go down first and hold the ladder for you.'

She had a moment of near panic as she sat on the edge of the platform and had to force herself to swing round and fumble for the rope ladder, but the panic passed and by moving slowly and carefully she got herself down.

'Just a minute.' Marcus did something with a piece of string that had the ladder rolling up again, then he put his arm round her shoulders and they made their way to the house. Even when they rejoined the others, he kept his arm round her shoulders and she wanted it there. Where was the independence she'd longed for? She smiled wryly and stole a glance at him, loving his determined air, his ability to get others to do what he wanted without her father's nastiness . . .

She realized that they'd reached Constable Yedhill, and forced herself to pay attention to what he was saying as they all went inside the kitchen.

He was incensed that such lawless behaviour could take place on his territory, but Marcus soothed him down. 'They'll be watching out for us going back into Tinsley, I'm afraid,' he ended. 'And they'll try to stop us there.'

The constable goggled at him. 'In daylight? *In England?*'

'Yes. They're desperate men.'

'Do you know who they are, sir?'

'I have my suspicions but until I can prove something, I'd best keep them to myself. We don't want anyone suing us for slander, do we? And rich men have a lot of ways of getting what they want.'

The constable looked from one to the other and pursed his lips. 'I reckon I know who you're referring to, sir.'

'Yes, I thought you would. Please keep it under your hat for now. The man in question is claiming that she's mentally incompetent.'

There was silence, then the old man said quietly, in a voice very unlike his usual hearty tone, 'We all know he's a tricky fellow, so you'd better get her away from here as quickly as you can. I'm only a constable and I don't always have the power to do what I think right.'

Marcus shook his hand. 'Thank you.' Then he turned to Serena again. 'I think you and I should catch the milk train into Manchester and get married as soon as we can. The next attempt to get control of you may prevent our marrying.'

'May I offer you both my best wishes for a long and happy time together.' The constable's tone was so grandfatherly and his smile so broad that Serena had a sudden urge to laugh, even though they were still in danger.

'Come on.' Marcus tugged her arm.

'I'd prefer to escort you to the station myself, sir, see you safely on the train.'

'That would draw too much attention to ourselves and . . .' Marcus's grin was suddenly full of mischief. 'It just occurred to me that if you escorted Vic and Pearl to the police station, dressed in our clothes, hiding their faces, Serena and I might stand a better chance of getting away without anyone noticing us. We'll have to hurry, though, because I still can't walk fast.'

Constable Yedhill puffed out his chest a little. 'I think I can help you there, sir. Jack Dabney takes his milk to the station in the next village so that he can call and see his mother and he goes right past the end of your drive. He's a good friend of mine and I'm sure he'd give you a lift if I asked him. You can catch a train in the opposite direction to Tinsley then.'

'Excellent idea. Serena, how quickly can you pack?'

'I haven't unpacked.'

'If you could lend Pearl something to wear . . . I'll go and get my things together at the Lodge and Vic can wear some of my clothes. Constable, could you bring the ladies to the end of the drive as soon as they're ready? Vic and I will meet you there.'

In the bedroom, Serena looked at Pearl and shivered. 'I can't believe what happened tonight.'

'Never mind that. And remember tomorrow to buy something pretty to wear. You surely don't want to wear that horrible thing you're wearing?'

Seven

Marcus and Serena waited near the end of the drive then climbed on board the milk float and let a grinning Jack Dabney cover them with a blanket.

'I feel a fool,' Marcus muttered as the blanket, which smelled rather strongly of horse, came down over them.

'As long as we get away safely.'

'You have your birth certificate and all that?'

'You've already asked me and the answer was yes. It still is.'

'Sorry.'

Jack reined in a little way from the station at Lower Horton and they climbed down, then he waved to them and clicked to his horse to move on.

Before they arrived at the station, Serena stopped. 'Here, let me tidy you up.' She reached up to pull a piece of straw off Marcus's lapel, then walked round him, brushing off other pieces of debris, after which he did the same to her.

The stationmaster had to open up the ticket office for them. 'We don't usually get people taking this train,' he said chattily. 'Too early for most folk, this is.'

'Family emergency,' Marcus said. 'We need to get to Manchester.'

When they were on the train, he turned to Serena. 'I don't intend to go as far as Manchester. I've an old friend in Oldham who'll help us. Will you trust me?'

She had no need to think about that. 'Of course.'

Constable Yedhill walked into Horton, carrying the suitcase for 'Miss Fleming' while Vic walked beside them, trying to limp very slightly in the same way Marcus did. He thought he passed someone keeping watch in the shadows, but wasn't sure.

Once they were inside the police station Pearl asked, 'What happens now?'

'We have a cup of tea,' the constable said firmly. 'And we wait. I don't know if you two noticed but there was someone watching us from the doorway of the village shop.'

'I saw him,' Vic said. 'I'm just hoping it was too dark for him to realize we're not Marcus and Serena.'

'I find it hard to believe they'll come after you here, though,' the constable said, lighting his gas ring and setting the kettle on it.

Just as dawn was breaking, there was a hammering on the door of the police station. The three looked at one another.

'Well, I'll be blowed! The impudence of them!' The constable drew himself up, seeming almost to swell with indignation. 'Why don't you two go into the back room? No need to make things easy for them, is there?'

'You're a good egg, constable.' Vic followed Pearl through the door at the rear of the public area.

Left to himself, Constable Yedhill was guilty of the small vanity of peering in the mirror and checking that his appearance was in order. Let them wait till he was ready! Who did they think they were, treating the law like this?

Only when the third round of knocking began did he open the door a little.

The man outside tried to push it fully open, but Reginald Yedhill was made of sterner stuff. 'Stop that this minute!' he roared, shoving the man so hard he staggered to one side. 'Who do you think you are, trying to push a police officer around?'

Mr Fleming moved forward, saying smoothly, 'I apologize for my man's eagerness, Sergeant.'

'Constable.'

'Constable, then. My man was simply trying to help, knowing how worried I am about my poor deluded daughter.'

'That doesn't give him the right to be disrespectful of the law.' For a moment he saw Mr Fleming's face take on a vicious expression, then it was wiped off and a conciliatory smile replaced it, curving up the thin lips but not lighting the eyes.

'May we come in, Constable?'

'If you have business here, certainly. But if *that fellow* has no business here, he can stay outside.'

'Wait here, Hudd!' Ernest said without turning his head. 'Don't let anyone in or out.'

Reginald Yedhill saw his opportunity to delay still further. 'If he tries to stop anyone coming in or out of *my* police station, I'll arrest him for obstructing a policeman in the course of his duty.'

Another gentleman who'd been standing further back moved forward into the light. 'Quite right, officer. May Mr Fleming and I come in now, though? It's rather a cold morning.'

Reginald inclined his head to the other man, whom he recognized as a doctor who treated mainly the more affluent citizens of Tinsley, and turned back, going behind the counter and lowering the flap into place, then standing waiting, hands resting on the polished wooden surface. Let them speak first.

'Where are they?' Fleming asked at once, staring round.

'Where are who, sir?'

'My daughter and that scoundrel who's trying to take advantage of her.'

'There are no scoundrels in my police station, and your daughter isn't here either.'

'You're lying!'

The constable was surprised. People said that Fleming was a cold fish, but today the fellow seemed very agitated about something. He turned to the other gentleman. 'I know who Mr Fleming is, but may I ask who you are, sir?' He knew the man by sight, but he wasn't going to admit that. Besides, he was enjoying causing these delays, enjoying it very much. He'd suspected during the latter part of the war, after rationing had been set up, that Fleming and a few others of the town's so-called leading citizens had been obtaining extra food on the black market, thus swelling the coffers of war profiteers, something he couldn't abide. Sadly, he'd never been able to prove that. But this felt like striking a blow against them and their like. Who were they to ride roughshod over those who'd put their lives at risk to protect England?

Fleming spoke in a tense, clipped manner. 'This is Dr Tolson, who has come to assess my daughter's condition. I'm afraid she's not been herself since her mother's death, and I'm very worried about her.'

'Oh? When I saw her yesterday, Miss Fleming seemed perfectly sensible and rational to me.'

The doctor took another step forward, speaking in a patronizing tone, 'These cases can be like that, Constable, seeming sane one minute then the next quite irrational. We're worried that without treatment Miss Fleming may do herself harm.'

Reginald Yedhill decided then and there that he was completely on Miss Fleming's side. If he'd ever seen wickedness wearing the cloak of respectability, here it was now. 'Well, I'm still convinced that she's as sane as the next person, and so I'd say in a court of law, if I had to.'

Behind the door, the two listeners smiled gleefully at one another and Vic mouthed, 'Good man!' at Pearl.

'Could I see my daughter, please?' Fleming asked.

'As I've already told you, she isn't here, sir,' Reginald repeated.

'She was seen coming in.'

'Oh? Who by? I arrived here in the small hours of the morning, when most *respectable* people were in their beds.'

'I don't take kindly to this prevarication, Constable.'

'I'm telling you the simple truth, Mr Fleming. Your daughter is not here.'

Ernest looked round and his gaze settled on the door at the rear of the room. 'Are you hiding someone in there?' He pointed his finger.

Reginald decided that he too could speak as if the others were lacking normal understanding, so slowed down and exaggerated each word. 'I've got no one *hidden* in there, Mr Fleming, just two people who are helping me with inquiries, and your daughter certainly isn't one of them.'

Fleming looked at the doctor and rolled his eyes to show his disbelief, then turned back and spoke very quietly and icily. 'You'll have to prove that to me, Constable.'

'Are you calling me a liar . . . *sir*?'

'I'm saying that my daughter was seen coming into this police station. I've had a man watching it ever since and she hasn't come out, therefore she must still be in here somewhere.'

Reginald Yedhill had been called upon to keep calm in the face of insults, adversity and violence during his long career in the force. He was glad of that now, because this gentleman had gone too far – definitely too far. He looked up at the picture of King George, something he occasionally did in moments of stress. His monarch's calm, slightly smiling face, with its neat moustache and beard, looked back at him, as if to say, 'You are *my* representative here, invested with *my* authority.' That gave Reginald courage, as it always did. 'I take exception to your accusations, sir.'

'And I take exception to your concealing my daughter from me.'

Reginald had a little think, drumming his fingers on the counter and considering his options. He couldn't keep this up for much longer without being accused of deliberate obfuscation.

Behind the door Vic looked at Pearl. 'Time to go out?'

'Yes. I don't want Uncle Reginald to get into trouble.'

Vic opened the door. 'I'll go first.'

He walked out into the police station. 'We couldn't help overhearing what you were saying, Mr Fleming. I don't know why you think your daughter is here, but it's simple enough to prove she isn't.' He gestured to Pearl, who came out to join him, wearing Serena's lumpy, ill-fitting coat quite openly. 'This is my fiancée.'

Ernest lost control of himself, something that rarely happened, pushing past the constable with a growl of anger to enter the room at the rear. It took only a moment to check that no one else was there, and that there was no door through which Serena could have escaped. He stood for a moment breathing heavily, then turned and went back out to say in a tight, clipped voice, 'It seems we were mistaken, Constable. I apologize for any inconvenience caused.'

The doctor lingered to say placatingly, 'He's very worried about his daughter. I'm sure you'll excuse him for any . . . less than tactful utterances.'

Reginald leaned forward, hands on the counter and looked the doctor straight in the eyes. 'I still can't see why he should be worried about her. She's a nice young lady, who seems perfectly normal to me. As *you* ought to be able to confirm, you being a doctor, sworn to help people and – what's the phrase now? – do no harm.'

The doctor stared back at him in shock, then swung round and left without a word.

Vic looked at Reginald and whistled. 'You didn't mince your words.'

'I'm too old for that. And what can he do to me, after all?'

Pearl had gone across to look out of the window. 'They're both getting into Fleming's car.' She watched the car move a hundred yards down the road and stop in front of the railway station, then called, 'Just come and look at this.'

The others both joined her.

'Well, he won't find any sign of them there, either,' Pearl said.

'Clever idea of yours, Constable, to send them off to the next station,' Vic commented.

The older man smiled. 'If I do say so myself, I've helped your friends. It'll be up to Miss Fleming's husband now to protect her, but if I can ever be of assistance – to any of you – remember that I might have come out of retirement because of the war, but I'm not too old to smell a rat.'

Pearl went over to give him a hug. 'Thanks, Uncle Reggie.'

The two men shook hands, then Vic and Pearl left.

'What do we do now?' she asked as they walked back towards the Hall.

'We wait. But if you'd care to start your new job by taking over the cooking, I for one will be very grateful, because I'm going to move into the Hall. I'm not leaving you and the other women here unprotected.'

'I'll enjoy doing the cooking. As long as Mrs Lonnerden isn't too fussy. I'm a plain cook and can't do fancy stuff.'

'Marcus says his aunt doesn't leave her bedroom these days. Anyway, Ada said she liked your cooking.'

'Ah, so you only love me for my cooking.'

He swung her round and pulled her close. 'You know that isn't true.'

She sighed and lifted her lips for a kiss. 'The sooner we get married, the better, Victor Daniel Scott.'

Marcus smiled at Serena as the train gathered speed. 'Don't settle down. We're getting off two stations down the line to catch another train. How do you fancy being married in Oldham?'

'Anywhere. Do you know, your lip is bleeding?' She reached inside her pocket for a handkerchief. 'Stick out your tongue.' She dampened a corner of the handkerchief on his tongue and used it to clean him up, something her mother had done with her as a child. But it was very different dealing with a man like Marcus. Her breath caught in her throat as she touched him and he responded by growing very still, only his eyes moving as he studied her face. When they lingered on her lips, she felt as if he'd touched her.

As the train began to slow down for the next station, he took a deep breath and moved across to the window. 'I'll just keep an eye on what happens here . . . Nothing but a trio of farmers loading milk and eggs . . . and no one got on or off the train. I think we're clear of them.'

At the second station, he checked carefully before opening their compartment door and helping her out. 'Wait here.' He went across to speak to the porter and a coin changed hands, then the waiting room was unlocked for them.

They had to wait half an hour for their train and it seemed to stop at every tiny station en route.

'I've never been to Oldham,' she said. 'I've never been anywhere much, except in the books I've read.'

'I've an old friend living in Oldham. He's recovering from war wounds, too, lost three fingers on one hand, but at least he's still got the thumb and one finger so it won't hold him back too much.'

She always marvelled at how soldiers who'd been wounded seemed able to make new lives for themselves and just . . . carry on.

'I wonder . . . can you manage to get out on your own? If

anyone's following us, they'll be inquiring about a couple. Travelling separately may help confuse them.'

His words shocked her. 'Do we need to be that careful?'

'It doesn't hurt to take every possible precaution. Here's your ticket.' When she nodded, he opened their inner compartment door, took down their bags from the net luggage rack, then picked his own up and vanished along the corridor.

On the platform in Oldham he walked straight past her and went to deposit his suitcase in the left luggage office, so she did the same. She turned away from the counter and for a moment couldn't see him. Panic washed through her in a great wave. She took a few steps to one side, saw no sign of him, moved forward and caught sight of him studying the newspapers on the bookstall. He looked up, gave no sign of recognition but paid for a newspaper and walked out of the station. She put the left luggage ticket into her purse then followed him outside, her heart thudding in relief.

Not until they had turned a corner did he stop and grin at her. 'Thank goodness for an intelligent woman!'

She couldn't smile back. The way he'd behaved this morning showed how certain he was that Fleming would try to pursue her, and that sent cold shivers all over her body, not just up her spine, because she knew how tenacious he could be.

Marcus's voice was soft in her ear. 'Cheer up, Serena. It's simply a question of being cautious until we're married. After that, he'll not be able to do anything, so will probably leave us alone.'

She didn't even need to think about this. 'I doubt it. I've heard him boast many a time about how he's got his own back on someone, even though he's sometimes had to wait years to do it.'

'In that case, we'll stay on our guard.'

'I can't believe he'd treat me like this. It's like some penny dreadful tale.'

'I can believe anything after what I've been through in the past few years.' For a moment or two he stared into space, looking sad, then smiled at her and pointed across the road. 'Look, there's a café over there. I'm hungry if you aren't.'

She wasn't in the least hungry, but she was thirsty and drank three cups of tea while toying with a piece of toast. Marcus finished his meal off and hers too.

Afterwards they went into the registry office and arranged to be married by special licence the following day.

'Don't want to wait an hour longer now the war is over,' Marcus told the clerk cheerfully.

'There are a lot of folk saying the exact same thing, sir. May I wish you both well?'

'Thank you.'

That was the moment when all this seemed suddenly real for Serena and she swallowed hard as she looked at him. Tomorrow she was going to marry this man, share his bed . . . How did you really know what a person was like? Most people would have thought Ernest Fleming a good husband and provider. She knew better. He'd been a domestic tyrant – and perhaps worse.

She realized Marcus was looking at her questioningly and said quickly, to distract him, 'What shall we do about a room for the night?'

'We'll go and see my friend. I'm sure Den will be able to put us up. Denholm Rawlins is his proper name, but he always shortens it to Den. Before we go to see him, though . . .' He looked at her speculatively.

'What?'

'Do you have to keep wearing those dowdy clothes or can you come out of hiding now?'

This was one thing she was sure about. 'I'd love to come out of hiding.'

'What are you wearing to get married in?'

'Pearl's lent me one of her frocks.'

'You don't sound very enthusiastic about that.'

'Well, it's – not my sort of colour or style. It's a bit – bright. Though it *is* better than any of the clothes I've got.'

'Why don't we go and buy you a pretty new outfit of your own, then? There must be something ready-made. You've a nice slim figure under all those lumpy clothes.'

'Ought we to spend our money until we know how we stand?'

'We definitely ought when it comes to a wedding outfit.

You only get married once. Call this my wedding present to you.'

'I've nothing to give you in return. And I've left my bank book with my things at the Hall.'

'You're giving me yourself. That's more than enough.'

She looked at him, doubtful that she was much of a gift to anyone, but he couldn't be faking a smile as warm and friendly as that . . . could he? Then she remembered her annuity and wondered, with a sinking feeling, if he was thinking about that. He'd made no bones about the fact that her money would be useful.

'We'll also book in at a photographer's and record ourselves for our descendants to laugh at.' He hesitated for a moment, then said quietly, 'I do want children, don't you? Not straight away, but eventually. I was always sorry to be an only child.'

It was the expression on his face as he said that which relieved her mind, rather than the words themselves. The longing showed quite clearly, a longing she had shared for years. 'Oh, yes. Though I had Frank when he wasn't at boarding school, and we got on really well, even though he was five years younger than me. I still can't believe he's dead.'

'Nothing can take away the years you had together.' He hesitated then took a strand of her hair and fingered it. 'And perhaps we could do something about your hair as well as your clothes? Have you ever thought of having it bobbed? You've so much hair it sort of swamps your face, even though this style is better than that damned hard knot you used to screw it up into.'

She could feel herself stiffening. Did he think she *wanted* to look like this? Especially now. 'Yes, *of course* I've thought of having it bobbed. What modern woman wants to struggle with this much hair? But *he* held very strong views on women's hairstyles and you know that I didn't want to make it easy for him to find me a husband.' She looked at him and couldn't help smiling as she added, 'Apart from the infuriating laugh that makes people wince, I can be extremely dull and boring about my church activities and my worries that the church needs new hassocks and prayer books.'

He chuckled. 'Sounds a very sensible thing to do, given the

circumstances, though I hope you'll stop using the laugh from now on. But what about the *real* Serena? What's she like?'

She hesitated. She'd asked herself that so many times and never found an answer. 'I don't think I even know. I've never been able to . . . be myself, you see, have always had to be on guard. All I clung to was that, once I turned thirty, I could become independent.'

He seemed to understand what was worrying her. 'I shan't chain you down or dictate to you, I promise. I'm not like that.'

She raised her eyes and gave him a little nod. 'No, I don't think you are.'

'Right then, let's make a start today on finding out who you are.' He tucked her hand into his arm and began walking. 'They told me at the bookstall that the best shops are on Yorkshire, Henshaw or High Street. And there must be a hairdresser's there too, surely?'

She'd never been inside a hairdresser's shop, because, like most women, she dealt with her own hair. First her mother, then Ruby had always cut it for her, chopping off the bottom inch or two every few months. Some women never cut their hair and were proud of being able to sit on it, but hers grew so thickly and fast it was too heavy, so she'd had it cut as short as she dared.

She'd lingered outside the one hairdresser's in Tinsley sometimes, after it had been bought by a woman who had trained as a hairdresser in London. Madame Clara's Salon had looked so splendidly modern under its new owner. The former owner had made most of her money selling false hairpieces or buying 'heads of hair' from poorer women in desperate need of money, and had sent out her customers with masses of hair piled on their heads in the old-fashioned way. But with the new owner you could get your hair washed, trimmed or bobbed into the short modern styles some younger women were adopting. Sadly, a flattering hairstyle had been the last thing Serena wanted then, but she wanted one now, wanted it quite desperately, to show Marcus she wasn't as dowdy and plain as the mirror said each morning.

Fleming had said that only women of a certain sort frequented such places as hairdressing salons or painted their faces, but that wasn't true. Several of her mother's friends went to Madame Clara's and used rice paper on their cheeks, too.

Serena and Marcus strolled along, looking in the shop windows, and that in itself was very pleasant, especially when other women looked at her enviously because of her companion. The scars on his face didn't stop him being tall and strong-looking, and the beard lent him a certain mysterious charm. They found several ladies' dress shops and studied the contents of the windows, settling on a particularly nice one on High Street. After she'd tried on several ready-made garments, they decided on a tailored costume in navy blue. It had a box-pleated skirt which should have ended several inches above the ankle but was longer on Serena. There was a matching jacket with belt, also with a pleated skirt to it, reaching to about sixteen inches below the waist. Unlike the garments she was wearing, it didn't make her look lumpy, but emphasized her slender waist.

Serena watched in amazement as the owner, who had said at first that it'd take several days to have the skirt shortened, succumbed to Marcus's cajoling and to the idea of dressing the bride of a returned soldier, promising to have the skirt shortened for her within a couple of hours.

They took the jacket with them and went into a blouse maker's, where they bought two blouses, one pink and one pale blue. There was a milliner's nearby and as they lingered to look at the hats displayed in the window, Marcus said, 'Not till after you've had your hair done. And the minute you do have a pretty hat, I'm going to throw away that lumpy object you're wearing on your head.'

The hairdresser's had a picture in the window of a young woman with bobbed hair. 'Shall we see if they can help us?' he asked and went in with her to make sure of that.

Two hours later, Serena looked up shyly as he came back to pick her up. He stared at her, not saying a word, and indicated with a twiddle of his fingers that she should turn round. This made her worry that she looked even worse now. She couldn't tell, she was so nervous.

Marcus was astounded to see the pretty younger-looking woman who had emerged from her disguise. Serena's hair was a lovely shade of brown – why hadn't he noticed that before? The shorter style suited her face and the horrible frizzy fringe was gone, leaving only a light feathery fringe which showed off her fine blue eyes with their long, dark lashes.

'There, sir. What do you think of her?' the hairdresser asked.

'I think she looks wonderful. You've done marvels.'

The woman beamed at him.

Serena turned to look into the mirror again and finger the hair at the side. She felt as if she didn't recognize herself any more. The hairdresser had cut her hair to hug her head and lie neatly in the nape of her neck before turning up a little. It had enough natural curl for that, revealing a glimpse of her neck.

'I didn't realize,' he began, stopped, then said it, 'that you were so pretty.'

'I am?'

'Yes, truly you are.' He saw tears well in her eyes and heard the hairdresser give a sentimental sigh. 'Your father was wrong to insist on you keeping your hair long.'

She smiled at him, such a wobbly, uncertain smile, he guessed then what a big step this was for her, and on top of a hectic couple of days, too.

He held out the parcel from the dress shop. 'They've done the hem. Is there somewhere here that you can change?'

The hairdresser smiled from one to the other. 'Come through to the back, miss.'

When Serena returned, the transformation was almost complete. In the new tailored costume, she looked trim and very feminine. The only jarring note was the hat. He stepped forward, removed it from her head and trampled it underfoot.

The hairdresser giggled.

Serena looked down at it in dismay. 'But I'll have to walk down the street without a hat!' She'd never done that in her life, not even when she was a child.

'Better that than put the ugly blob on again,' he said firmly. He brushed a piece of fluff off one lapel. 'I shall be proud to marry you tomorrow.'

They hurried down the street to a milliner's shop and there Serena found a very flattering hat, with a wide brim and neat crown, and a fluffy feather to one side of the crown.

'We make these especially for the ladies with bobbed hair,' the milliner said with a smile. 'You don't need such wide crowns without all the hair.'

'She'll have that one,' Marcus said firmly. 'Perfect for our wedding.'

'Very good choice, sir.' The milliner turned back to Serena and studied her. 'You look very smart and modern now, miss, if you don't mind me saying so. I saw you looking in the window earlier. I wish you both happy.' Tears stood out on her lashes for a moment as she added quietly, 'My husband didn't make it back, but we had a few happy years together, at least.'

Serena couldn't help hugging her, she looked so sad. And that was something the old Serena would never have dreamed of doing.

As they walked down the street, she stole glances at herself in every shop window they passed. He'd said she looked pretty. And she did look . . . rather nice.

'We'll pick up our luggage and catch a cab at the station,' Marcus said.

'Are you sure we should impose on your friend?'

'Very sure. He and I served in the same regiment all through the war. That makes the survivors as close as brothers, believe me.'

As they sat in the cab he took her hand again. 'There's something I have to tell you about my friend.'

'Yes?'

'Den's a doctor. He's been staying with his parents while he recuperated. His father's also a doctor and . . . well, I think it'd be a good thing for them to check you carefully while we're there, so that they can swear there's nothing wrong with you. Two doctors against one if your father ever makes it necessary, which I hope it won't be.'

The euphoria of her transformation into a modern young woman left Serena abruptly and reality returned to sit heavily on her shoulders. 'Oh.'

'Even after we're married, I want you to be safe. You say your father won't give up easily. And if he *is* in serious financial trouble and wants your annuity, well, who knows what he's done with your inheritance? We'll ask Justin Redway to check up on that. And we'll leave your mother's jewellery in the bank for the time being, shall we? We'll have enough to live on with my money, if we're not extravagant.'

She nodded, but he could see the sparkle had gone out of her.

'Ah, Serena, I hate to see you look like that. I won't let him get hold of you, I promise.' Marcus took her hand and they sat quietly for the rest of the journey.

He was such a kind man. And he did seem to like kissing her.

But not nearly as much as she liked kissing him. She wished he'd taken the opportunity to kiss her again.

The Rawlins house was a commodious residence to the south-east of the town centre, situated on Queen's Road and over-looking Alexandra Park.

'Wait here. I won't be long.' Marcus slipped out of the cab, closing the door quickly but still letting a gust of chill air inside.

As Serena waited, she worried about them turning up with-out warning like this. And what would these people think of her, running away to get married at her age?

The front door of the house opened and Marcus came out, accompanied by a man who was his opposite in many ways, being short and sturdy with gingerish hair. He was beaming and gesticulating as the two walked along the path, clearly happy to see his friend, so she immediately felt better about being here.

Marcus flung open the cab door. 'Here she is! Serena, my dear, this is Den Rawlins, my very good friend.'

She got out of the cab and was pulled into a hug by this complete stranger, who then held her at arm's length and asked, 'What on earth's a pretty girl like you doing getting married to this ugly devil?'

She couldn't help smiling again, his cheerfulness was so infectious. 'It seemed the kindest thing to do.'

He offered her his arm. 'Let's leave Marcus to supervise the bags and get you inside out of this chilly wind. My mother's out but she'll be back soon, then she'll find bedrooms for you both.'

'Are you sure it won't be too much trouble?'

'She loves having visitors, especially friends of mine. Says they keep her young. You'll see.'

They went into a chaotic sitting room which looked as if people used every inch of it.

'We aren't a tidy family,' Den said with a grin. 'Hope you don't mind.'

'I love it. I come from a rigidly tidy home. This feels much more comfortable.'

They sat down and within minutes a smiling maid brought them a tea tray. Serena poured, content to listen to the two men catching up with one another's news.

When they'd finished the tea, Marcus looked at her. 'All right if I tell Den about your little problem?'

She could feel herself going stiff and could only manage a nod.

When Marcus had finished his explanation, Den looked at her, his expression serious now. 'This must be dreadful for you.'

'Yes.'

'Tell me about your father.'

She couldn't bear to call him that any longer, so out it came again, the fact that Ernest wasn't her real father and the name of the man who was. She also found herself telling Den how she'd made herself look unattractive for many years and even how she was terrified of bringing trouble to Marcus now. When the words ran out she sat there with her head bowed, unable to face the two men who would, she was sure, think her a foolish creature, if not worse.

Marcus stood up. 'I'll leave you with Den for a few minutes, Serena.'

As the door closed behind him, she looked at the doctor apprehensively, wondering what this was about. Surely Marcus didn't think she was really unstable mentally?

Den came to sit on the sofa next to her and clasped her hand in his. 'You must be a very strong person to have survived a life like that.'

She blinked in shock. '*Strong*?'

'Yes. To have coped with it – and survived – and managed to escape. You've done so well.'

This was the last thing she'd expected to hear. 'You really think so?'

'I wouldn't say it if I didn't mean it. What I wanted to ask privately was whether you feel forced to marry Marcus or whether you'd feel better if we made some other arrangements and you didn't have to marry anyone until you were ready?'

'Oh no! I *want* to marry him!' Doubts suddenly shook her. 'Unless he's asked you to – to tell me *he* doesn't want to.'

'From the way he looks at you, I think he's very happy to be marrying you, and both as friend and doctor, I'm delighted to think of him having someone of his own. He had a very lonely boyhood, you know, and it wasn't till he joined the Army that he made lasting friendships.'

'How do you know?'

'Men talk sometimes during quiet nights on watch, perhaps saying more than they would in normal times. And Marcus and I always did get on well. You must have been lonely too.'

'I was some of the time, but I had Frank. It was much worse after he joined up. And although I had my mother, she was always terrified of *him*, always worrying about upsetting him.'

'So you're happy to marry Marcus?'

'Very happy indeed.'

'That's wonderful, then. I hereby propose myself as witness tomorrow and I daresay my mother will come along as well. She dearly loves a wedding. Let's bring Marcus in to join us again, shall we?'

She grabbed his sleeve. 'You're absolutely certain I'm all right?'

'Utterly, Miss Fleming. And I'm sure of something else . . .'

Of course she couldn't resist asking, 'What?'

'That you're a very intelligent woman as well. Marcus needs that. He never did bear fools gladly.'

It seemed a strange thing to say, but he knew his friend better than she did, so she didn't challenge that statement. 'Thank you. And please, call me Serena. I hate the name Fleming, shall be delighted to discard it.'

That same night a man broke into Ernest Fleming's office and brought out his Ever Ready tubular electric torch with a wry smile. When he was a young fellow, he'd had to use a lantern to break into places, but modern progress had provided him with far better equipment for his burglaries, for which he was duly grateful.

He went through the desk's contents quickly, not finding what he was looking for. He studied the rest of the room, his gaze settling on the oak filing cabinet, each of its four drawers supplied with highly polished brass cardholders to help him find what he needed. It was locked, of course, but a child could have picked such a simple lock. He proved that in a few seconds and went through the papers, finding the file he'd been asked to steal almost immediately. He grinned. This was one of the easiest jobs he'd ever done.

Then he heard a noise and switched off the torch, cursing under his breath. Surely someone else wasn't breaking in here tonight? Of all the bloody coincidences! He stuffed the file down his jacket and crept across to the heavy velvet curtains, concealing himself behind them and taking care to turn his feet sideways so that his toes wouldn't show.

The door opened and a thin line of light showed under the curtains, so faint that the other man must also be using a shielded torch or lantern. The watcher frowned and prayed not to be noticed.

There was a smell he recognized. Paraffin. A splashing sound, then someone struck a match and there was a whoosh as something caught fire. The light beyond the curtains was suddenly much brighter.

Torn between fear for his own safety and a strong desire not to be caught, the watcher hesitated. When he heard someone run across to the door and close it, he opened the curtains a crack and saw to his horror that the room was rapidly being overrun by flames. He pushed aside the curtain and ran towards the door, trying to avoid the blaze. But it seemed to have been started in several places at once and he had to pass through a barrier of flames to get out.

His heart was in his mouth as he went out into the hallway, but whoever had set the fire had now left. He went quickly towards the rear, eased up the window through which he'd entered and slipped out through the back yard, his face stinging where the flames had burned him.

He ran home as quickly as he could, not wanting to be caught out on the streets when the fire brigade came to put out the fire. They'd not be in time to save the contents of the filing cabinet, though. He patted his chest, where the papers were safe beneath his jacket. Good thing he'd already got what he'd gone there for, or he'd not have earned his fee for this strange job.

Eight

Marcus and Serena sat in the waiting room at the registry office with Den and Mrs Rawlins, who had indeed insisted on coming with them to act as the second witness. Serena felt as if she were in a dream, floating along happily, surrounded by people who were kind and *normal.* She looked sideways at Marcus, who had shaved off his beard in honour of the occasion and who looked younger without it. He must have been very good-looking before his face was damaged and he was still an attractive man. Well, she found him attractive.

His hand was resting on his thigh. As she watched, he lifted it to cover hers, which was lying on her lap, hesitated, then let it drop back on his leg.

She'd have liked to hold his hand, but didn't dare take the initiative. Then she got angry with herself for thinking like that. She'd vowed to be a modern woman, had she not? So she reached out for his hand and, though he shot a surprised look at her, she felt his fingers curl round hers, saw a smile lift the corner of his mouth.

'Not long now,' he whispered.

'Mmm.' She stared down at their joined hands and he went back to staring straight ahead. But he didn't let go of her. And she didn't try to pull away.

Another couple came in with their witnesses. The bridal pair were arm in arm, beaming at one another. There was a whole crowd of people with them, all looking relaxed and happy. Serena wished she felt relaxed. Instead, her stomach was churning with nerves and she hadn't been able to eat much at breakfast.

A woman poked her head round one of the big double doors and called, 'Graye and Fleming.'

As they stood up, Marcus pulled her hand through his arm.

The other young woman waiting to be married called, 'Good luck!' and smiled at them.

Serena nodded but couldn't manage to speak.

It was left to Mrs Rawlins to say comfortably, 'And good luck to you too, dear.'

After a few formalities, an elderly man with a long thin face asked them to repeat a few phrases after him, then suddenly and shockingly declared them to be man and wife.

Marcus turned Serena round and kissed her quickly on the cheek, whispering, 'All right?'

She nodded. But she wasn't all right. She felt totally lost, as if she didn't know who she was any more. Thank goodness she had him to hold on to.

'My turn to kiss the bride!' Den leaned forward and smacked a quick kiss on her lips, then his mother kissed the air above her cheek.

'Come along, Mrs Graye,' Marcus said. 'Let's go and have our photo taken.'

'Mrs Graye,' Serena whispered, and the name echoed several times in her head as they walked out. Oh, the relief of not being Miss Fleming any longer! Suddenly the day seemed brighter, the wind less chill and she didn't care if it rained or snowed.

She was married! She didn't have to pretend to be Ernest Fleming's daughter any longer, nor did she have to use his name. And if that was a strange thing to think on her wedding day, then too bad, because it was very important to her to cut all ties with *him.*

When they came out of the photographer's, Mrs Rawlins stopped in the doorway. 'Where is . . . Oh, yes, there it is.' She turned to Marcus. 'We've booked you two in at the pub in the next village. They're quite famous for their honeymoon suite and by great good fortune it's vacant tonight. It's our present to you. I do feel newly-weds deserve a treat, and though you'd have been welcome to stay with us, it's better for you to have some time to yourselves, don't you think? I packed your things secretly and here they are.' She pulled Marcus's head down and gave him a smacking kiss on the cheek, then kissed Serena, who was the same height as her.

Den shook hands with Marcus. 'You're a lucky devil. Let

me know if she has any cousins.' He turned to Serena. 'Look after him. You've got a good 'un there.'

Then the Rawlinses were gone and the cabbie was coughing to remind them to get in.

'How kind they are,' she said wonderingly.

'They're a wonderful family. I spent a few of my leaves with them. Cheered me up no end. They lost another son on the Somme and I know they all miss him dreadfully, but they haven't let it blight their lives. As Den says, you have to keep on enjoying life while you can.'

She nodded and when Marcus didn't say anything else, she pretended to look out of the window, but in reality she was starting to worry about sharing a bedroom with him tonight. She was so ignorant about what really happened between a man and woman, even though she understood the anatomy of it from her first-aid course. Anatomy didn't tell you how it felt, how much it hurt the first time – which everyone said it did – how your new husband felt about touching you so intimately.

He'd think she was such a fool, for all her fine new clothes.

The Travellers' Inn was an old-fashioned building just outside the town. It was very rambling and the landlady showed them up two flights of stairs and along a twisting corridor to get to the 'bridal suite'. This was really only a large bedroom with a four-poster bed, which the landlady was obviously very proud of from the way she smoothed down the silky green counterpane.

'Shall I . . . unpack our things?' Serena asked when they were alone, but her voice came out scratchy and higher-pitched than usual and he noticed, she could see he did.

'You do yours and I'll do mine. It's only worth getting out our nightclothes, really, because we'll be off again tomorrow morning.'

'All right.' It didn't take long to get her things out and put them under the pillow, then she fidgeted with the bedcovers, straightening them, wondering what to do next.

Marcus got his pyjamas out, then looked at her across the bed. 'I've asked Den to phone Justin and let him know we're all right and safely married. Justin will phone Constable

Yedhill. There are only two phones in the village. The other is at the Hall, but I'm not keen to leave a message with Gladys or Ada.' He smiled. 'Come and sit down. These chairs are very comfortable.'

She took the other big armchair and held out her hands to the cheerfully blazing fire, leaning her head back against the chair. She surprised both herself and him by laughing.

'What's so amusing?'

She rolled her head from side to side. 'I was thinking how much more comfortable bobbed hair is, especially after that bun, and shorter skirts . . . but most wonderful of all is being with normal people.'

He leaned back, smiling. 'I hope to keep you happy.'

She was suddenly serious. 'No one is happy all the time, I'm sure, but if I can stop being afraid . . .'

They sat quietly for a while, then there was a knock on the door and the landlady brought in a big tray.

'I usually serve the bridal couple up here,' she said as she set the contents of the tray out on a small table near the window.

The food was good but Serena wasn't hungry.

'You don't eat enough,' Marcus said.

'I'm really not hungry.'

'Try a little more, to please me.'

So she forced down a few more mouthfuls of meat and potatoes, then pushed her plate aside. 'I can't eat any more. I'm – feeling a bit nervous. About tonight.'

Marcus set down his knife and fork. 'I said we could wait to consummate our marriage and I meant it.'

She swallowed hard but still her voice didn't sound normal to her. 'I'm sorry. It's just . . . well, I hardly know you and so much has happened that I don't feel to know myself either. Please don't be angry with me.'

'The only thing that would make me angry would be you assuming I'm as unreasonable as your father.'

'Call him Fleming,' she said quickly. 'I don't want to call him "father" any more.'

'Fleming, then. Most men aren't unreasonable, you know. And I promise I won't lay a finger on you until *you* feel the time is right.'

Her eyes strayed to the double bed and he followed her gaze. 'I can sleep on one of these chairs, if you prefer it. I've slept on far worse.'

Suddenly her fear of him left her. 'No, that would be silly. You need a good night's sleep too.' She couldn't hold back a yawn. 'I'm sorry. I didn't sleep well last night or the night before, and I'm exhausted.'

'So am I, actually. I'm getting better, but I'm still not my old self. Look, why don't you go and use the bathroom, then you can change into your nightdress while I go.'

He was being so kind, she took heart, but she still made haste to take her clothes off and get into bed while he was out.

When he came back, he was wearing his pyjamas and a checked woollen dressing gown. He put his clothes tidily on one of the armchairs, broke up the fire to save the unburned pieces of coal, and turned off the lamp. In the dying glow of the fire his silhouette seemed very large as he walked across to the bed, and for a moment her heart skipped a beat or two. Would he change his mind?

But he got into bed without touching her, said, 'Good night,' in the same pleasant tone and settled down beside her.

With a sigh of relief she snuggled down.

He heard the sigh and it soon became obvious that she was asleep. She was frightened of him, for all her brave talk. Fleming had done that, he was sure, given her a fear of men. During the day she'd relaxed a little, but as soon as they'd come into this bedroom she'd turned into a stiff, careful stranger.

The trouble was, she looked so pretty he couldn't stop his body reacting to her, so now he was all too conscious of his unsatisfied desire and a longing simply to touch her and enjoy the softness of her skin. He smiled grimly. He wouldn't do that though. He didn't intend to frighten her off.

But one day he would make love to her and she would enjoy it. That he swore.

The following morning Serena woke with a start to find Marcus bending over the bed, shaking her shoulder lightly and smiling.

'I'd have liked to leave you to sleep longer, but they stop serving breakfast in half an hour.'

'Oh, goodness!' She sat up abruptly, realized she was only wearing a nightdress and tugged the sheet up, feeling her cheeks go hot with embarrassment, though the garment was as modest as any blouse.

'I'll go and wait for you downstairs in the dining room. Don't be long. I'm ravenous.'

Again she was grateful for his understanding, and when he'd gone, she scrambled out of bed and had a quick wash. She put on her wedding outfit again, because she was so ashamed of her other clothes. As soon as they got back to the Hall, she intended to alter everything which wasn't too nasty a colour.

Downstairs she found Marcus leaning on the lounge bar, talking to the landlord, but he turned when he heard her footsteps and led her across to a small side room where a table was set ready for them.

'We have a special breakfast for newly-weds,' the landlord said, chuckling when Serena blushed. 'Bacon, a whole egg each, fried bread, and as much toast and jam as you want.'

Serena didn't think she could eat so much and started to say so. 'I'm not sure I—'

Marcus put his fingers across her lips. 'You hardly ate anything yesterday. I don't want you fainting on me.'

'I'll . . . try.'

Marcus ate his food, persuaded her to eat most of hers, then finished the rest for her, after which he sat back in his seat and sighed in satisfaction. 'I don't think I've been so well fed since I came home. I have a hearty appetite, I'm afraid. Now, I think we'd better go back and sort things out in Tinsley, don't you?'

She couldn't stop herself from shuddering. 'Yes, though I wish we didn't have to.'

'Fleming can hardly knock us over the head in a public place and carry us off.'

'He tried to do that to me before, remember? Well, not knock me over the head, but carry me off from a public place. And he'd have succeeded, too, but for you and Vic.'

'Well, it'd be a futile effort now, because I'm officially your next of kin, and I know you're of sound mind.'

She nodded, trying not to let him see how afraid she was. But something told her that Fleming wouldn't easily give up.

'Come on. Let's find out about trains, then I'll pay our bill and take you home.' He pushed his chair back and went to move hers to let her stand up.

'"Home",' she said wonderingly.

'I hope the Hall will soon feel like home, Serena.'

'It can't feel less like it than my old one did.'

'And don't forget, it'll soon be Christmas. I'm determined to celebrate in style this year, our country's first peaceful Christmas for so long, and the first for us as a married couple.'

She knew he was trying to cheer her up, so she didn't say anything else. But all the way back to Tinsley she was wondering what sort of reception they would have, wondering if Marcus really would be able to protect her from Ernest Fleming.

PART TWO

Nine

On the afternoon of November the eleventh, the chief nurse came into the ward and smiled round at the men. 'It's happened at last, boys!'

They turned towards her expectantly.

'The war's over.'

There was silence, then some ragged cheering. One man turned his back to hide the tears in his eyes, another sat motionless, staring down at the floor.

The orderly, who was a former patient, walked across to the window and let the sounds of the long, narrow ward wash around him. He didn't feel like cheering or weeping . . . or anything much really.

'You all right, Aubrey lad?'

He turned to Jim, who'd become a close friend over the months they'd both been here, and smiled. 'You think you'll go mad for joy when it happens, but all I can think of is how many people have lost their lives. Was it worth it?'

'We didn't have much choice.'

'*You* did. You came all the way from Australia to fight with us – and you suffered for that.'

'Ah, I'm getting right again now. And who was there to miss me back there?' He studied the younger man. 'You've not . . . remembered anything else?'

'I think I have, actually. It's the name of a town. Tinsley. But I only remember the name, not anything about the place. Maybe that's where I lived. Who knows?' The doctors said Aubrey's memory might never return, and because no one knew who he really was, or even what regiment he was from, because of mix-ups in the field hospitals, they weren't sure enough of him to let him go back to active duty. He didn't mind them setting him to work here, as he didn't want to get himself killed. The ones he felt sorry for were the lads who did have to go back, but he knew what he did here was useful, more useful, to his mind, than the killing he'd been forced into before.

He saw Jim frowning and managed a smile. 'What I'd really like is to get out of here. You've only one more operation to go now. I'll miss you, though. You've been a good friend to me.' It was the nearest he could get to saying out loud that this man had become like a father to him. Jim had no family of his own back in Australia and was older than the rest of them. His body was now a patchwork of scars and new skin, and his thinning hair was streaked with silver, but his eyes were bright with life and, more importantly, he was both wise and kind, knowing when to listen quietly and when to tell a chap to buck up and get on with his life.

'We can keep in touch afterwards, if you like,' Jim offered, rubbing the toe of his slipper in circles on the floorboards. 'I could even come and visit you in Tinsley before I go back to Australia.'

'I'd really like that. Promise!'

'Cross me heart an' hope to die.' Jim looked at him thoughtfully. 'Dr Fitton might be able to help you get out of the Army for good now the war's over. Why don't you ask him?'

Aubrey nodded. In July 1917 he'd been found naked, unconscious and badly injured, with even his identification tag missing, after the battle they now called Passchendaele. He'd not remembered how his injuries had happened, or much else either. No one had recognized him, so the nurses had given him the name Aubrey Smith. He liked it so much he'd arranged to keep it officially when they brought him back to Blighty to the blessed quietness of this long-term convalescent home in Surrey.

He'd done little except sleep the first month, then gradually his body had recovered enough from his injuries for his mind to start functioning better, but he still had no idea who he was, except that he had a northern accent – probably Lancashire, they said. Sometimes he thought he remembered a young woman, rather plain but with a lovely kind smile. He didn't remember her name, though. He'd wondered at first if she was his wife but that hadn't felt right, so he'd come to the conclusion that she was either a relative or a friend, because she was definitely too young to be his mother. Unless he was very lucky and bumped into her or someone else who recognized him, he reckoned he'd never know.

And would anyone recognize him now? The face that looked back at him from the mirror was serious and not bad looking, but he seemed to catch fleeting glimpses of another face, that of a much younger man, rather nervous and *soft-looking* was the only way he could describe that face. He didn't look soft now, few men did after what they went through in the trenches.

And what he'd seen in the convalescent home had made him appreciate how lucky he'd been. He'd only lost his memory and sustained a few superficial wounds. He still had both arms and legs, all his fingers and toes. Some men had lost so much of themselves, physically or mentally, that they'd have to be cared for like babies for the rest of their lives.

He did keep wondering who he was, though. How could you not? The book he'd borrowed from the doctor about his condition said that such complete memory loss was often caused by things too painful to bear.

What had been so painful about his previous life?

Ah, who knew anything? He fixed the smile back on his face and turned to clap Jim on the shoulder. 'Come on! Let's join in the celebrations.' He took a sip or two of the beer one of the orderlies had smuggled in, then passed the glass to Joe, who had no legs now but was determined to walk again one day, not ride on one of those little trolleys some legless men used. Joe was another whose example kept Aubrey going. There were a lot of grand fellows here.

The following day Aubrey went to see the doctor in charge of their unit to ask how quickly he could be demobilized.

'Why? Have you remembered something?'

'A town called Tinsley. I've looked it up on the maps and it's a small place in Lancashire, north-east of Oldham, so that fits with my accent.'

'Do you want us to make inquiries on your behalf with the authorities there?'

'I'd rather do it myself, sir. It's more than time I went out into the world and stood on my own feet again, don't you think?'

'I do. I'll sign you off as "unsuitable for further service" but suitable to be released.'

'Thank you, doctor.' Aubrey hesitated, then had to ask, 'You *do* think I'm fit to be released, don't you?'

'Oh, yes. I have done for a while, but I was waiting for you to ask me yourself. That was my final test.'

'Good.' Strange what a difference it made, a doctor saying it. But he'd known it really.

'Will you be all right for money, Smith?'

'I've been saving my wages since I started working as an orderly, sir. Well, there isn't much to spend them on here, is there? So I can manage for a while then find myself a job. After all, I'm a trained orderly now. If I had any money, I'd like to become a doctor and help people, but I can't afford the training.'

'There are other ways of helping people. It's a long training to become a doctor. If we reckon you at about twenty-five, which seems reasonable, you'd be into your thirties before you were qualified to practise.'

The doctor didn't say that they had no idea of the education Aubrey had received, no idea of his qualifications or training, though they'd guessed that he'd had a sound education from the ease with which he read and the things he said. Sometimes, when he felt particularly desperate about all the uncertainties with which he had to live, he wondered how you could build a whole new life on a few months' memories and no family of your own.

The doctor tapped the papers on his desk. 'I reckon it'll take a couple of weeks to get the paperwork sorted out, so you may as well continue working here until we hear from the powers that be.'

'That's all right, sir. As long as I know it's in the pipeline.'

It wasn't all right, of course. Having made the decision, what Aubrey desperately wanted was to get the hell out of here and find this Tinsley place, see if he could retrieve his past. He'd looked at the town on the map so many times. Why didn't he remember what it looked like, for heaven's sake, if that's where he came from?

He went off to find his friend and tell him the latest news. As the days passed, he had plenty of time to say his goodbyes and plan what to do. The Army didn't make it easy for you to get away from them, and even with a doctor's recommendation, you had to wait on their convenience.

A month later Aubrey said goodbye to Jim and left the convalescent home, driven to the nearest main-line station by one of the lady volunteers from the village. He listened to her gentle prattling with one ear, saying 'Mmm' and 'Yes' at intervals while trying to get used to the idea that he wasn't ever going back again. That thought was both terrifying and exciting.

When she left him at the station, he felt bewildered for a moment or two, so unused was he to making his own decisions, but a fatherly porter seemed to sense his uncertainty and quickly directed him to the correct platform.

The train was quite full, so he got into a compartment with a group of four soldiers sprawled about in it. As they made room for him, one of them cocked an eye in his direction, noting the Army greatcoat over civilian clothes. 'Just been demobbed?'

Aubrey nodded. 'Yes. Released from the convalescent home today, actually.'

'Going back to your family, son?'

'Lost my memory. Don't even know who I am.' He'd decided to be open about this. Well, he'd only give himself away if people asked him for details of his background.

'Bad luck, that. Where are you going, then?'

'Place called Tinsley, in Lancashire. I remembered the name so I'm going to find out if I come from there.' And suddenly he could see the town in his mind's eye – well, see the main street anyway. He caught his breath and sat very still, letting the vision roll through his mind, his head beginning to throb, as it did whenever he remembered something important.

'You all right?'

He summoned up a smile. 'Just remembered something else. It always gives me a bit of a headache to remember, but that'll soon pass. I'd put up with any number of headaches to get my memory back.'

He wasn't sorry to part company from them and have the compartment to himself, friendly as they had been. It was good to watch the peaceful English countryside, with fields, farms, small towns and villages passing in quick succession. The neatness of it all gave him a sense of sanity after the madness of war.

By the time he got out of the train at Tinsley, Aubrey was too exhausted to care about anything except finding a bed for the night. It was dusk and outside the station people were hurrying home from work. The gas lamps along the street made pools of light, seeming feeble at the moment as they competed with the last of the daylight. Rain was falling straight down from a leaden sky.

He found a cab and asked if the driver knew where he could find a room for the night. 'I've just been demobbed. Don't have any family to come back to.'

The cab driver took him to a pub where a motherly landlady no sooner discovered he was a returning soldier than she gave him a right royal welcome. Aubrey let her show him up to a bedroom, tried very hard to answer her well-meaning questions, but wanted only to lie down and sleep.

She seemed to understand how he felt. 'Look at me, nattering my head off like this, Mr Smith. Don't go to sleep quite yet. I'll bring you up a cup of tea and a sandwich. I'm betting you've not eaten for a while.'

He blinked and tried to remember when he'd last had a meal. 'You're right.' He opened his knapsack and found the package. 'They gave me some ham sandwiches, but I forgot to eat them. Maybe you could toast them for me?'

'Yes. We mustn't waste good food, must we? But don't go to sleep yet. You've got to eat to keep up your strength.'

He wasn't hungry, but he was desperately thirsty so he sat upright on a chair and waited for her to come back. He'd recognized the main street near the station, at least he thought he had, so surely he was in the right place? If he was very lucky, during the next few days or weeks, someone in the town would recognize him.

Or would that be unlucky? What if he was coming back to turmoil and trouble?

The landlady returned and stood over him while he drank two cups of tea and ate the sandwiches, which she'd fried up nice and crispy. Then she looked at his white, exhausted face and unpacked his pyjamas for him, laying them ready on the bed.

'I'll wait outside the door, Mr Smith, and you can pass me out your dirty clothes. It'll be my pleasure to wash them for you and dry them overnight.'

He was touched by this. 'Why are you being so kind to me?'

Tears welled in her eyes. 'I lost my son in the war. So whenever I can help someone else's son, I do.'

He hugged her. That made her tears flow in earnest and she hugged him convulsively before pulling away and smiling mistily at him. 'See you in the morning, Mr Smith. Breakfast can be served any time you wake up.'

'Yes. And thank you, Mrs Beamish. For everything.'

He had no trouble getting to sleep, woke once to use the chamber pot under the bed, then slept right through until ten in the morning by the wristwatch Jim had given him as an early Christmas present. Aubrey hadn't felt so wonderfully rested for months, if not years, and lay there for a few moments, enjoying the simple luxury of not having to jump to it at someone else's bidding.

When he went downstairs he found the landlady talking to her cellar man, who looked old enough to be her father. She swept her lodger off with her to the kitchen and cooked him a large breakfast. As he ate, she sat companionably across from him, sipping a cup of tea, and he found himself telling her his story.

'I'd not be much help to you because I'm not from round here and I only took over this pub at the beginning of '16. You should go to the newspaper, the *Tinsley Telegraph* it's called, and ask them to publish your story with a photo. Someone's bound to recognize you then.'

He stirred his tea, watching the whirlpool in the centre of the cup, thinking over her suggestion. 'I'm not sure I like the thought of making a public spectacle of myself. I'd rather have a poke round, then if I find some relatives, it'll be my choice whether to approach them or not.'

She looked at him in surprise.

'The doctors say I may have an unhappy past and that's why I don't remember, so I'm not rushing into anything.'

'Eh, lad, I hope there's no trouble waiting for you here.'

'Whatever it is, I'll cope. Anyway, I just want to stroll round the town today and see if that wakes up any memories. All right if I stay on with you here for a day or two longer? I'm not short of a bob or two.'

'Stay as long as you like, love. I'm happy to give you a weekly rate and it'll be nice to have a young fellow around. This pub is on Yorkshire Road, which is the main street, so you'll have no trouble finding your way back here. It's not a big place, Tinsley.'

Aubrey stood outside the pub and stared down the road. From what he could see from here, the town was long and narrow, built on one side of a valley on the edge of the moors. Shops lined the main street and there were one or two larger buildings. The terraced houses on the uphill side of Yorkshire Road zigzagged from side to side up the hill, buttressed by solid retaining walls, looking as if stubbornness was the main thing that kept them there. Those streets cut off from the main road at sharp angles.

On the other side, narrow streets led down a much gentler slope, set at right angles to the main street. The next street along from the pub had barely room for one vehicle and the pavements on either side were only wide enough for one person. He knew, with another of those blinding flashes, that these streets led down to a river. A name dropped into his mind, the Tinnen. So he followed the street downhill to check that out, not even considering seeking shelter, though it had begun to drizzle and was a miserable, grey sort of day. His old Army greatcoat kept him warm and dry, shabby as it was. He fingered the front of it as he buttoned it right up. Its rough wool was familiar and comforting to the touch.

At the bottom of the hill he found he'd been right. A narrow strip of public garden ran alongside the river, and in the bare earth of the flowerbed, there was a painted wooden sign standing on two legs that said, *Merry Christmas To All!* It had painted holly at each corner, so badly done that he smiled.

After a quick calculation of dates, he realized there was only a week or so to go to Christmas. He wished he'd thought to get a present for Jim before he left, wondered when he'd see his friend again.

Further along the river there was a shelter for cabbies and the man who'd driven him from the station the previous day was sitting there, staring out at the weather.

'Mind if I join you?'

'Be my guest.'

Aubrey sat down.

'I picked you up at the station yesterday, didn't I? Took you to the Weaver's Arms?'

'Yes. Good place to stay. Thanks for that. I'm Aubrey Smith.'

'Vic Scott.' He shook the hand Aubrey offered. 'Which regiment were you in?'

'I don't know. Got blown about by a shell and lost everything, including my memory.'

'Rotten luck.'

'Worse things happen.'

'Yes.' Vic looked down at his leg. 'I lost the bottom half of this. I don't know which is worse.'

They both sat silent for a minute or two, then Vic asked, 'What brings you to Tinsley, then?'

Aubrey shrugged. 'The name of the town seemed familiar and I do have a northern accent, so I thought I'd have a look round, see if anything rang a bell.'

'And does it?'

'Maybe. I'm not sure.'

The cabbie looked at his watch. 'Have to go now, picking up some friends of mine at the station. Good luck with your hunt.' He glanced up at the sky. 'Can I give you a lift back to the town centre? The rain seems to be setting in. You're going to get soaked if you walk about.'

'Thanks. Is there somewhere I can get a cup of tea?'

'Rose's Tea Rooms just along Yorkshire Road from the station. I'll drop you off there.'

'No, don't bother. I'll get out at the station and walk along, look in the shop windows.'

Ten

The cab drew up just as the train chugged into Tinsley station and Aubrey got out, calling, 'Thanks for the ride!' He hurried across to get out of the rain and buy a newspaper from the lad huddled near the main entrance, then stood watching the few passengers come out of the station. He was in no hurry to get anywhere, which felt strange and unsettling, but he enjoyed watching people – ordinary people – going about their business. It was another of the things that made peace seem a reality.

A young woman and a man with a scarred face walked past him arm in arm, and he turned his head to look at the woman again. Did she look familiar or was he just imagining things? At that moment she turned sideways to smile at the tall man beside her and Aubrey sucked in his breath sharply. It was such a charming smile, so . . . familiar. Could she possibly be the woman he'd remembered a couple of times? Her hair was different, but then of course it would be. A lot of younger women had had their hair cut short in the past few years.

The two went across to the cab he'd just left and he heard the driver, who sounded to be a friend rather than a hireling, exclaiming at her appearance, not just her hair but also her clothes. Aubrey took a step towards them then stopped. He'd promised himself to be cautious, not to rush into anything.

The driver stowed their luggage and asked if they wanted to go straight back to the Hall. Aubrey couldn't make out their answer, but it didn't matter. He knew now where she lived, could find her again if he chose. He stayed where he was as the cab pulled away, lost in thought, and then was rudely jostled aside by two men who were staring after the cab.

'Did you see 'em?' one asked the other.

'Aye.'

'I didn't recognize her for a minute, Mr Hudd. What's she done to hersen?'

'Had her hair cut. We'd best go and tell Mr Fleming them two are back.'

Aubrey let them walk away, leaning against the wall as pain washed through his head.

'You all right?' A man carrying a big parcel stopped to look at him in concern.

'Just a dizzy turn. I've been doing too much, I expect.' He rubbed at his temple.

The man looked at him shrewdly. 'Just come back from the war?'

'Yes. Does it show?'

'The greatcoat rather gives it away.'

Aubrey tried to dredge up a smile, but he was still feeling sick and dizzy and the attempt failed.

'You're not well. Come and have a sit down in my shop. It's just over there.'

Aubrey wanted to be on his own but his body was still betraying him. His head was throbbing and great waves of dizziness were washing through him. The world didn't steady around him till he'd been sitting down for a minute or two in the shop, then slowly he got in control of himself again. 'Sorry.'

'Have you had any other turns like that?'

'One or two. I got caught in an explosion, lost my memory. Every now and then something stirs up something from the past and then this happens. I've not had it as bad as this since the early days, though.' He looked round with pleasure. 'A bookshop.'

The man nodded. 'New books and old, stationery and pens, whatever will turn a penny into twopence. It's the second-hand books that make the most profit, strangely enough. People who won't pay out two bob for a new book will happily give threepence or sixpence for an old one, and the ragged books on my penny tray sell like hot cakes.' He stood up as the shop door tinkled. 'Ah, Mr Redway. Come to pick up your new book? I bet it's in this parcel.' He removed the wrapping, folding it carefully, and looked at the titles of the books inside. 'Yes, here it is.'

An older man with silver hair and a thin, intelligent face picked up the book, eagerly scanning the cover. 'Yes, this is the one. Thanks for that, Ted. How much do I owe you?'

He paid for it, nodded farewell to Aubrey, frowning slightly and hesitating by the door as though he wasn't sure whether he recognized him or not, then shook his head as if to dismiss the idea and left.

Aubrey didn't try to detain him, didn't want to be recognized at the moment, because he was still trying to come to terms with the fact that he'd recognized the name the two men outside the station had used. *Fleming.* Well, of course he'd recognized it. It had been his own name once. But something had held him back from speaking to them, maybe the sort of men they were – both had brutal faces, though one was quite well dressed. But fear of their employer had shown in the way they spoke about him. This Fleming fellow didn't sound like the sort of person you'd want for a friend, and Aubrey intended to be very careful whom he claimed as a relative.

'Here you are, lad. That'll perk you up. You can't beat a cup of hot tea on a rainy day.' The bookshop's owner set down a steaming cup on the counter and smiled at him.

'Thanks.' Aubrey picked it up, enjoying its warmth as he cradled it in his hands. 'It's a raw day out there.'

'Yes. There's no hurry for you to leave. You look chilled to the marrow and you're not in my way.' He poked the small fire next to which Aubrey was sitting.

Suddenly a woman burst into the shop, bringing with her a whoosh of cold, damp wind. 'Ted, your Margaret's had a fall. You'd better come quickly.'

'She's all right?'

'Yes, but she needs your help to get home from the infirmary.'

Ted looked across at Aubrey. 'I wonder if you'd mind keeping an eye on the shop for me? I had a delivery yesterday, and once word gets round, customers will be coming in to buy Christmas presents. All the prices are marked inside the books in pencil, same in the second-hand ones. It's only the ones I've just picked up that aren't marked.'

'I'm happy to look after things,' Aubrey called after him, getting a wave of the hand in reply.

He stayed where he was till he'd drunk the tea, took the empty cup through to the kitchen, saw the teapot and peeped inside. The tea in it would only go cold and stewed, so he poured himself some more and walked slowly round the shop with it in his hand. The place had electric lighting, so it was very bright inside. There was a small counter, a section near the entrance displaying stationery and pens, and everywhere else shelves and shelves of books. Paradise! The new books were near the front and many of them had bright covers; the rest of the wall space was taken up by used ones, which looked much duller, and there were piles of books on the floor in a corner, as well as on the edges of the steps that led to the next floor.

He walked down the side wall, reading a few titles, taking one off the shelf because it had been an old favourite of his. It was ragged and well worn, but was holding together well enough. He looked inside and saw that it contained a book-plate inscribed *Frank Fleming*. His head throbbed again and he stumbled across to the chair near the counter and collapsed on it.

Frank! His real name was Frank. Not only that, but this had been *his* book. His family must have received one of the *missing presumed dead* telegrams and got rid of his things. He hugged the book to him, feeling choked with emotion, and it was a few minutes before he calmed down enough to open it again. The price was pencilled in on the flyleaf next to his name: *3d*. He could definitely afford threepence to retrieve an old friend like this. He went behind the counter and found the till drawer, opening it and depositing a shiny golden three-penny bit inside, then sat down and began to read the book, *his* book again now.

A few minutes later a clergyman came in, looking mildly surprised at the sight of a stranger behind the counter. 'Oh. Are you working here?'

'Just looking after the shop for Ted for an hour or two.'

'Well, I heard there'd been a new delivery and was wondering if my book had come in.'

'Which book is that, sir?'

'PG Wodehouse. *Uneasy Money*, it's called. I know it's frivolous stuff, but the fellow makes me laugh.'

'Do you know where it'd be kept?'

With a smile the man came behind the counter and indicated a shelf with several books lying sideways on it, markers sticking out of them. 'There! That's mine! And the price of those books is always on the cover. See.'

'That'll be one and sixpence then, sir.' Aubrey took the silver florin the customer held out, giving him a sixpenny piece in change. 'Do you want me to wrap it up for you?'

'Yes, please. Don't want it to get wet, do we? Looks as if the rain's set in to stay.' He pointed to a roll of brown paper. 'Ted uses that.'

Aubrey made a neat parcel and handed it over.

'New to the town, are you, young fellow?'

'Yes, sir. Just been demobbed.'

'Do you come from Tinsley?'

Something still whispered to Aubrey to keep quiet about himself. Clergymen met a lot of people and this one seemed very talkative . . . He avoided telling a direct lie. 'Just looking for somewhere to settle.'

'I wish you luck, then. Don't forget to come to church on Sunday. You'll be made very welcome, I promise you.'

Aubrey smiled and made a non-committal noise, glad when his chatty customer left. He sat on the high stool behind the counter and let his thoughts tiptoe gently back to his name. *Frank Fleming.*

But why did the thought of his surname fill him with anger? And could he be closely related to the Mr Fleming the two men at the station had feared so greatly? He hoped not.

After some thought, he decided he preferred his new first name as well as the surname Smith, which was so nice and ordinary. He'd continue to call himself Aubrey Smith whatever he did about his family, because it felt like his name now.

It was over an hour before Ted returned. 'Sorry to leave you alone like that, and thanks for taking over.'

'How's your wife?'

'Resting at home. They had to put some stitches in her leg. Everything all right here?'

'I've sold three books for you, including this one to myself. Threepence.'

'Oh, take the book as a thank you. Never mind paying.'

'I've paid already.'

'Well, take the money out of the till again.' Ted handed over the threepenny bit then hesitated. 'Have you found yourself a job yet?'

'No, not yet. Don't know what I want to do, since I haven't the faintest idea what I did before.'

'You wouldn't fancy working for me, would you? Only, I'm not as young as I was and I'd like to ease off a bit, spend more time with Margaret. I can afford an employee – just. I can't pay much, but there are a couple of rooms upstairs. You could live there for nothing.'

Aubrey stared at him and felt the genuine warmth of the other man's smile. 'I'd like to have a go, see how it suits me – and see how I suit you, for that matter. Would that be all right? I'm not sure yet whether I want to stay in Tinsley or not, you see. How about we give it a couple of months, then we'll both know how we feel.'

'Good idea. I could tell you were a book lover the minute you stepped inside, from the expression on your face as you looked round.' Ted glanced at the book Aubrey had bought, then flicked open the front cover. 'I thought so. One of Frank Fleming's books. Poor fellow was posted missing presumed dead. The father got rid of all his things. I have some other books of his here.'

'Oh?' Aubrey tried to hide his eagerness. 'Well, if they're as much to my taste as this one, I'll probably end up buying them. If you know where any of them are, that is . . .'

'Oh, I know where all the books are. This place may look untidy – well, it *is* untidy, I admit that – but it's all up here.' He tapped his forehead. 'Right then, when can you start?'

'I thought I'd started already?'

Ted beamed at him. 'Excellent.' He frowned. 'You look a bit familiar, as if I ought to know you.'

So Aubrey explained about his lost memories. He guessed that, like many soldiers, he'd left home as a boy and grown up over the years of war, so he'd probably changed a lot in appearance. Which was a good thing, he felt.

He was pleased that chance had brought him into this shop. It'd give him somewhere to live and an excuse for staying in

Tinsley. Now that he knew about this Fleming fellow, he felt even less like rushing into anything.

When Vic stopped the cab at the foot of Bridge Lane, Marcus helped Serena out and called, 'We won't be long. I just want to let Justin know we're back and married, so that he can communicate this formally to Fleming.'

Vic beamed at them. 'I didn't want to ask at the station because you never know who's listening, but I guessed you'd got wed. I'm really glad for you both and I wish you happy.'

'Thanks, old chap.'

Serena walked up the street with Marcus, marvelling at how much her life had changed since the day she'd first come to find Justin Redway.

When they went into his rooms and asked to see him, he came hurrying through from the back office, calling, 'If that's who I think it is, I want to see them this minute.' He gestured to them to go through with him. 'I've got my cousin here and she was just asking about you, Serena.'

Evadne stood up and came to take Serena's hands. 'My goodness, you do look well!' When Justin indicated chairs, however, she remained standing. 'I'd better leave you to talk privately, but it's nice to meet you again, Miss Fleming.'

Serena blushed. 'I'm Mrs Graye now. This is my husband Marcus. Marcus, this is Evadne Blair, who helped me when I was trying to escape from . . . Fleming.'

'And clearly you succeeded. I'm delighted for you.' She shook hands with Marcus, then offered her cheek to Justin. 'I'll see you tonight for dinner, coz.'

When they were alone, he asked, 'I gather everything went all right, then, if you two are married?'

Marcus took out the marriage certificate and offered it. 'Here's the proof of Serena's new status.'

'Excellent.'

'Do you want to inform Fleming for us?'

'Yes, it'd be better to leave that to me. But I shall wait a little, because he's rather busy at the moment with other things. There was a fire in his office last night and the whole place burnt down. Very convenient way of hiding the evidence of what happened to Serena's inheritance, don't you think?'

She looked at him in dismay. 'I can't believe it!' Then she looked down and admitted, 'Yes, I can. He can be very cunning.'

Marcus put his arm round her but didn't say anything.

She took a long, shuddering breath and asked the question closest to her heart. 'Do you think there's going to be any of my money left at all? My f— Fleming, I mean, told me that he'd lost all the income he'd saved for me over the years in a bad investment.'

'We'll see about that. I'd be surprised if he could touch the annuity itself, but there should be quite a bit of money from all these years he's been looking after it for you. If he's telling the truth about losing it in bad investments, there should be bank records to substantiate that, even if his office records have been destroyed . . . though the bank manager is a friend of his and may prove awkward about letting us see them. We also have to deal with Hammerton and the last remaining cottage. He hasn't answered my letter yet.'

'That place *is* still mine, isn't it?'

'I'm not sure yet. But even if it has been sold, we'll have first right to the money Fleming got for it. He can't have lost that if it's only just been paid.'

She sighed. 'I can't believe what he's done to me. In anyone else, it would be called stealing and the person would be arrested.' She looked at Marcus, worried that he would find her less appealing as a wife without the money he'd expected her to bring to him. But to her relief all his face showed was concern.

'I've enough for us to live on, Serena, though not in luxury, I'm afraid.'

'I don't need luxury to be happy.' Then a thought occurred to her and she brightened a little. 'I still have my mother's jewellery, at least. That must be worth a few hundred pounds. He didn't get hold of that, because I lodged it in the Yorkshire Penny Bank before she died.'

'That was very sensible,' Justin said approvingly, 'and I'd advise you to keep it in the bank until other matters have been settled. If Fleming would try to kidnap you like that, who knows what else he'd do? I wouldn't put it past him to try to steal the jewellery from you if you took it out of safe keeping.'

Marcus nodded agreement. 'Now, is there anything else you

need us to do, Justin? No? All right, we'll leave you to tell Fleming what's happened when you see fit. We need to settle in at the Hall, then I'll rent out the Lodge.'

As Marcus stood up, Serena suddenly remembered something. 'Oh! There are some boxes of my things still here, aren't there? I must get a carrier to bring them out to the Hall.'

'I'll arrange that for you, my dear. Now you two go away and enjoy settling into your new home.'

As she and her husband walked slowly down to the river, Serena explained about the things she'd taken from her old home. 'I'm hoping I can alter some of my mother's clothes.' She looked regretfully down at her smart new costume. 'I can't wear this all the time.'

'If not, we'll buy you something else.'

'I don't want to be a burden to you, especially if I haven't the money you thought I had.'

He stopped walking and set his hands on her shoulders, turning her to face him. 'I didn't marry you for the money, truly I didn't, though I admit it'd come in useful. I married you for two very selfish reasons – firstly, I didn't want to be alone any longer, and secondly, I was attracted to you. And since you needed help, it seemed to me we'd both benefit.'

'Do you really mean that?'

'Of course I do.'

He was attracted to her! Happiness curled through her. 'I thought . . . it was the money and just that you needed a wife.'

'No, Serena. I did want a wife, but I wanted it to be you.'

And she was crying suddenly, burying her face in his shoulder and sobbing as if her heart would break.

'What have I done? Serena, look at me. What have I done to upset you?'

She raised her face and sniffed, but there was a soft glow to her cheeks as she said, 'I'm not upset, I'm happy.'

He threw back his head and laughed. 'I'm glad you told me. I thought women cried when they were unhappy.'

'They cry when they're happy, too. Especially when someone has just taken a load off their mind.'

He clipped her up in a quick hug, delighted when she hugged him back. 'Come on then, woman. Let's get you home.'

*   *   *

When they'd left his rooms, Justin picked up the marriage certificate, slid it carefully into his inner pocket and went out into the rain, whistling cheerfully beneath his umbrella as he strolled up to Yorkshire Road. He made his way to the magistrate's rooms and only had to wait ten minutes to see Marley.

'I thought you ought to see this.' He passed the certificate across. 'Apart from the fact that this makes her Graye's responsibility, she signed it the same way as the others, with that dot after her name.'

'Interesting. Can you keep it somewhere safe?'

Justin frowned. 'I'm wondering just where could be considered safe. Fleming is a close friend of my bank manager.'

'You don't think Dewison would . . . ?' Gerald stared at his friend. 'You *do* think that!'

'It's possible. Where do you bank?'

'At the Yorkshire Penny Bank. I never did like dealing with Dewison. Do you want me to put the certificate in my safety deposit box for you? We can use it for evidence in the other matter as well.'

'Might be a good idea. That marriage gives Serena her freedom from her so-called father, and he won't accept that without a struggle, if he's as desperate for money as we suspect.'

'So-called father?'

Justin let out a little growl of exasperation. 'Damn! I hadn't intended to let that information out yet. We have no way of proving it, but Serena's mother told her on her deathbed that another man had fathered her.'

'Do we know who?'

'Someone called James Lang.'

Gerald stared at his friend in shock. 'But I knew James! We were at school together.'

'Ah. You don't happen to know what became of him, do you?'

'No. He just vanished, was supposed to be meeting me but never turned up, which wasn't like him. Then I heard he'd got some girl in trouble and run off. That wasn't like him either. And I always thought it strange that he never even wrote to let me know he was all right, nor did he contact his family that I heard of. I presumed he was dead, had been killed in an accident or something.'

'Well, I'd be grateful if you'd keep that information to yourself for the time being.'

Justin was very thoughtful as he walked home, taking a detour to view the blackened ruins of Fleming's rooms, which had been very thoroughly burnt down. There wasn't a hope of salvaging any of the fellow's papers and records.

He wondered if Westin had managed to break in and find anything before the fire. Why hadn't the fellow been in touch?

It wasn't until Justin was about to close the place up and go home to get ready for his dinner at Evadne's that a short, thin man wearing a muffler over his lower face slipped into his rooms.

'I'll deal with this gentleman,' Justin said at once to his clerk. 'It's a personal matter, not business, so you may as well leave early. No one else will be coming out in this foul weather.'

When the clerk had gone, Justin locked the outer door and only then did he turn to the man patiently waiting in a corner. 'Come through.'

In his office, he stared in shock as his visitor unwound the muffler. 'What happened to your face, Westin?'

'Got burnt getting out of that place. Someone came in and set it alight – deliberate it was. I had to hide behind the curtains till he'd gone, but he'd started fires all over the building, so I had trouble getting out.' He hesitated. 'I won't be able to go to work till this is healed, so I was hoping you'd see fit to give me a bit extra, Mr Redway, because I did get what you wanted.'

'Show me.' Justin studied the folder, which was covered in dirty finger marks and was charred at one corner, letting out a low whistle as he saw the contents. He looked up. 'You did well. I'll pay you wages for a week or two till you're fit to go back to work.'

'Thank you, sir. Any time you want me to do a little job for you, you just ask. You're a gentleman, you are!'

Eleven

The cab drew to a halt at the front door of the Hall and Marcus helped Serena out. When he'd opened the door, he turned and took her by surprise, picking her up and carrying her over the threshold. As he held her, they stared at one another, then he bent his head and set a very gentle kiss on her lips. 'Welcome to your new home, Mrs Graye. I hope you'll be happy here.'

There was a round of applause from the back of the hall and Pearl stepped forward, with Gladys a few steps behind her, looking nervous. 'We heard you drive up. Congratulations.' Then it seemed to sink in how much Serena's appearance had changed and Pearl squealed loudly. 'Oh, you look *wonderful*!'

Behind her Gladys nodded her head.

Ada appeared at the top of the stairs.

'They got married,' Pearl called up to her.

'Good. I wish you both happy.' She gestured to them to come up. 'The bedroom's ready.'

'Come on. See what we've done.' Pearl took Serena's hand and hurried her up the stairs, with the two maids following. She led them to the room at the front of the house which she and Serena had shared two nights previously and flung open the door with a flourish of one hand.

Ada must have worked hard, Serena thought, because the room had that newly cleaned feel to it, not the dustiness it'd had two nights before. There was a cheerful little fire burning in the corner fireplace and an easy chair near the window to tempt you to rest for a moment or two and enjoy the view.

She stood by the door and tried to look pleased. But she wasn't, not really! She was so very conscious of that huge bed dominating the room that all her worries rushed back.

Everyone expected her to share this bed with Marcus and that made her feel nervous.

He came to stand behind her, his hands resting lightly on her shoulders. 'The room looks lovely, doesn't it? Thank you so much, Ada. As if you didn't have enough on your hands.'

'Getting married is special, sir, and anyway it'll be lovely to have the house running properly again.' She looked expectantly at him.

'We'll certainly do our best to set things in order, but I'm not sure yet how much money there will be, so, apart from Pearl and Vic, I daren't hire any more staff.'

'That's double what we had before,' the maid pointed out.

'And I'm not going to sit down and expect to be waited on,' Serena said quietly. This was one thing she *was* sure of.

'Nor I,' Marcus said.

'Well, then, there you are,' Ada said again. 'Things can only get better.'

There was the sound of a hand bell ringing, then ringing again.

'Drat her!' Ada muttered under her breath. 'She knows we're trying to get you settled in.'

Marcus took a quick decision. 'How about making something for us to eat, Pearl?'

She nodded and went off, followed by Gladys.

He looked at his wife. 'Come along and meet my aunt, Serena. She may not be polite, but it's proper that she meet the new mistress of the house.'

He gave Serena a little tug and escorted both women along to the other wing. 'You go in first, Ada. Call out if she's not decent, but otherwise, just announce us.'

She rolled her eyes and went into the bedroom, leaving the door slightly ajar. 'It's Mr Marcus and his new wife, ma'am, come to see you.'

'I'm too tired.'

'We won't keep you a minute.' Marcus led the way inside, determination clear in the set of his face. 'Aunt Pamela, I've brought my bride to meet you. Serena, this is my aunt.'

Serena was shocked by the old lady's appearance. Pamela was sallow and so thin that she looked more like a skeleton dressed in skin. Her eyes had a yellowish tinge to them and weariness showed in every line of her body. 'I'm sorry you're not well. I didn't mean to . . . trouble you.'

Mrs Lonnerden stared at her. 'Well, you've got good manners at least.' After chewing the side of her lip, she asked, 'Serena who?' When her visitor didn't reply, she added sharply. 'Who were you before you married, girl?'

He waited for Serena to speak, and when she didn't, said it for her. 'She was a Fleming, Aunt.'

'You've married *that man's* daughter?'

'Yes. But Serena had run away from him and she doesn't like him any more than you do.'

Pamela scowled at them. 'Well, blood will out, and I'm sorry to be connected to him in any way. He's a rogue and opportunist, if ever I met one, and it was he more than anyone who got my Lawrence into trouble. How could you *do* this to me, Marcus?' She tugged out a sodden rag of a handkerchief and mopped her eyes with it, but more tears followed.

Serena went over to the bed. 'Don't cry, Mrs Lonnerden. Fleming isn't my real father.'

Pamela stared at her open-mouthed, so once again Serena explained.

When she'd finished, the old lady nodded and closed her eyes. 'That's all right, then.' She let her head drop back against the pillows. 'I'd like something to eat now. That new girl who's doing the cooking has a nice light hand with the pastry. And I'm too tired to talk any more.'

As they moved towards the door, she added, as if speaking to herself. 'I'm so glad you're not *his* daughter.'

They shut the door quietly behind them.

'She looks ill,' Serena said. 'Very ill.'

'She's a bit better than she was,' Marcus said. 'I think she wanted to die after she lost Lawrence, but we'll feed her up a bit. Give her another month or two and she'll be telling us how to run our lives.'

Serena wasn't so sure. His aunt had the same look in her eyes that Serena's mother had had for the last few weeks – a distance, as if she was no longer quite of this world.

When informed that Hudd and another man were asking to

see him, Ernest nodded to Ruby and told her to show them in. He waited until the door was closed to ask, 'Well?'

'Your daughter's come back, sir,' Hudd said. 'She got off the train only half an hour ago with Mr Graye. Went off in a cab but fortunately I looked down Bridge Lane as we were walking here along Yorkshire Road and saw them going into Redway's rooms.'

'Hmm. Go and keep watch on Redway then, and let me know who else goes to see him. He's up to something and I want to know what. One of you can bring me the information while the other keeps watch. It's only a five-minute walk from here.' He waved his hand in dismissal and when they'd gone began to tap his pencil on the desk. So, she'd come back, had she? That was rather stupid of her. And what was she doing with Graye?

Hudd would find out for him. Very useful fellow, Hudd.

A few hours later, Ruby knocked on her master's door and showed Hudd in again.

He barely waited for the door to close before he said, 'Ches Westin just went in to see Redway, sir.'

'Who is Ches Westin?'

'A burglar, been in prison for it. Redway defended him last time, got him a reduced sentence on compassionate grounds.'

'Wait for Westin to come out and persuade him to tell you what he was doing there.' Fleming smiled, or rather the corners of his mouth turned up, but his eyes stayed cold.

'Yes, sir.'

Half an hour later, Hudd was back again, this time sporting a bruise on his chin.

'What happened to you? I hope you didn't draw attention to yourself.'

'We took Westin down the back alley. He – er – struggled a bit. You'll not believe what he told us, though, sir.'

'I won't if you don't tell me.'

'He burgled your offices just before the fire. Got his face burned, he did, getting out. Arnold's keeping him safe in the cellar of your other place in case you want to question him yourself.' He grinned. 'Good thing that didn't burn down, eh?'

'Did the fellow take anything from my rooms?'

'A folder, sir, with information about Miss Fleming in it,

he said. He gave it to Redway just before we caught him. Pity, that.'

Fleming sat very still and quiet, even though inside he was extremely angry. He'd not have expected Redway to break the law. And if the lawyer reported him to the police and it came out what was inside the folder, that'd be . . . difficult. Damnation! He should have kept that folder in the cellar of the other place. 'I want to question Redway and get that folder back. Wait till he's closing the office tonight and keep him in his rooms, then send for me.'

'Yes, sir.'

'One moment.'

'Yes, sir?'

'If he should get hurt, just a little, in the struggle, I should not mind. Come and fetch me when you have him safely held.'

Hudd nodded and left.

Ruby knocked on the study door. 'Your meal is ready, sir.'

'I'm not hungry. Tell Cook to put something cold on a plate for me for later. I've a headache, so will just sit quietly in here for a time. Don't disturb me. I'll ring when I want you.'

She backed out quickly and quietly, wondering what he was up to now. He had *that look* on his face, the one that usually meant someone was going to get into trouble. She'd seen it time and again over the years of working for him. Going back to the kitchen, she passed on the message to Cook.

'You and me will eat his dinner, then,' Cook said at once. 'I know how to appreciate a good piece of roast beef even if he doesn't.'

But Ruby couldn't eat her meal in peace, because the door-bell rang again, and the same man went in to see her master. Fed up of all this, she hesitated, then bent her head to the keyhole.

What she heard had her backing away in dismay.

Justin sat on after his visitor had left, reading through the folder's contents very carefully. Not until the town hall clock chimed seven did he realize what time it was. He locked away the folder in his bottom desk drawer and only then noticed the piece of paper that had fallen out. Unwilling to delay a minute longer, since he was already late for dinner at Evadne's, he picked the paper up and put it on the side table, slipping it under some other bills for safety, then going to lock up for the night.

He looked up the stairs as he went out and wasn't surprised to see that all the lights were switched off. He must be the last one out of the building tonight. Not for the first time.

As he was locking the front door, the world exploded in pain and darkness and he could feel himself falling . . .

He regained consciousness to find himself securely tied to a chair in his office, with a man standing guard, wearing a muffler round his face to hide his identity. Justin had a fair idea of who the fellow was, however, and knew with a sickening lurch of his stomach why he'd been captured.

Groaning, he closed his eyes again, and let his head loll as if he wasn't fully conscious. Footsteps came in, someone heavy.

'Is he unconscious?'

Fleming, as Justin had expected.

'Came to a minute ago, then groaned and went off again.'

'You hit him too hard. Give him a shake. I need to ask him a few questions.'

Justin suffered the shaking and let himself open his eyes, feigning bewilderment and dizziness.

Fleming thrust his face close and asked in that chill, quiet tone that rarely changed, 'Where is it?'

'Where's what?'

'You and I both know what I'm talking about, but if you wish my men to beat the information out of you, then they'll no doubt oblige.'

For a moment Justin held silent, but he couldn't see any way of avoiding Fleming finding the folder. 'It's in my bottom desk drawer. The key is in my pocket.'

Fleming extracted the bunch of keys and went round to the other side of the desk. The first two keys didn't work, but he calmly continued inserting them until he found the key that did. Opening the drawer, he took out the folder, glanced at its contents and nodded.

At the door he beckoned to one of the men and murmured something quietly.

Justin looked at him in sudden fear as he caught the words 'better dead'. Surely Fleming wasn't going to have him killed?

The door closed behind Fleming and the man came back in, beckoned to his companion and whispered to him in turn. The second man looked absolutely terrified and Justin heard him say, 'No! I'm not committing murder for him or anyone.'

'Don't be stupid. You're in it now and you'll be in worse trouble with *him* if you don't do it than if you do.'

Hudd's voice. The man who did all the dirty jobs for Fleming. Justin's guts suddenly turned to churning liquid terror as Hudd went out and came back with an oil lamp from the storeroom. He opened the oil reservoir and scattered its contents on the rug.

'I'll pay you anything you like to let me go instead!' Justin said.

The two men looked at him and the one who had protested looked pleadingly at the other, but he shook his head and muttered, 'Much as my life's worth.'

All too quickly Hudd set the rug on fire and left the room without a word. Justin tried desperately to pull free from his bonds, but his arms were tied very tightly behind him to the chair and he couldn't loosen them at all, nor could he move the heavy chair more than an inch or two with his feet tied to it. He looked round in rising panic . . .

The newly-weds were fêted by their staff and friends, and there was even a small wedding cake, thanks to Pearl's mother, though it didn't contain many currants and the layer of icing sugar was so thin as to be almost transparent. Still, they made a ceremony of cutting it and eating a piece each. Then the staff left them alone.

As the time for them to go to bed grew closer and closer, however, Marcus could see Serena glancing at the clock, then glancing again two minutes later, her face wearing that glassy expression he'd seen slide over it in her father's presence. There could only be one explanation: she didn't want to share his bed.

And he didn't want a woman who was merely 'doing her duty', as the saying went. Either they made love because they both wanted to or they didn't make love at all. He was quite sure in his own mind about that. And yet, before they married, he could have sworn there was something between them, some spark of attraction which could be fanned into a blaze if they both gave it a chance.

But perhaps Ernest Fleming had spoiled her for that sort of thing, made her feel marriage was a prison, rather than a partnership . . . perhaps she had only married Marcus because she felt he was the lesser of two evils. He didn't know, couldn't seem to work it out. First he thought one thing, then the other. What did he know of women anyway, after spending the last few years mainly with men? And he was tired, so very tired, with other things to worry about as well, so much responsibility lying on his shoulders.

Eventually he could stand her nervousness and monosyllabic conversation no longer. 'It's about time we went to bed, isn't it?'

'What? Oh, yes! Yes, of course.'

'I wonder, would you mind changing the dressings for me first? I hate to keep asking you, but it's necessary.' Relief showed on her face. It was definitely relief.

'Of course I don't mind. I'll go and get a jug of hot water from the kitchen while you – um – get ready.'

She was up and out of the room before he could speak. That decided it. He wanted her but he wasn't going to force himself on her. He'd never do that to any woman. She needed more time to get used to him, and who could blame her? Her life had been turned upside down in the past few days.

Wishing things were different between them, he turned off all but one of the oil lamps, wondering if it would be possible to get modern gas lights this far out of town. Picking up the lamp from the nearby table, he went into the hall, where he met Serena carrying a ewer of steaming water and some clean cloths. 'I'm just in time to light you upstairs.'

They went up in silence, leaving the lamp which always stood on the hall table burning low.

In the bedroom, Marcus removed his trousers and put on his pyjamas, while she avoided looking at him by fiddling with the bowl. He rolled up the pyjama leg and let her tend to the largest wound, which was still unhealed in the centre but was getting smaller every week, with pink healthy flesh building up again where the jagged crater had been.

'It's looking a lot better.'

Strange, how normal her voice sounded when she wasn't facing the possibility of him asking for a husband's rights. He watched her tend the wound, loving the feel of her gentle fingers on his skin.

'Shouldn't I check the ones on your body as well?'

He nodded and unbuttoned his pyjama top, wincing as she pulled the sticking plaster off.

'This one got bruised during your scuffle at the cottage the other day. It still looks red and tender, must be very sore.'

'I suppose so. You get used to the pain after a while, and unless something happens to remind you, well, you just get on with things.' He watched her. 'You're very good at that, deft I think the word is. Better than some of the nurses I've had.'

'Am I really?'

She smiled at him, a real smile this time.

'I wouldn't say so if I didn't mean it. Serena . . .'

Her expression grew wary. 'Yes?'

'I think we should wait longer to consummate our marriage . . . until you feel more comfortable with me. I can see that you're still nervous.'

She gave him a long look but it revealed nothing of her feelings. 'Whatever you feel best.'

He didn't know what was best, dammit, only that he wasn't going to force her, and that he wanted to make her happy in bed.

She began gathering together the things she'd used. 'I'll just take these downstairs again.'

She stopped halfway down the stairs, swallowing hard, desperately willing herself not to weep, because the others were still sitting chatting in the kitchen. Marcus definitely didn't want her, wasn't the slightest bit interested in making her his wife, however much he dressed it up as waiting till they knew one another better! He'd probably only married her for her money and for the convenience of having a wife to run his house. Well, why else would any man want her, with so many younger, prettier women around?

And she didn't know how to tell him that she thought they should make love, that she both wanted to and was afraid to, but that she wanted to feel she was really his. She knew she grew stiff when she was afraid or upset.

Why should he want her? No other man ever had in any sense, not her real father and definitely not her pretend father.

The baize-covered door into the servants' quarters opened and she summoned up a smile, starting down the stairs again.

'I'll hold the door open for you, love.' Pearl smiled at her.

'Thank you.'

In the kitchen, Gladys was yawning, but she came to take the bowl and cloths from Serena.

'I can manage it. You look tired, Gladys.'

'No, no! That's my job. You get to bed, ma'am.'

So Serena went slowly and reluctantly back up the stairs. She stopped outside the bedroom to take a deep breath and will herself to tell him what she was thinking, then went inside.

But Marcus was asleep, one hand flung across his eyes, his chest moving up and down slowly. She tiptoed across to the bed and picked up her nightdress, not bothering to go behind the screen because he wasn't awake to see her.

From the shadow of his arm, Marcus watched as his wife took off her clothes. That at least he could allow himself. She had an attractive body, small and slender, with well-formed breasts and just a hint of a curve to her belly, as a normal woman should have. He could feel his body reacting to the sight of her and hoped she wouldn't notice, because he was quite sure the sight of him erect would terrify her. She put on a lawn nightdress, which for some reason made her look both virginal and sensual. It was hard to keep breathing slowly and steadily, hard to pretend to be asleep, because he wanted her quite desperately. It had been so long . . .

Blowing out the lamp, she sighed and got into bed, such a deep, weary sigh that he was glad he'd held back. Only when she was lying there with her back to him did he allow himself to move, turning away from her and making a small noise as if merely stirring in his sleep.

But he couldn't turn his back to the images of the lovely curves of her soft woman's body, which played and re-played in his mind.

And he couldn't turn off his need for her.

It seemed a very long time before he got to sleep.

Twelve

As the flames began to lick around his trouser legs, Justin rocked the chair to and fro, calling for help as loudly as he could in between coughing and choking from the hot, smoke-filled air. Breathing was becoming increasingly difficult. He managed to move the chair backwards away from the flames, still trying desperately to free his hands, but then the chair hit something and would go no further.

Suddenly a voice spoke beside him, 'Did you mean what you said about paying anyone as set you free?'

'Of course I did.'

'How much?'

'A hundred pounds.'

'Two hundred.'

'All right, all right.' Justin's feet felt hot, he could smell singeing wool, and sweat was pouring down his face.

'Get me out of here quickly then, or I'll be in no state to pay you anything.'

The ropes tying his wrists suddenly fell away and the man bent to slice through the bindings on his ankles. With a sob of relief, Justin pushed himself to his feet and grabbed his briefcase from the floor near the filing cabinet. He hesitated, then braved the flames for a few seconds more to snatch at the pile of papers on it, which were curling up and turning brown from the heat. Stuffing them down his jacket front, he prayed he'd got the one that had fallen out of the file.

The man was tugging his arm. 'Come *on*!'

Struggling for breath, Justin stumbled through a nightmare of flames and smoke. He'd have lost his way but for his companion, and as they pushed the door into the street open, the flames behind them blazed higher with an angry roar. 'Shut the door!' he rasped, his throat feeling as if it had been sandpapered.

As a bell began clanging in the distance, the man looked at him, eyes pleading. 'The fire brigade mustn't find me here.'

'Meet me at number ten at three o'clock this afternoon. Go in through the back yard.' Justin pointed up the street towards the headquarters of the WSPC. 'I'll have the money waiting for you there.'

'Swear it!'

'I promise! You saved my life, didn't you? Think I'm not grateful?'

'I'll be there.' The man slipped away into the smoke-filled darkness just as the fire engine rumbled down the street and stopped outside the offices.

Justin had been one of those who'd pressed for the purchase of a Merryweather fire engine several years ago, but had never thought to need it himself. The modern motorized vehicle didn't have to wait for horses to be harnessed and could transport five or six trained men to a fire anywhere in the town within minutes of the warning being given.

'Stand clear, sir.' Working rapidly and efficiently, the uniformed men found the nearest water main, attached a hose and began pumping water into the building.

Justin watched in shuddering relief as they extinguished the fire before it could destroy the whole place.

As the flames died down inside, they left a black, sodden, stinking mess, with windows broken, sprouting fringes of blackened glass shards, and smoke still curling up here and there. The captain of the brigade came to stand next to Justin. 'You're lucky this place is close to a fire point.' He squinted sideways by the light of a street lamp. 'Mr Redway. Do you know how the fire started, sir?'

'Yes, it was deliberately started by two men who broke into my rooms and robbed me.' He'd decided on this story because he had no way of proving it was Fleming who'd arranged it, but wanted it made obvious that someone in the town was committing crimes. 'I was dazed and I think they thought I'd perish, but I got out in time.' He shook his head. 'It spread so quickly. I can't believe how quickly. I was never so glad to see anyone as you and your men, and may I congratulate you on your speedy arrival?'

'Someone saw the fire and sent to warn us. The lad who brought the message slipped away before we could take his name, though, so we don't know who your saviour was.' He scowled at the mess. 'Looks like we've got a firebug in town, what with Mr Fleming's offices going up, then yours. Both were definitely deliberate.'

'You're sure of that?'

'Oh, yes. Fleming says he can't believe it, but I know what I found and there was a smell of paraffin. You can't hide that completely, sir. It lingers even after the fire.'

A policeman turned up just then and Justin had to go through it all over again with him, though his voice was little more than a croak now.

Then Evadne came running down the street and flung her arms around him. 'Oh, I'm so glad you're safe!'

'So am I,' he said shakily.

'There was I thinking you'd let me down for dinner, when we heard the fire-engine bell. A passer-by told our maid there was a house burning in Bridge Lane and I knew, somehow I just *knew*, that it was yours. Are you all right, Justin? Really, are you?'

He held on to her for a minute, because he most certainly wasn't all right. Now that the emergency was over, reaction had set in. 'I'll t-tell you about it l-later.' He couldn't stop shaking, couldn't even get another word out properly, because it was sinking in how close he'd come to death. Flames still seemed to be burning round him, people's voices coming and going in his ears.

Evadne took charge. 'Constable, my cousin is very upset after his narrow escape, so I'm taking him home with me. You can find him at my house if you need to question him further. He'll be spending the night there.' She put her arm round Justin's waist and they walked slowly up the lane and out from the town towards her house.

Once there, she took him into the sitting room and he collapsed into a chair, putting his head in his hands. When she closed his fingers round a glass, he looked down and saw it was a brandy. He took a gulp, then another. Gradually the shuddering stopped, and when he looked round, she too had a glass in her hand. Although she gave him a half-smile, she didn't press him to talk until he was ready.

Then, in jerky sentences punctuated by shudders and silences, he fumbled for the words to tell her what had really happened.

She stared at him in horror, not speaking till he'd finished. 'But you have to tell the police, Justin. You can't let Fleming get away with this.'

'I've no proof. He'd charge me with slander. But I will have a word with Marley. He knows what's really going on, though he's as helpless as me to stop the man without proof.'

'You will be careful from now on, won't you?'

He nodded.

'Surely you're not going to pay this man who untied you? He should be locked up, not rewarded.'

'He didn't want to harm me, I heard him say so, and he came back and saved my life. I find I value that rather highly.'

'Well, have it your own way. You usually do. But you're staying here tonight, where I can keep an eye on you.'

'Thanks.' He definitely didn't want to be on his own tonight – or any other night until Fleming was dealt with.

Surely there must be some way to stop the man?

Ernest heard the fire engine's bell clanging away as the ancient apparatus made its way to Bridge Lane. He looked at the clock and smiled as he ate the last piece of beef sandwich with great relish. Redway should be nicely toasted by now, and serve him right for poking his nose where it shouldn't go. He hoped the man had died in agony. He looked down at his empty plate and rang for it to be cleared away.

Ruby worked in silence as usual, which he much preferred.

He watched her go out then settled down with the newspaper. The folder with all the papers in it was now in his home safe, which was in the wall behind a singularly ugly portrait of his late wife's mother. He scowled as he thought about Grace. He supposed he'd better find himself another wife and try once again for a son, though he'd make sure he selected someone young and healthy, best of all a widow with a child to raise, who had already proved she was fertile and would be grateful to find another protector. He'd have a look round. There were plenty of young widows, thanks to the war.

Pity Frank had been killed. Ernest didn't really want to marry again. Women were such a nuisance, and if he found one from a good family, she'd be expensive too, and he was just a trifle short of money at present. Though that was going to be remedied.

He stood up and began to pace to and fro, wondering exactly how to deal with Serena. Married or not, she definitely wasn't going to keep that damned annuity when he needed the money so much more. He'd have to stop gambling with Hammerton, though. The fellow was so lucky you had to wonder if he cheated.

He smiled as he thought of the fire. Well, at least Redway wouldn't be poking his nose in where it wasn't wanted now. He was still smiling about that as he fell asleep in his cosy bed.

The customers coming into the bookshop the following day all talked about the latest fire. Aubrey listened to them patiently, getting the same story several times over, with details that changed each time. At one stage, Ted grinned at him. 'You'll do for me, son. You not only love books, you listen to folk, and customers like that.'

'Thanks. It's strange, though, isn't it? No big fires in the town for years, then two houses burn down within the week, one of them completely destroyed.'

'I wish that bugger had been destroyed with it.'

'Fleming?'

'Aye. Who else? Redway's a decent sort of chap, for a lawyer, but Fleming's a nasty sod. He owns quite a lot of property round the town. I'm thankful this building belongs to me, though he's had a go at me a few times, trying to persuade me to sell to him. As if I would!'

'What do you mean, "had a go"?'

'Come in to persuade me himself, hinted at problems I might encounter if I don't sell. Though he hasn't set fire to the place yet, at least. Luckily I'm just opposite the police station here. Easy enough to call for help, eh?'

Aubrey frowned at this and Ted grinned even more broadly.

'I bet you haven't heard the rumour that he set fire to his own office to hide what he's been doing? It's not the sort of thing people say publicly, but it's being whispered in private.'

'No, I haven't heard it. Is it true?'

'Could be. He's a gambler. Him and a few other fine gentlemen of this town, in that fancy club of theirs with its private rooms. There's two unlawful things that go on in those private rooms: women and gambling. I wonder why Fleming doesn't want folk finding out what he's been doing. They say that daughter of his can't even get her own inheritance money out of him. There must be some truth in it.'

Aubrey's head was spinning at these revelations about his father. 'I didn't know Fleming was a gambler.'

'Well, how could you? You've only been in Tinsley for a few days.'

'And you say he has a daughter?' Suddenly Aubrey had a mental image of the woman with the kind smile, and a stab of pain went through his head. 'Where is she?'

'Rumour says she ran away from home a couple of days ago. She's not living with him any longer, that's certain.'

The room spun round Aubrey for a moment or two. 'Serena,' he said suddenly. 'She's called Serena, isn't she?'

'Yes, that's her. Poor dowdy thing, she is.'

Aubrey stared at him in puzzlement. 'Dowdy? I think I saw her at the station and she looked very modern, smart, with bobbed hair and shorter skirts. In fact, I'd call her pretty.'

'Can't have been the same person,' Ted said dismissively. 'She's a real frump, Fleming's daughter. Who was she with?'

'A man, tall, with a badly scarred face. They got into a cab together going to the Hall, so I assumed they were married. They had two suitcases and, well – they just seemed married.'

Ted stared at him in surprise. 'She was with a scarred man? Does he have a bit of a limp?'

'Yes.'

'A chap called Marcus Graye inherited the Hall recently, and he was badly injured down one side of his face and body. Surely *he* hasn't married her?'

Aubrey shrugged. 'I don't know. I just saw them together at the station.' He was puzzled about all this, wanted to think about it, see if he could remember any more.

Ted clapped the younger man on the shoulder. 'Come on, we'll make a start on clearing out the upstairs while there's a lull. Though I don't think you should move in until after Christmas. It's a lonely time to be on your own, Christmas is. I'd invite you over for a meal, but to tell you the truth, my Margaret isn't up to visitors.'

'I like being on my own.' Aubrey could see that Ted didn't believe him, but it was true. He'd spent most of the past few months living cheek by jowl with other people, and the thought of being absolutely on his own was very appealing.

He followed Ted upstairs to the three rooms on the first floor. Two of them were filled with boxes and miscellaneous piles of books, and above them were two attic rooms with sloping ceilings. He'd been up here before but this time he looked around with a proprietorial feeling. The front room was empty and very spacious, with a big window looking down on the station end of Yorkshire Road and, as Ted had said, the police station opposite. He'd have this room for his sitting room, could imagine a big armchair in that square bay window, a small table with a pile of books on it nearby.

'I'll still need the big back room for storage,' Ted said. 'But with the middle one for your bedroom and one of the attic rooms at your disposal, you'll even be able to put up a friend, if you want.' Even as he was speaking, the doorbell of the shop tinkled.

'You go and get it, lad. You've got younger knees than I have.'

Aubrey went down to find one of the two men who'd pushed past him at the station standing there. 'Can I help you?'

'Need to see Mr Bailey. Urgent. Tell him it's Jem Pitterby.'

Aubrey called up the stairs, 'It's for you.' He waited in the shop until Ted came down and even then he didn't go up the stairs, because for some strange reason the man made him feel uneasy.

'Message from Mr Fleming. There's a house to clear out. Old lady in Cooter's Lane hadn't paid her rent for a few months, so Mr Fleming is taking the furniture in lieu. Wants you to make an offer on the books. There are a bloody lot of 'em cluttering up the place, should be worth something to you.'

'All right. Where is it?' Ted wrote down the address. 'I can come there with you now if you want. I've got a new assistant, so I don't need to wait till after the shop closes.'

The man nodded, his eyes sliding sideways to Aubrey, his brow wrinkling as if something puzzled him.

As Ted went for his coat, Aubrey walked forward to ask the fellow, 'What's happening to the old lady's furniture?'

'What's it to you?'

'I need to furnish some rooms. Might suit me to take it off your hands. Might suit your employer too. What's the furniture like?'

'Clean. Old-fashioned but solid enough. She'd known better days. You'd have to clear it out straight away, though. He's got someone waiting to move in tomorrow. Shortage of decent houses, there is.'

So, after Ted came back from valuing the books, Aubrey walked the few streets up to the house in question and looked over it with the man breathing down his neck.

'How much?' he asked at last.

'Fifteen pound.'

'Ten.'

He saw the other study him calculatingly and folded his arms. 'I'm not made of money and I'm not going much higher because it isn't worth it. How about splitting the difference? I'll give you twelve pounds ten shillings.'

'All right, but you'll have to take everything and move it today. Mr Fleming allus sells house contents to a dealer in one lot. Says it's not worth the trouble of splitting it up, except for the books.'

'Always? Does he do this often?'

The man grinned. 'As often as necessary. He gets his rent money one way or the other. Clever fellow, Mr Fleming. Well? I can't stand here all day waiting.'

'All right. I'll arrange for the whole contents to be collected.'

'I know a fellow as'd do it for you.'

'Thanks, but I know someone too.' He didn't, but when he got back he asked Ted who would shift the stuff, and then walked down the street to the address Ted gave him and arranged to have it moved that very afternoon. As Ted said, who was to know what Pitterby would take for himself if the house contents were left lying around?

'Are you always so suspicious?' Aubrey asked.

'Only when I'm dealing with Fleming and his men. Wouldn't trust any of them as far as I could throw them.'

'Yet you do business with them.'

Ted shrugged. 'I'm not stupid enough to show them how I feel. That'd really be asking for trouble.'

Which gave Aubrey even more to think about.

The day after his brush with death, Justin hired Vic and his cab to drive him out to the Hall. He felt safer with a man he knew had no link to Fleming. That sod was walking round town looking like a cat that had swallowed a plump canary, for all that his offices had burned down recently.

'You all right, sir?' Vic asked, shocked by Justin's pallor.

'Sort of. When we get out there, can you come in and join us while we talk? I reckon everyone who lives at the Hall is involved in this, whether they want to be or not.'

'What, even old Mrs Lonnerden?'

'Even her.'

Which made Vic worry all the way out of town. He left his horse and cab with Hill and raced up to the house to find out what was going on.

Everyone was in the sitting room, which Serena and Pearl had cleaned thoroughly the previous day and which still smelt faintly of grate blacking and Ronuk polish, a brand Gladys swore by. Even Mrs Lonnerden was there, sitting in a big armchair with a rug across her knees.

As soon as Vic joined them, Justin began telling what had happened to him. When he had finished relating his narrow escape, Marcus turned to Serena, who was looking white and shocked. Without thinking what he was doing, he took her hand. 'I won't let Fleming get hold of you, I promise. Forewarned *is* forearmed, you know. I'm going to get out my service revolver and keep it handy.'

She looked down at their joined hands, and though she didn't pull away, she didn't meet his eyes either. 'Fleming can be a very determined man. I don't want to put you in danger.'

'So can I be determined,' Marcus said. 'And I look after

my own.' He turned to Vic. 'Be careful who you take as passengers from now on, especially after dark. In fact, don't you think you'd better stop working after it gets dark? This is a time to be rather careful. I know we agreed you could do some part-time work with the cab, but maybe it isn't wise.'

'I was just thinking that I'd get out my own revolver and keep it handy when I drive out.' Vic grinned. 'I used to be a crack shot, actually. They used me as a sniper for a time.' He smiled across at his fiancée, but even Pearl's usual ebullience seemed dimmed by the news and she didn't return his smile.

'We'd better be even more careful about locking up here,' Serena said. 'I'll have a word with Gladys and Ada, if you like.'

Aunt Pamela stared at them bleakly. 'Fleming is getting out of hand. Something needs to be done about him.'

'He's a little difficult to pin down, Aunt.'

'Hmm.' She went back to staring into the fire.

Serena realized Justin was sitting quietly, waiting to speak. 'Sorry, Mr Redway. We're being very rude to you.'

He smiled. 'You've just had some bad news. I do have some good news for you, though.'

They both looked at him questioningly.

'The magistrate has ruled that the sale of the final cottage is null and void, so it and its contents are yours to keep, sell or do whatever you wish with.' He hesitated, then said, 'There is some doubt about the validity of the forged signature.'

Serena brightened. 'Really?'

'Whenever you sign something, you put a dot nearby, like a full stop. You did it when you gave samples of your signature for Marley and when you signed papers for me. We said nothing at the time, but he feels you'd have a good case for challenging Fleming about the sale of the other cottages. But, of course, it'd cost money to do that and the result could not be guaranteed.'

She turned to Marcus, smiling. 'Well, at least I'm bringing you something.'

'I keep telling you: all I want is you.'

She stared at him and swallowed hard.

'I mean it,' he added very softly.

'I'm still glad I'm not coming to you penniless.'

Justin coughed. 'Unfortunately, your father is saying he can't give details about what happened to the money from your annuity over the past few years, because the records have been burned. No one believes him, but he's sticking to his story and he smiles as he repeats it. Marley has ordered Dewison at the bank to disclose details of Fleming's accounts, but I'm guessing there won't be anything showing in his personal account, and who knows what other names he uses? I doubt Dewison will disclose those.'

Serena sighed. 'Fleming's a thief, isn't he?'

'It seems likely. No doubt he'll concoct a story to cover the losses, so you may never retrieve anything, but the annuity itself should still be intact. Even there he's stalling, has a doctor's letter from Tolson saying he's too ill to do business – though that clerk of his goes to work at Fleming's house every day and the men who deal with his properties are coming and going as well.'

'How can he keep doing this?' Serena asked, eyes flashing.

'It's a question of proof.' Justin looked at the clock. 'I'm sorry, but I can't stay much longer. I'd rather drive back by daylight, for obvious reasons.'

Vic stood up. 'I'll go and bring the cab round.'

When he'd gone, Justin said, 'You've got a good chap there, Graye.'

'I'm well aware of that. He's more a partner than an employee though. We have a few plans for the future and they don't include him driving a cab, but at the moment he's saving hard to get married, so wants to earn every extra penny he can, and I've not really got going here.'

On the way into town, on a stretch of road where there were no houses and where high banks hid the road from view, a battered-looking motor truck drove towards the cab, swerving at the last minute to block the road and causing Dolly to shy and nearly land them in the ditch.

Vic reined the horse in hastily, trying to calm and hold her while reaching for his revolver.

The door of the truck opened and two men got out, their faces covered by mufflers. They left the motor running and turned to face the horse cab. 'Need a word with your passenger,' one called. 'Stay where you are and you won't be hurt, driver.'

Vic didn't like the looks of them. 'It's you who'd better stay where you are. If you take one step further I'll shoot.' He let them see the revolver, pointing it at them and praying that Dolly would stay still. There was no sound from Mr Redway inside the cab.

The men stopped moving, glancing at one another then back at him. 'You wouldn't dare!' one said and took a step forward.

Vic took careful aim and managed to hit the man in the fleshy part of the leg. Cursing, both men scrambled back into their vehicle. 'I was trained as a sharpshooter,' he yelled after them. 'If you don't drive away, I'll shoot out the windscreen next and whoever is driving will get it in the face.'

For a moment there was silence except for the puttering noise made by the truck's motor, and he wondered if they too had guns with them. In which case he would be in trouble, exposed as he was on the raised driving seat.

'We'll be back!' one of them yelled.

'Good. I'd like another shot at you.'

The truck backed down the road cautiously, then the men turned it round in the gateway to the next field and drove off.

Justin got out of the cab, looking white and shaken. 'Has Fleming run mad? Does he think no one will notice what he's doing? This is *England*, not a battlefield.' He shuddered. 'I don't think you're safe driving this cab around any more.'

'No. I wonder whose truck that was. It's not one I recognize from round here. I wish I had a car or motor bike and I'd have chased after them.' Vic shrugged. 'Let's get you into Tinsley now.'

'How are you going to get back to Horton safely from there, though?'

'I'll keep my revolver beside me. If I come straight back after I've dropped you, and take a different route, maybe they'll not have had time to think up any more nasty surprises.'

Justin went back to Evadne's. She took one look at him and

shut the door hastily, tugging him into her sitting room. 'I can see from your face that something else has happened. Tell me.'

He explained.

'I'll just finish giving my cook orders for the day, then we'll decide what to do.'

He was glad of a few minutes' peace to pull himself together. By the time she came back he had had a few thoughts. 'Can I stay on here with you, Evadne? I don't think you'll be in danger, or I wouldn't ask, but I don't have live-in help and I think I'd be at risk living on my own.'

'Of course you can. What are you going to do about Fleming, though?'

'I can only work legally.'

She made a scornful noise. 'That won't get you very far.'

'I do have a friend in Marley. In fact, I need to see him. Can you take a message to him from me when you go out?'

'I'll do better than that. I'll get the lad next door to take it now. No one will think of stopping him. But shouldn't you report this to the police?'

'I suppose so.'

'It's not like you to be so indecisive. Are you sure you weren't hurt?'

He shrugged. 'It's really shaken me. For the first time in my life I'm feeling my age.'

'Pooh! You're only sixty-three. Plenty of life in you yet.'

Aubrey was pleased with his new furniture, which he'd helped the carter to carry up the stairs late that afternoon. It might not be stylish but was more than adequate for his needs. The only thing missing was a mattress, since the old one had been badly stained. The bed frame was in good order, though.

He felt guilty at going through the old lady's personal possessions, but someone had to do it. In the drawers of a heavy mahogany sideboard, which had been the very devil to get up the stairs, he found old photographs no one would ever recognize again, and letters from her parents written decades ago, faded, full of admonitions to behave modestly and save her money. She seemed to have been a governess.

He spent quite a while studying his own face in the dressing-table mirror, fingering the grey streaks which ran along each side of his auburn hair now. That made him look older, and the scar on his chin didn't add to his attractions.

But he was beginning to worry that eating Mrs Beamish's hearty meals had filled in the hollows in his cheeks and made him look more like his old self. It was only a matter of time before someone recognized him, and yet he didn't want to reveal himself to a father who seemed to be universally detested by decent folk. Maybe the best thing would be to leave Tinsley for good?

Only, he had a sister, wanted to meet her, because she had a nice smile. If he was to keep in touch with her, how could he leave? He looked at his watch, wishing he had Jim to talk this through with, then went back to the Weaver's Arms for tea.

'When are you going to show me round your new place?' Mrs Beamish asked.

'As soon as I've got it arranged and tidy. I have to find a mattress for the bed yet, and I'm not sure I can get hold of one before Christmas.'

'You can have one of mine if that's all that's stopping you. We've a couple of new ones in the attic.'

'I can't do that.'

'Call it a Christmas present.' She smiled at him. 'Think I haven't noticed how eager you are to leave here?'

'Not eager to leave here, just wanting my own place. I've spent a long time in institutions, first the Army, then the hospital. You long for a private, family life again.'

'Promise you'll come to me for help if you need it.'

He gave her a hug. 'Of course I will. And I'll come and visit you too. What's more, you'll be invited to take tea with me one day, cream cakes and all.' He saw her eyes go suspiciously bright and gave her another hug. He hadn't remembered anything about his mother, but had grown fond of this woman, who was cheerful and got on with her life in spite of her personal tragedies. She was a lesson to him, he reckoned, and if he'd believed in a beneficent fate, would have thought he'd been sent to meet her on purpose. She was another reason why he didn't want to leave Tinsley.

She patted his cheek, sniffed loudly and said, 'Come on. No time like the present. We'll get that mattress down then find someone to help you carry it to the shop. If you buy them a beer, they'll be happy to do it.'

He couldn't help it, he planted a smacking great kiss on her cheek, and though she told him not to be impudent, he could see she liked it.

Thirteen

The following day, which was Saturday, Aubrey nipped out from the shop several times during lulls, to buy groceries, soap, a dozen small items for his new home. He was aware at one stage of a man staring at him and later a woman at a market stall asked who he was, saying he looked familiar.

He'd be using the kitchen downstairs behind the shop, but it suddenly occurred to him that he didn't know how to cook, so he went to look for a cookery book in the second-hand section. He chose one designed to provide young women with the basic information on budgeting and shopping, to enable them to care for their husbands and families.

This seemed to afford Ted great amusement and he waved aside his offer of payment. 'Call it my housewarming present to you. But I want a slice of your first sponge cake.'

Aubrey blew a raspberry at him, a loud noise that echoed in the shop. 'I shan't even try to bake cakes, thank you very much, not when there's a cake shop a few doors away. But I would like to cook myself proper meals, things to my own taste.' He knew men didn't usually bother with cooking, but after the bland food of the convalescent home, he had a craving for stronger flavours.

He kept thinking about his sister, and fate played into his hands later that morning, as Marcus Graye came into the shop to find a book for a Christmas present for his wife. Aubrey hesitated as Marcus inspected the new books, then went to ask Ted in a whisper, 'That is Marcus Graye of the Hall in Horton, isn't it?'

'Yes.'

'He married Fleming's daughter recently, didn't he?'

'So the gossips say. There hasn't been an announcement in the *Tinsley Telegraph* yet, though.'

'Mind if I take him upstairs for a word once he's chosen his book? I've remembered something else and I need to ask him about it.'

Ted nodded, so Aubrey dealt with Graye's purchase. 'Excuse me, but could I have a word with you? It's private, to do with your wife. We could go to my sitting room upstairs, if you've a minute.'

'All right.'

Aubrey led the way, got the other settled on the sofa and plunged into speech. 'I don't know any tactful way to say this, but I think I'm your wife's brother. I was injured in the war and lost my memory, but remembered the name Tinsley so came back. When I heard the name Fleming, I realized it was *my* name too. I already had a vague memory of a woman smiling, and when I saw you and your wife at the station a couple of days ago, I felt as if I recognized her – though her hair's different to what I remember. I gather she's Fleming's daughter, so I was wondering—'

Graye's voice was cool and unfriendly. 'Shouldn't you go and see your father first?'

'No. I haven't heard anything good about him and – ' Aubrey rubbed his forehead – 'I feel uncomfortable when I try to remember any more about him. To be frank, I'm not sure I want to get in touch with him at all, and I'd appreciate your keeping my existence a secret until I decide.'

'What do you feel when you remember your sister?'

'I don't remember much, but I see her smiling at me. I've been seeing her face for months, actually, but didn't know who she was. And it's never brought on a headache, so I'm assuming I got on well with her.' He saw that Graye was studying him, frowning, clearly undecided what to do, so gave him a moment or two to think.

'Are you absolutely sure you're Frank Fleming?' Marcus

said at last. 'I'd hate to raise false hopes in Serena. She loved her brother greatly and I don't want you hurting her.'

'I'm quite sure. Coming back here did the trick and I began to remember.'

'Well then, Frank—'

'Not Frank, not now!' He realized his voice was quite sharp and took a deep breath before continuing. 'When I couldn't remember my own name, the nurses gave me another – Aubrey Smith – and that's my official name now, on all my papers. I don't feel comfortable with Frank Fleming as a name, which is another reason I've waited to contact my father.'

'Why have you waited to contact Serena?'

'I didn't want to give her a shock, then you came into the shop, so I thought I'd speak to you first, ask you to break the news to her.'

'I don't know what to say. If you're telling the truth, it sounds like Serena *is* your sister, and when she talks about you, it's obvious she loved you dearly, but . . .' Marcus hesitated, wondering how much to tell Aubrey Smith, then looked at the other man's clear-eyed gaze and decided to risk it. If Smith was faking this, he was an amazingly good actor, but Marcus had had a lot of experience in assessing men and he didn't think the other was lying.

'But what?'

'There's something you need to know first. We don't think Fleming *is* her father.' Marcus explained how matters stood. 'And at the moment we seem in some danger from him. We guess he must be desperate for money. You may prefer to wait to reveal who you are until he's accepted how matters stand and we've sorted out her inheritance, which he's withholding.'

Aubrey sat there feeling dumbfounded. 'It sounds like something you'd read in a novel or see at the cinema.'

'Unfortunately, it's really happening. I don't know why the man thinks he'll get away with it, but he seems to have been lucky so far.'

They sat in silence for a moment or two and this also made Marcus feel more at ease with the other man. He hated it when people gabbled on for no reason.

'What do you advise then?' Aubrey asked. 'Should I come and see Serena yet – or not?'

'You still want to?'

'Of course I do. Let alone it's not pleasant being alone in the world, I have fond memories of her.'

Marcus could understand that. Even a short time of living with Serena had taught him to appreciate her. 'I'd guess Fleming will try to get you under his control again once he finds out who you are.'

'I'm not a boy any more, and I'm not dependent on him. He'll never control me again.'

'Don't be so sure. He doesn't seem to care what other people want and doesn't hesitate to exploit their weaknesses, from what I've heard.' Marcus hesitated again, but didn't think this the time to tell Aubrey that his father might have tried to commit murder.

'We'll cross that bridge when we come to it. Look, I was going to walk out to Horton tomorrow. Could I come and see Serena then?'

'Come and have lunch with us.'

'You'll . . . tell her about me, prepare her?'

'Yes, of course.'

Aubrey walked down with him to the shop door, where they shook hands.

Ted cocked one eyebrow at him when he went back to stand irresolutely next to the counter. His friend clearly wanted to know what was going on.

'It's a complicated story and involves others, so I can't tell you about it yet,' Aubrey said. 'Hope you don't mind.'

'It's to do with finding your family?'

'Yes.'

'You're Frank Fleming, aren't you?'

Aubrey stared at him in dismay. 'How did you know?'

'You've looked familiar ever since you came to work here. You used to come in quite often as a lad, spending your pocket money on books. You've changed a lot so I wasn't sure at first. If you want to conceal your real identity, that's your business as far as I'm concerned, but I should warn you that one or two people have told me you remind them of someone. I said you had relatives in the town.'

'I appreciate you keeping this to yourself.'

Ted came to clap him on the shoulder. 'I always felt sorry

for you when you were a lad. You weren't happy. Fleming kept trying to change you into something you weren't. But I think you've grown up now and are your own man.'

That compliment pleased Aubrey greatly. It was how he felt, his own man, but of course the proof of that would come when he met his father again.

He knew he had to do that soon, couldn't run away from his past – not if he hoped to build a better future for himself.

Marcus walked slowly home from the station in Horton, still thinking about his encounter with Serena's brother. At the Hall, he went round to the kitchen door, rapping twice, then once again, to let them know it was a friend. What was the world coming to when you had to keep your door locked in the daytime? Was this a 'fit country for heroes to live in' as Lloyd George had promised? It didn't feel like it at the moment. Well, he'd had just about enough of Fleming and intended to do something about the fellow after Christmas, with Redway's help.

It occurred to him that a few things might be thrown into the balance once Aubrey revealed himself to his father.

Serena was on the other side of the big kitchen chatting to Pearl, and he just had time to slip the parcel behind a plate on the shelf near the door before she turned round. Gladys saw what he was doing, so he winked at her and she gave him a shy smile before going on with what she was doing.

He went across to kiss Serena on the cheek. She didn't stiffen as she usually did, but smiled and said, 'Come and see what Pearl and I've been doing.' Taking his hand, she pulled him through the hall to the sitting room, which now had bunches of holly to brighten it up, with a couple of bright red bows on the bunches at either side of the fireplace. 'Your aunt told me where to find the ribbons. I wanted our first Christmas to be – a bit special.'

He noticed a bunch of mistletoe hanging above the doorway and swung her back under it, pulling her into his arms and kissing her quickly before she could protest. When he drew his head back, she went a bit pink but smiled shyly at him, so he didn't let go of her. 'I've been dying to kiss you properly ever since we got here. You don't mind, do you?'

Serena drew a deep breath. Today, when they were making beds, Pearl had teased her about her 'frozen' expression and she'd suddenly realized that she'd fallen into her old ways of hiding her feelings, so afraid was she of being hurt by Marcus, because he had far more ability to hurt her than Fleming had, since she was already starting to care for him.

After that, she'd made an excuse of having some mending to do and stayed in her bedroom for half an hour, not noticing the chill, glad that Marcus was out. She didn't do any sewing, just sat staring out of the window, wrapped in her mother's old lilac shawl, thinking long and hard about what Pearl had said. And in the end she came to the conclusion that she was being cowardly, and promised herself to be more open with her husband. It was more than time things were settled between them. Either they were married or they weren't. 'I don't mind at all, as long as you really want to kiss me.'

He'd been waiting patiently for her reply, but when she said that, he gaped at her. 'Of course I want to! You're my wife.'

'But you haven't – we haven't . . .' She broke off, could feel her face flushing, but kept her eyes on his face.

'We haven't consummated our marriage?' he finished for her.

She nodded.

'I thought *you* didn't want to.'

'Oh. Well, *I* thought *you* didn't want to. But I must admit I'm glad we didn't rush things, glad we waited a day or two. It all happened so quickly I panicked – well, I hardly knew you.'

'Have we waited long enough now, do you think? Have you stopped panicking?'

She nodded, staying within the circle of his arms and leaning her head against his shoulder. His words and the promise behind them made her feel breathless and excited in a way she'd not known before.

'That'll be the best Christmas present I've ever had, a real wife,' he murmured from just above her right ear. Then he remembered. 'Come and sit down. There's something I have to tell you. It's good news, at least I hope it is.' He pulled her towards the sofa and told her about the encounter with the young man working in Bailey's Bookshop.

She burst into tears before he'd finished, losing herself in a tangle of disjointed phrases and sobbing against him for a while. When she pulled herself together, she accepted his handkerchief and blew her nose, then nestled against him once more. 'You don't think it's a hoax, do you, Marcus?'

'No. He seemed a nice fellow.'

'What did he look like?'

'Just a little taller than you, hair rather like yours in colour, now I come to think of it, but with grey in it, especially at the sides, and a scar on his chin.'

'Frank's going grey?'

'That's the other thing. They gave him a new name when he couldn't remember his old one. He calls himself Aubrey now – Aubrey Smith. And he says he feels more Aubrey than Frank.'

'Does Fleming know?'

'No. Aubrey's not even sure he wants to get in touch with his father, doesn't like what he's been hearing about him, doesn't feel good when he tries to remember things about him.'

'I'm not surprised. If my so-called father loved anyone, he loved Frank, but he had a strange way of showing it, always nagging him. Nothing Frank did was ever good enough, and he was bad at sport, which made things worse. And he absolutely hated the boarding school he was sent to. When he was younger, he used to cry when it was time to go back there.' She sighed. 'I felt so sorry for him, but there was nothing I could do except write to him and send him parcels of food.'

'You'd better go easy on reminiscences when you see him. He says he finds it painful to recall some things, Fleming especially. Anyway, Aubrey's coming here tomorrow.'

'That's wonderful! The best Christmas present I could have!'

Her eyes lit up and she looked so pretty, Marcus couldn't resist kissing her again. 'The way you smile makes me want to kiss you. You do it so rarely. No wonder Aubrey remembered it. You have the most beautiful smile.'

'That's the nicest thing anyone's ever said to me.'

The gong in the hall sounded and she jumped to her feet. 'Oh, dear, I was supposed to be helping with dinner.'

'They won't mind when we tell them the news about your brother.' And he kept his arm round her as they went to join the others in the kitchen. He saw Pearl nudge Vic and grin, but he didn't care. He wanted to show the whole world that he loved his wife. He blinked as that thought slid into his mind. *Loved her!* Yes, he did.

But how exactly did she feel about him? Would it be rushing things to tell her he loved her? He didn't know, didn't understand women well enough.

That night when they were getting ready for bed, Serena suddenly froze, paralyzed with the fear that he'd find her lacking in bed, that she really was, as Fleming had said so often, a poor excuse for a woman.

Marcus seemed to understand that she was afraid, because he put his arms round her very gently, saying only, 'I'm not going to pounce on you the minute you lie down, you know. I need to cuddle you before anything else, holding you close will be a lovely way to begin, don't you think?'

That made it easier to slip into bed beside him and let him take her in his arms. She sighed and rested her head against his shoulder. When he stroked her hair and pulled her face round for a kiss, she found herself enjoying it. He began to caress her gently, and his hands seemed filled with their own magic. It felt as if he set a glow on her skin wherever he touched it. She tried to speak, but he laid one finger on her lips.

'Shh, darling. Let me love you. We've nothing to rush for, only ourselves to please.'

And so she lay back and shyly let him explore her body, amazed that this man's lightest touch could send warmth flooding through her, make her want more touching. When he kissed her again, a deeper kiss that went on for a wonderfully long time, she kissed him back, daring to stroke his head, her fingers lingering on the scars in his check. As he stiffened, she moved to kiss those scars. They were badges of honour as far as she was concerned. And that seemed to make him relax. It also gave her the confidence that she could learn to sense his needs, learn to love him, that he could *need* her love.

But her thoughts soon grew as tangled as her emotions, for

his clever fingers continued to play across her body. She'd been afraid of his touch, now she craved it and her fingers took on a life of their own, caressing his body in turn, avoiding the sore places, enjoying the strength and firmness of him.

The world blurred around her, narrowed down to Marcus, so that all led gently and naturally to an intimacy that both shocked and delighted her. It didn't hurt, as gossip had hinted, though it didn't take her to ecstasy either. But he seemed to lose himself in her and it was wonderful that she could give him this pleasure, hear him cry out in joy as his rhythmic movements came to a climax. Once he'd stilled, she held him tightly, not wanting to let go of him ever.

After a while his voice sounded in the darkness beside her. 'It'll be better for you next time, I promise.'

'It felt wonderful.'

'My lovely Serena.'

That endearment above all brought tears to her eyes.

He felt the moisture against his chest and asked urgently, 'What's wrong? Tell me. Did I hurt you?'

'There's nothing wrong. I'm just . . . happy.'

With a soft chuckle, he relaxed against her. 'I'd forgotten how you cry when you're happy.'

Soon he was breathing evenly and deeply.

She lay there for a while – feeling wanted, feeling married, feeling so much love for this man whose heartbeat was close to her ear that it filled her with amazement. She had not expected this much joy in her marriage.

Aubrey woke before it was light, filled with such a sense of anticipation that he couldn't bear to stay in bed. When he went out to use the lavatory at the bottom of the yard, he was delighted to find it wasn't raining. Later, when the sun rose, the world was briefly filled with the sparkle of sunlight on melting frost and he went out to watch that. The air was free of smoke today because the mills weren't operating, and that added to the brightness of everything.

He was going to see his sister!

The mere thought of that made him happy and nervous at the same time. Would she like him? Would he feel comfortable with her? Would he remember anything painful while he was with her? Questions tumbled through his brain one after the other as he tried to occupy himself by arranging more of his new furniture upstairs. He must definitely get another bed, because Jim had promised faithfully to come and see him before he returned to Australia. He'd written to give his friend his new address and hoped to get a reply before Christmas.

He began making a list of things to do, even the simplest item making him feel happy, because he could *choose* for himself, not have someone else choose for him.

Not wanting to be early, he didn't let himself set off until ten o'clock, then strode out briskly in the direction of Horton, breathing in deeply and enjoying the fresh air. It was so good to be out of doors. He studied the winter landscape he was passing through with a keen eye, eager to know it again. Had he gone for walks round here before? He loved walking in the countryside. It had been his one chance to be on his own when he was working at the convalescent home. He'd loved to watch plants blooming and dying in their eternal cycles, birds nesting, insects humming busily around. Most of all he'd enjoyed the sky, the cloud formations, the glorious freedom of that great space above him into which his thoughts sometimes seemed to soar like birds.

When he reached the village of Horton, he stopped to ask directions to the Hall and then, for the first time, his feet slowed and he began to feel nervous. Did his sister care about him as he felt he had cared about her? Or was he wrong about her?

Serena had also woken early that morning, eager to see Fr—no, she must remember to call him Aubrey now. *Eager to see Aubrey*, she corrected herself mentally.

'Are you awake already?' Marcus inquired from beside her.

'Yes.'

'You won't make him arrive any earlier by lying and worrying about him.'

'How did you know I was worrying?'

He ran one hand down her arm. 'I can feel the tension in you.'

'I might as well get up then. I didn't want to wake you.'

'We'll get up together and share a pot of tea before the others join us.'

The kitchen was chilly, but Marcus soon got the fire blazing and as they sat there together she smiled at him. 'I feel really and truly married now.'

'So do I. And I like it.'

A short time later Gladys peered in through the door and Serena tried not to let her amusement show. The elderly maid was having difficulty adjusting to such an egalitarian household and rarely entered a room without first peeping in to see whether she'd be intruding on anything.

'Come and join us!' she called. 'I've just made a pot of tea. You sit down and I'll pour a cup for you.'

So Gladys sat there shyly, hardly saying anything, but clearly enjoying the luxury of having a warm room and hot drink waiting for her.

Vic came out of the rooms he would share with Pearl after they were married, and at almost the same time his fiancée came down from the servants' quarters. Soon Ada was with them too.

'It only needs my aunt to join us for there to be a full household,' Marcus joked.

Ada looked round apprehensively. 'Well, Mrs Lonnerden did say she might come down for dinner tonight if you could find time to lend her your arm down the stairs, sir. But *she* wouldn't want to eat in the kitchen with us, I'm sure.'

Serena answered for him because he was sitting frowning. 'Of course he'll help her down, Ada. It's good news that she's feeling better.'

The maid hesitated. 'She's not better, exactly, still very weak, but she says she's tired of staying in bed.'

'Anyone would be,' Pearl said. 'Shall I clean the morning room and set the table there for luncheon, Mr G— Marcus?' She still had trouble calling him by his first name.

'Yes, I suppose so, though I'm sorry to add another room to the cleaning roster. Don't think I don't appreciate how hard you're all working. But I think we'll eat in the kitchen tonight.'

'*Mrs Lonnerden?*'

'Yes, my aunt as well. Start off as we mean to continue.'

After breakfast everyone set about their chores without

being told, and Serena found it comforting to know that they were each supporting her in their own way. Pearl was in charge of preparing a lunch worthy of the occasion, and Gladys helped Serena make sure the smaller sitting room was immaculate, so that she and her brother could chat in private. As they lit a fire, its cheerful blaze seemed to add the finishing touch.

A few minutes before eleven the front doorbell rang and Serena clutched Marcus's arm.

'We'll answer it together,' he said reassuringly.

She stood beside him as he opened the door, not moving for a moment, just looking at her brother, instantly sure that it was him, though he looked a lot older. Then she couldn't bear just to look and flung herself into his arms, weeping hysterically, saying, 'It *is* you! It *is*!' Realizing how stiffly he was holding her, she pulled back. 'I'm sorry. You don't really know me any more, do you? But I'd have known you anywhere, even with the grey in your hair. Come in, do.'

But he was feeling dizzy as more memories cascaded into place. It was Marcus who guessed what was happening and stepped forward to lend him an arm, supporting him into the small sitting room.

'Sorry,' Aubrey muttered.

She followed them, terrified she'd done something wrong.

As he sank down on the sofa, Aubrey smiled at her, his old, wry twist of a smile. 'Don't look so worried, Serena. I get a bit dizzy sometimes when I remember things, that's all. This wasn't painful stuff, just rather a lot of memories flooding back at once. Come and sit beside me, let me look at you.'

Marcus winked at her and let himself out of the room, then she turned to Aubrey and took the hand he was offering.

'Why don't I remember you as pretty?' he said in puzzlement.

'Because I deliberately screwed up my hair in a bun and made myself as ugly as I could. Otherwise *he* would have married me off to someone as horrible as himself.'

'Our father?'

'*Your* father, not mine.'

'You're sure of that?'

'Oh, yes. It was the last thing Mother told me. She wouldn't lie, not when she was dying. I don't feel guilty now about always hating him.'

'I can't remember much about him, except that I don't feel as if I *want* to remember. I feel as though I was glad to shut a door in my head on something painful. Does that sound foolish?'

'No. He's an evil man.'

'*Evil*?'

She nodded. 'He tried to have me locked away in the asylum to keep hold of my annuity, and he tried to kill my lawyer to stop him pursuing the matter.'

'You're sure.'

'Oh, yes. I want you to stay, Fr— Aubrey, but I can't help thinking you'd be happier and safer if you left Tinsley and went somewhere he could never find you.'

'Like Australia?'

'Yes.'

He studied her silently for so long that she had to ask, 'What are you thinking?'

He pulled her to her feet and went to stand with her in front of a big, gold-framed mirror, one arm round her shoulders. 'Look at us. We may be only half-brother and sister, but we're very much alike.'

'That's because we both take after our mother.'

'Tell me about her, and about yourself. Tell me everything you can think of.'

'If you'll tell me what's been happening to you.'

An hour later Marcus knocked on the door. 'May I come in?'

Serena turned to him with an expression of glowing happiness on her face and he felt a sudden spurt of jealousy, wishing he had been the one to put it there. 'Come and have something to eat, you two. You've not even offered your brother a drink, Serena.'

'It was more important to talk,' Aubrey said.

They went into the morning room, eating in style today, served very formally by Gladys. Only as the meal ended did Aubrey say, 'I don't know what to do, whether to go and see my father or not. I'm tempted to leave it till after Christmas, but I'm afraid someone will recognize me and tell him I'm back.'

'You've decided to stay in Tinsley, then?' Marcus asked.

'For the time being. I have a job I like and I'm making friends. I'm even enjoying having my own flat.'

'You're not lonely?' Serena asked.

'No. I've been craving some peace and quiet for months. When you're in the Army, there's always someone ordering you around. I'm expecting a visit from a friend, though, and I will be glad to see him. I wrote to let him know where I was and he's promised faithfully to visit me. Jim won't go back on his word. I'll have to find a bed for him to sleep on, though.'

'Take one from here,' Marcus said at once. 'There are several spare ones not being used. I'll find someone to carry one into town for you.'

When Aubrey left, Serena stood at the door watching him walk down the drive, not moving even after he'd disappeared from view.

'Come inside, woman, or you'll catch your death of cold,' Marcus said from behind her.

She turned into the house, wiping away a tear.

'Happy or sad?' he asked.

'Both. He never saw Mother again or she him.' She shivered suddenly. 'Why do I feel that something awful is going to happen?'

He shook his head, wanting to dismiss that feeling out of hand, but not able to. He also felt a sense of foreboding and had learned during the war to pay heed to his intuition.

As a result of that, he sent a telegram the next morning as soon as the local post office, which was situated at the rear of the village store, opened. He didn't intend to sit and wait for Fleming to act, but take action himself, first to protect his own, then, when a suitable opportunity presented itself, to expose Fleming for the villain he was.

Fourteen

Aubrey walked slowly back to town, feeling happier about the future than he had for a long time. To have found a sister when he'd had no one . . . it brought tears to his eyes even to think of that. And if it was unmanly to be so emotional, well, he didn't care.

As he was walking through the town centre, he was stopped by a man he thought he recognized, but couldn't remember from where. A stab of pain in his forehead made him guess that some bad memory was returning. The man's outline seemed to blur and waver in front of him as pain throbbed through him.

'Excuse me, sir, but are you all right?'

'Pain in my head.' Aubrey reached out for the nearby lamp post and clung to it while the street wavered around him.

'Are you ill?'

'Just . . . give me a minute. It'll pass.' Images whirled in his brain and the man's face seemed to come and go among them. 'Hudd.' It was a few seconds before he realized he'd said it aloud.

'You know my name, then.'

He blinked and tried to focus on the man. 'You're . . . Sam Hudd.'

'Yes. And you're Frank Fleming.'

Aubrey took a deep breath, then another, not wanting to confirm his identity, not able to deny it either. 'I need to . . . sit down. Excuse me. I live nearby.'

'Do you want to lean on me?'

He didn't but the world was still spinning round him, so Aubrey found himself grateful for support from the man who had once brought him back forcibly when he ran away from school, and hadn't been gentle about it, the man who had been his father's second in command for a long time, a man much hated in the town. The irony of this would have made him laugh if he hadn't been in such pain.

It was only when he stopped for a rest that he realized they were heading away from the town centre towards a house he recognized. 'I wanted to go *home*.' He tried to tug his arm away, but Hudd kept tight hold of it.

'That's where I'm taking you, sir. Home.' He indicated a side street.

'That house is *not* my home!'

'Of course it is.'

Aubrey found himself being force-marched for another few unwilling steps. 'Let go of me!'

'I'm only taking you to see your father.'

After struggling in vain to get free, Aubrey saw a policeman walking along the other side of the street and called out, 'Constable! Constable, I need your help.'

The policeman hurried across to him. 'Is there a problem, sir?'

'Yes. This man is trying to force me to go with him and I definitely don't want to do it.'

The policeman looked at Hudd and his expression said he knew and disliked him. 'Is this true?'

'The gentleman was ill, couldn't stand up on his own. I was taking him to my employer's house for help.'

'All the help I need is help getting to my own home,' Aubrey said. 'I work in Bailey's Bookshop and live above it.'

The policeman gave Hudd a suspicious look, then turned to Aubrey with a smile. 'Let me help you home then, sir.'

Hudd hesitated then stepped back, scowling at both men.

It wasn't very far to the bookshop and by the time they got there, Aubrey was already feeling better.

The policeman looked at him thoughtfully. 'Could you spare me a moment, sir? I'd like to ask you something.'

'Why don't you come inside?' Aubrey unlocked the door and led the way into the interior, which looked dark and mysterious with the shop's window blinds down. He switched on the electric lights to dispel the feeling of apprehension that was still lingering inside him. Nothing like bright lights for chasing away the demons of the dark! He saw the policeman studying his face and guessed what was coming next.

'I've been thinking I recognized you, and then seeing you with Hudd brought it back to me. You're Frank Fleming, aren't you?'

Aubrey gestured to the officer to follow him across the shop and subsided gratefully on one of the chairs near the fireplace, waiting till the other man was seated before admitting, 'I used to be.' Once again, he explained how he had become Aubrey Smith. 'Sometimes when I remember things it makes me dizzy.'

'And Hudd was trying to force you to go to your father's house?'

'Yes. But I don't want to face *him* when I'm feeling under the weather, and even then the meeting won't be in that house if I can help it. I'm starting to remember living there and the memories aren't pleasant, believe me.' He saw the officer struggling to maintain a calm expression and couldn't hold back a snort of bitter laughter. 'It's all right. You don't have to pretend to be impartial. I learnt soon after I got back how people regard my father. And I know now that *I* wasn't very fond of him either, that I was glad to enlist in the Army and get away from him.'

After a moment's consideration he added, 'I intend to remain Aubrey Smith. I have all my documents in that name now, so it's quite legal. You're welcome to check them if you wish.'

'Well, it might simplify matters if I could tell my sergeant I'd seen them. If you don't mind, that is, sir?'

'Why should I mind? I'll fetch them down. Won't be a minute.'

When he got back, he said casually, 'I've just come back from having lunch with my sister, Mrs Graye she is now. She got married recently.'

'So I hear. In fact, there's rather a lot of gossip going on about your family, what with the fire burning down your father's office and all. I did hear from my colleague, Constable Yedhill, that they'd had an incident or two with your father's men out at Horton, as well.' The officer hauled himself to his feet. 'If you have any more trouble – with anyone – just nip across the road to the police station and let us know, sir. We're here to protect people – when we can.'

No one liked his father, Aubrey decided, feeling somewhat despondent about that. He was glad he'd come back because of being reunited with his sister, but he knew he couldn't postpone the meeting between himself and his father for much longer – even though he wished he need never see the man again. But that would be a coward's course and he wasn't going to follow it.

The next morning Ted came to work looking so blessedly normal and happy that Aubrey found himself cheering up.

The shop was busy and, as Ted had said, the cheap penny books sold well to the poorer customers. Some of the richer folk clearly wanted to buy books that looked expensive as gifts, no matter what was inside them, but the true book lovers didn't seem to care what a book looked like as long as it was a good read.

During the afternoon a man came in who didn't even pretend to look at the stock. He walked straight across to the counter and stared at Aubrey. 'Your father said I'd find you here, Frank.'

Aubrey stared back at him. 'Dr . . .' The man's name escaped him, but he remembered the face, with its high colour and plump cheeks.

'Don't you know my name?'

'As you must be aware, I lost my memory in an explosion and can only remember things patchily, you hardly at all.' Which wasn't quite true. He was feeling intense dislike toward this man, together with a memory of fear and pain.

'I need to speak to you privately, Frank.'

Aubrey didn't even have to think about that. 'No. You're not my doctor now, and I'm busy.'

'It's very foolish of you to behave like this – irrational, even.' He pulled out a notebook and began writing.

A customer who had been hovering, waiting to pay for a book, edged away and put the book down. 'I'll – um – come back later.'

Ted came across to stand beside his assistant, annoyed by this loss of a sale. 'If you're not here to buy a book, I suggest you leave, Dr Tolson. *We* have work to do today, even if you don't.'

The doctor smiled and leaned on the counter. 'Oh, but I am working.'

Aubrey knew there was a threat in those words, but before he could open his mouth to tell the man to go to hell, Ted went and flung the door open.

'Get out or I'll bring in the police! You're upsetting my customers and staff, and I'm not having it.'

Dr Tolson's plump face turned an even brighter red, and as he stuffed his notebook in his pocket, he said to Aubrey, 'You're definitely behaving irrationally, and so I shall report to your father. You need help, young man.'

When he'd gone, both men looked at one another.

'I know who was behaving strangely here and it wasn't you, lad. What the hell did he mean by that?'

Aubrey sighed. 'I'd guess that my father intends to gain control of me again, any way he can. He's already tried that "behaving irrationally" stuff on my sister. I'm sure it wouldn't stand up in court.'

'Trouble is, Dr Tolson doesn't always go to court,' Ted said slowly. 'He's in charge of the asylum and there are tales of young women from good families ending up there simply because they were expecting babies – and a couple of them haven't come out again.'

Aubrey looked at him in horror, then pulled himself together and went to finish tidying a nearby shelf. But he couldn't concentrate and after a few minutes turned round and said urgently, 'Look, if my father kidnaps me under the pretence that I'm in need of care, will you do something for me, Ted?'

The older man nodded.

'Will you send for my sister and her husband and ask them to get me another doctor, any doctor except Tolson.'

Ted nodded again. 'You can rely on me, though I hope it doesn't come to that.'

Aubrey went back to work. His father wasn't going to frighten him into compliance. Indeed, such incidents only made him more determined to live his own life. Immediately after Christmas he'd find another doctor and explain the situation. No one was going to pretend that Tolson was his physician.

* * *

That same morning, Justin went to see his old friend Marley again. This time he used the rear entrance, hoping none of Fleming's men had seen him.

'This is getting serious.' Marley tapped the page of notes Justin had rescued from the fire. 'Have you reported it to the police yet?'

'No. Not sure if it's worth bothering.'

'It's definitely worth it.' He studied his old friend. 'They've got you worried, haven't they?'

'Yes. Try nearly being roasted to death and see how courageous you feel.'

'All the more reason to stop them.'

'Dammit, man, the police have known for years about the gambling and the coercion that's been going on, not to mention the sharp business practices of a certain group of men, and they haven't managed to put an end to any of it! I can't see this case being any different.'

'Fleming's overreaching himself – and don't tell me Hammerton isn't deeply involved, because I won't believe you. If we resist and push them hard, they may make a mistake. Good thing the cab driver had a revolver, eh?'

'It's his old service revolver. I don't think it's licensed or anything.'

Marley grinned. 'I shan't pursue that point. I reckon a man who's fought for England and lost his leg in the service of his country has a right to defend himself.'

As a result of this conversation, an earnest young constable came round to see Justin and take copious notes on the 'incident' for his sergeant's files.

'We will look into this, sir,' he said as he left. 'But we have to tread carefully.'

Justin didn't feel optimistic about Fleming getting caught.

Later that day, Constable Yedhill puffed his way along the lane to the Hall and went round to the stables, where he found Marcus and Vic chatting.

'Why didn't you report that incident on the way back to Tinsley?' he demanded of Vic.

'What good would it have done? And how did you find out about it?'

'The sergeant in Tinsley is an old friend of mine. Did you recognize the men?'

'No.'

'What about the truck?'

'Not a vehicle I've seen round here before.'

'The sergeant intends to ring all the nearby police stations when we have the necessary information and ask them to look out for a vehicle like that with a bullet hole in it – or find out if anyone has repaired the bodywork of such a vehicle. It'll all take time, but you'd be surprised what we can come up with if we set our minds to it.'

Vic did not feel optimistic about the chances of finding the men who'd attacked the lawyer. They weren't local and could have come in from anywhere to do the job of frightening Mr Redway – or had they actually intended to kill him?

He felt angry every time he thought of what had been going on here for the past few years. War profiteering by men like Hammerton sickened him, especially as such fellows had sat safely at home while young Englishmen like himself risked their lives every day – no, every minute! – for their country.

On the Monday afternoon a large Humber, very highly polished, turned into the drive of the Hall and drew up before the front door. Serena, who had rushed to peer out of the window and see who it was, felt her heart start to thump with nervousness when she recognized the vehicle and its occupant – Fleming.

She hurried into the kitchen. 'Mr Fleming is about to pay us a call. Pearl, could you please answer the door and show him into the sitting room? Don't answer any questions about us. I'm going to change into my best clothes before I see him. Can someone fetch— Oh, there you are, Marcus. Fleming has come to call on us.'

'I saw the car coming up the drive.' A little breathless, Marcus looked down at himself. 'I thought I'd better change my clothes before I see him, so ran up to the house. I've been going through the things in the Lodge, so that I can offer it for rent.'

They both hurried up the back stairs as Pearl went to answer the door.

Marcus was ready first. 'I'll go and keep an eye on Fleming. Take your time, Serena. He hasn't seen you in your new clothes and it won't hurt for you to look your best.' He went downstairs, pausing in the doorway of the sitting room to stare at Fleming, who was warming his hands at the fire.

'You must be my son-in-law.' The visitor came forward, hand outstretched.

Marcus gave it the briefest of possible shakes. 'Won't you sit down?' He indicated an armchair.

Fleming sat in the chair, looking as calm as if he hadn't recently sent his men to this very house to kidnap his daughter, hadn't tried to kill Justin Redway.

Disgust for the man sat like nausea in Marcus's throat. He'd met one or two like him, icy manipulators who cared nothing for other people's feelings, and he hated to think that Serena had spent most of her life in this one's power. Only a very strong woman could have survived years of browbeating without becoming docile and cowed. He was thankful she still had an independence of mind and spirit, but her upbringing had marked her nonetheless. He knew she was unable to trust other people easily, but he felt he was winning her trust – and her love, too, he hoped. Hearing footsteps approaching, he stood up. 'Ah, there you are, darling.'

As Serena walked in, Fleming's eyes narrowed and he said nothing, just looked her up and down, not bothering to hide his surprise at her changed appearance.

Marcus went to put his arm round her shoulders. 'Come and sit down. Mr Fleming was just about to explain what brought him here.'

Fleming stood up and moved across to Serena. When she took a step backwards, he stopped. 'I wanted to see my daughter, of course, and to meet you, Graye, since you're married to her – even if it was against my wishes.'

'She's old enough to make up her own mind about that sort of thing.'

'Ah, but was she in a suitable frame of mind, after the loss of her mother, to choose sensibly? My daughter has always—'

Serena decided she wasn't going to be talked about like this, as if she had no mind or opinions of her own. 'We both know I'm not your daughter.' She could see that Fleming was surprised by her interruption, but Marcus gave her a nod and sat back, as if leaving her to take charge of this interview. The length of his thigh was pressed against hers, however, its warmth sending a continuing message of support that heartened her.

'We know nothing of the sort,' Fleming snapped. 'Are you suggesting that your mother was of loose morals, would have been unfaithful to her marriage vows?'

'I don't intend to discuss my mother with you, apart from saying I know she wouldn't lie to me when she was dying. You and I have nothing to say to one another now that isn't best said through a lawyer, so don't let us keep you. I can't think why you came out here. You must know how I feel.'

His voice suddenly rang with his old hectoring tone, the sharpness of which had reduced her to silence and obedience on many occasions. 'I came to try to put a stop to your foolishness, Serena, and you *are* being foolish, very foolish indeed. It isn't too late to have this marriage declared null and void, and whatever you say, you *are* in an unstable state mentally. That's very obvious to me, who knows you better than anyone. Why, look at the way you've changed your appearance, the way you're aping younger women. At your age! You look utterly ridiculous in those clothes and as for that short hair – it's so common! People are no doubt laughing at you behind your back.'

Beside her, Marcus twitched and shot a quick look sideways, eyebrow raised as if to ask whether she needed his help.

At that moment she realized that Fleming had lost some of his power to hurt her verbally. She wasn't dependent on him now and it was her own efforts that had set her free, which she was secretly proud of, so she answered him with the simple truth. 'Actually, I'm happier than I've been for many years and I'm delighted with my appearance. No need to dress dowdily now to avoid *your* men friends. I can be myself at last.' She took Marcus's hand. 'And I couldn't be happier!'

When her husband raised her hand to his lips and kissed it, she gave him a dazzling smile.

Breath whistled into Fleming's mouth and his expression turned grim, but he didn't move from his chair. 'I think you'll find this so-called happiness is an illusion. Graye is only after your money.'

'And you aren't?' she asked quickly.

He ignored that. 'I hear your brother Frank is back in town.'

'Oh?' She wondered how much he knew, so didn't comment.

'And I gather he's been out here to visit you.'

She still didn't answer, using his own trick of waiting until someone grew uncomfortable with the silence.

In the end Fleming leaned forward and snapped, 'Well, hasn't Frank been here?'

'He prefers to be called Aubrey now.'

'His name is *Frank*. Frank Fleming.'

'That's up to him now.'

'We'll see about that.' Fleming broke off for a moment, taking a couple of deep, slow breaths. The traces of anger vanished from his face, leaving it as cold as a statue's. 'You really should know me better than to continue annoying me like this, Serena. Your stupid insistence on finding out what happened to the annuity income will get you nowhere. As I've already told you, I lost that money through bad investments, which I deeply regret. But that's water under the bridge now. You will find life much pleasanter if you don't have to worry about such things, and you'll never be short of money in my house.'

Marcus stood up, amazed at the crudeness of this threat. 'We don't intend to discuss the matter of Serena's money without our lawyer present. And I too think you've said enough for now, more than enough. Let me show you out, Mr Fleming.' He gestured towards the door.

After a moment's hesitation the older man stood up, but before he moved, he looked Serena up and down once again. 'You're wasted on *him.* I could have found you a much better husband had I known what you could look like.'

'But I love Marcus,' she said quite simply.

'And I love Serena. We're both happy as we are.'

'Let's hope you stay happy.' Fleming stood up and walked towards the door. 'Life is a fragile flower, is it not?'

Marcus set Serena on one side and whispered, 'Stay here!' He followed their unwanted guest to the front door. Before he opened it, he said, 'Don't come here again, Fleming, or try to contact my wife.'

'She's still my daughter and I have her welfare at heart.'

'We both know neither of those statements is true. It's her money you want.'

The mask slipped for a moment. 'And I'll have it too – whatever it takes to get it. I'm owed it for what I did for her and her mother. I gave her a respectable name. What's more, *you* should remember that I always get what I want in the end, one way or another. If you continue to stand in my way, you shouldn't feel too confident about your own future.'

'You're admitting your theft, then? And offering us more threats?'

'Not where anyone can overhear us.' Fleming walked outside and sauntered across to the car, where Hudd was holding the door open. He got in without looking back.

Marcus didn't move until the vehicle was out of sight, then he shivered and closed the door, walking slowly back into the sitting room.

Serena was standing looking into the fire, one hand on the mantelpiece. 'I overheard what you were saying to him. He's not going to give up, is he?'

'No.'

'How does he think he can force me to go back to him? I don't understand that.' As Marcus came across to put his arms round her, she asked, 'What are we going to do? We can't spend the rest of our lives living in fear.'

'We're going to make plans of our own. Consult our friends. Demand an accounting from Fleming. And in the meantime we should prepare for Christmas.'

'Goodness, I'd forgotten all about that.' She forced a smile. 'Only two more days to go.'

As she started moving towards the door, Marcus pulled her back into his arms. 'I was proud of you just now. It can't have been easy to face up to him.'

With a sigh she leaned against him, loving the way his lips brushed lightly against her temple. 'It's easier to be brave when you're not alone.'

'You were brave when you were on your own for a good many years.' He lifted her chin with his fingertip. 'I really am glad we got married, Serena, and I really do love you.'

Breath caught in her throat and she gave a shaky laugh. 'I love you, too.' She put her arms round him and kissed him, then they stood for a moment or two, enjoying the closeness and warmth.

At length he stepped back. 'Once Christmas is over, we'll take the initiative against Fleming. I'm not sure how yet, but I'll think about it, work something out. In the meantime, let's enjoy the lull. I can't imagine him doing anything over the next day or two, can you?'

'I hope not. I can't remember the last time I enjoyed Christmas.'

Her voice was so wistful he hugged her again.

When she'd gone up to continue altering one of her ugly frocks, he went to stare into the fire. He wasn't sure there would be a lull over Christmas, though he didn't intend to tell her that.

But Fleming was wrong about no one overhearing what he'd said to Marcus. While the two men were talking in the hall, there had been a listener at the open window upstairs. Pamela might be old, but there was nothing wrong with her hearing and she'd heard and understood the implications of every word they exchanged.

She waited until Marcus had closed the front door behind him, then she went across to the bed and sat down on it, anger boiling hotly in her. *That man!* How dared he even come to this house? He had ruined her son Lawrence and now he was trying to ruin her nephew, who was the only person with Lonnerden blood left. Marcus was a poor second to Lawrence, to the man her son had been before the war anyway, but he was all the family she had left now. If it was the last thing she did, she'd make sure Fleming was stopped.

When Ada came in with her tea, Pamela was sitting in the chair by the fire.

'I didn't know you wanted to get up, madam. You should have rung for help.'

'I wanted to see if I could manage on my own and I did. I intend to get up every day from now on – while I still can.' She looked at her maid, hating the pity in the woman's eyes.

If anyone knew how bad she was, how little time she had left, Ada did. 'I'm grateful for your help over the past few years.' She saw the surprise in Ada's eyes and let out a rusty laugh.

'Thank you, madam. I'll get your clothes now, shall I, and help you change?'

'Yes. And after that fetch up a tea tray, with two cups, then you can sit down and tell me all you know about what that man Fleming is doing.'

'I only know what I hear in the kitchen. I haven't been into Tinsley for weeks.'

'Then you can tell me what the others are saying. They keep trying to protect me.'

Late that afternoon the five o'clock train pulled into Tinsley station. The two men who had fallen into conversation as they shared a compartment said goodbye and one got out. He pulled his hat down low over his forehead, then went to deposit his suitcase in the left luggage office before walking slowly out of the station. He needn't have bothered to try to conceal his face. Dusk had already fallen and the people he encountered were more concerned with getting home for tea than studying the faces of passers-by.

He strolled along Yorkshire Road, amazed at the changes that had taken place since the last time he had been in Tinsley many years ago. Before he did anything else, he wanted to renew his acquaintance with the town where he'd been born and call on his brothers. Since the left luggage office stayed open until the last train at ten o'clock, he had time to do that before keeping his promise to Aubrey.

The train chugged slowly along the line. At the next stop, the village of Horton, the second man got out and asked directions to the Hall. 'Is there a cab?'

'Sorry, sir. There's only one cab driver and he isn't working today.'

'I'll carry your bag on my bicycle rack and show you the way there for threepence, sir,' offered a youth who'd been unashamedly listening to them.

'You're on.'

Picking up his bag, the man followed his youthful guide

briskly through the village, enjoying the clear air with its hint of frost. The street lamps stopped before the end of the village, but he had his guide to follow and his eyes soon grew accustomed to the darkness. Quite an isolated place, the Hall. Out of sight and out of hearing of the rest of the village. Not a good position, strategically.

Fifteen

Later that evening there was a knock on the back door of the bookshop. Only the coalman and dustmen usually came round to the rear, and certainly not at this advanced hour, so Aubrey pulled the frying pan off the gas burner and went to peep out of the window before he answered it. It was too dark to make out more than the figure of a man, but he wasn't tall or burly and seemed to be on his own.

There was a second knock, so Aubrey took the precaution of arming himself with a stout walking stick before he opened the door just a crack. But what he saw by the shaft of light streaming from the scullery made him throw the stick aside and fling the door wide open! 'Jim!'

'I kept my promise, you see.'

'Come in, come in! Why on earth did you go to the back door?'

'I didn't want to be seen coming here.'

Aubrey frowned. 'Seen by whom?'

'I'll explain later.' Jim picked up his suitcase and came inside. 'For the moment, have you somewhere I can sleep? I don't care if it's on the floor, but I don't want to be seen in the town till I'm ready.'

'I can do better than the floor. I've got a spare bedroom and the bed's very comfortable. How long can you stay?'

'I'm not sure. A few days at least – if that's all right with you?'

'All right! That'll be wonderful! It means you'll be here over Christmas.' Aubrey led the way into the kitchen. 'Have you eaten?'

'No.'

He looked at the frying pan sitting next to the gas burner, with its tiny piece of liver. 'This won't go far. I know! I'll go out and buy us some fish and chips.'

'Buy one serving or people will wonder who the second lot is for.'

Aubrey stilled, staring at his friend in amazement. 'What's all the cloak and dagger stuff about? You're the last person I'd have thought would—'

'I'll explain as we eat. Now, go and get that fish and chips while I finish frying this.'

A quarter of an hour later the two men sat down at the tiny table to share a meal. Since both were hungry they ate steadily for a while before speaking, then Jim asked, 'Have you remembered anything else about yourself?'

'Yes, my name. I was born Frank Fleming, it seems.'

Jim's fork dropped from his hand as he stared at Frank in shock. 'Dear God, you can't be that man's son!'

Aubrey set down his knife and fork and looked pleadingly at his friend. 'I'm not proud of it, I must admit, but I can't change who my father is, so I hope it won't come between us.'

'No, of course not. I was just . . . surprised.'

'Why do you speak as if you hate him?'

Jim stared down at his plate, then said, 'He did me a disservice a few years ago, the worst thing anyone has ever done to me, and I came back to Tinsley to see him as well as you. I feel it's more than time to sort a few matters out, though it's too late for the main thing I wanted . . . Look, I can't explain the details yet because it's not my secret alone. Would you trust me and tell me all you know about him without asking too many questions? I'm still trying to work out what to do, how to approach him, you see.'

'You've only to stay here and he'll probably come to you. He's got men trying to force me to see him, which I don't want to do yet. I thought you were one of them when you knocked on the door.'

'Did you now? Why don't you tell me all about it, lad?'

'I'd like to, Jim. I really need some advice. And . . . and you feel more like my father than *he* does.'

'I wish you *were* my son.'

Both men stared at one another, half-smiles on their faces, then, embarrassed by these admissions and emotions they applied themselves in silence to clearing their plates. Afterwards they boiled a kettle to get some hot water, and washed up carefully before going to sit by the fire upstairs. Aubrey took up bottles of light ale from the crate of mixed beers Mrs Beamish had sent along as a Christmas present, and poured out two glasses.

Jim took a long pull and then set down his glass. 'Now, lad, tell me what's been happening since you came back to Tinsley . . .'

When there was a knock on the front door of the Hall just as they were all sitting down to their evening meal in the warmth of the big kitchen, Marcus went to answer it himself. He paused to pick up his revolver, just in case.

But the man grinning at him as he opened the door was nothing to do with Fleming. 'Den! Come in.'

'When I got your telegram, I thought it might be best for me to come straight here. You sounded to need reinforcements, so I told Mum and Dad about your little problem. I'd have been here a couple of hours earlier, but I needed to get a declaration from Dad signed by a justice of the peace.'

'Den, you ugly old devil, I can't think why I'm so glad to see you!' Marcus shook his hand vigorously. 'Thanks for coming.'

'Things looking bad?' Den asked softly.

'Not wonderful. Don't tell them why you're here. I don't want to upset Serena unless I have to.' Marcus too spoke quietly. 'Fleming actually had the cheek to come out here and make veiled threats. It upset her, but she stood up to him beautifully.'

'I like your wife. Now, hadn't we better join her?'

Marcus led the way to the kitchen. 'Look who's here! Den was visiting a friend nearby and decided to come and spend a night with us.'

Serena looked up and smiled at the cheerful young doctor. She hoped she kept the smile on her face, but she guessed at once why he was here. Marcus was protecting her again. Well, it made a nice change to be protected instead of used. She went round to offer Den her cheek while Pearl set a place for him at the table.

Aunt Pamela, who had insisted on joining them and was sitting nearest the fire, wrapped in a thick shawl, looked disapproving as Marcus brought Den round to be introduced. 'In my day we didn't entertain our friends in the kitchen.'

'I've eaten in worse billets, believe me, Mrs Lonnerden,' Den said easily.

'You're another soldier who's survived the war, I suppose,' she muttered.

He waggled one hand at her. 'Lost a few fingers, though. I was a doctor in the Army. Glad to be out of that sort of thing now, I can tell you.' He cast a professional eye over her yellowish complexion and extreme thinness, but said nothing. When he saw the changes in her nails and the slight tremor of her hand, he guessed what ailed her. He'd seen that look before. You couldn't mistake the symptoms of renal failure.

She looked at him with eyes that said she knew what he was thinking, then looked away with a sigh.

He set himself to cheer everyone up, and soon had even the two elderly maids laughing.

After the meal, however, Pearl stood up and said, 'I'll just go and get the fire blazing in the sitting room, shall I, then you can move in there?'

Marcus smiled at her. 'Thanks, Pearl.' A few minutes later he offered his aunt his arm and led her through to the sitting room, moderating his pace to hers because she didn't seem able to walk very fast these days. Den strolled behind them with Serena.

To everyone's relief, Aunt Pamela didn't stay with them for long and soon said she must seek her bed.

She was walking so slowly that Marcus started to get up to help her. Den tugged his sleeve, mouthed, 'I'll do it,' and went outside with her. She stopped at the foot of the stairs with a sigh, and he said gently, 'Let me carry you upstairs,

Mrs Lonnerden. You don't want to overtax your strength, and I gather you've been quite ill.'

'I wish I'd died,' she said bitterly, but let him sweep her into his arms.

'Have you seen a doctor lately?' he asked, after he'd set her down on her bed.

She nodded. 'I know what's wrong with me, young man, but I haven't told anyone the details and I'd appreciate it if you'd keep your knowledge to yourself.'

'Of course. But if there's anything I can do while I'm here, I'm at your service.'

'I thought you were just staying overnight.'

'No. Marcus thinks Fleming is going to make another attempt to control Serena, even set aside their marriage. I'm here in my capacity as a doctor, in case I'm needed to verify that she's in full possession of her mental faculties.'

'That man should be taken out and shot.' Acid edged her words. 'He was a bad influence on my son Lawrence, and if I could see him get his just desserts, I'd die a happy woman.'

'Fate doesn't usually tie things up so neatly, I'm afraid. But I won't let him lock Serena away, I promise you. And now, dear lady, let me send up your maid to help you to bed. I'll come and see you in the morning, eh?'

When he went back into the sitting room, his expression was still shadowed, and Marcus asked if anything was wrong. He shrugged. 'Your aunt isn't a well woman.'

'No, poor thing. But she's better than she was, at least. We'll have to try to feed her up.'

Den didn't contradict him on this. He preferred to let patients decide how much they told their families about their condition. Well, he did when they weren't soldiers trapped in a system overloaded with rules and regulations.

After that, the evening passed swiftly. At ten o'clock, Serena left the two men talking, and when Marcus went to open the door for her, whispered, 'Don't hurry up if you want to chat to Den.'

'Thank you. I thought I'd try to persuade him to stay for a few days. He'll cheer us all up. That all right with you?'

She smiled. 'Of course it is. But I know perfectly well why

you brought him here, so you don't need to pretend his arrival was an accident.'

'I shall have to learn not to underestimate you. You're still too quiet, and I forget that you're a clever woman – as well as a pretty one.' He kissed her cheek and watched her mount the stairs, appreciating the trim ankles showing beneath a dress she and Pearl had altered. As he went back to join Den, he decided that a man wanted – no, *needed* – to protect the woman he loved. Theirs might be a quiet love, for neither of them was demonstrative or outgoing, but love was growing between them nevertheless, taking root like a sturdy plant which would, he hoped, only grow bigger as the years passed.

Smiling at himself for such fancies, he went back to talk to his friend.

Evadne came home that evening full of excitement. 'I went to lunch with a friend and, Justin, you'll never guess who was there, looking awfully ill at ease.'

'Who?'

'Mrs Hammerton. It seems her husband has been putting pressure on some of my friends' husbands to get their wives to include her in women's social events. It won't work, you know. You can't make a silk purse out of a sow's ear, and she's an ill-educated bore. Just having her there put a complete damper on the group, I can tell you, because no one likes her husband. Mind, one can't help feeling sorry for her, she's such a poor drab of a creature, for all her fine clothes and jewels. And she knew we didn't want her there.'

'Did she say anything of interest?'

'Nothing specific, but she did let drop that her Cyril is angry about something Mr Fleming has done.'

'How on earth did you get her to say such a thing in public?'

Evadne winked at him. 'She didn't say it in public. I went up to powder my nose at the same time as she did, and I was so friendly she confided in me, saying she knew we'd been forced to invite her and was sorry about that. I told her she must come to my next luncheon and she accepted gratefully. Mind you, I doubt her husband will let her, because he's one of those anti-Votes for Women types and he was one of those who shouted rude things when we marched through town. He still glares at me if we so much as pass in the street.'

'You're a clever woman, Evadne.'

'I am, aren't I?'

What, Justin wondered, had Fleming done to make Hammerton angry?

Hammerton stared at his wife and resisted the urge to thump her, because it wouldn't do any good. When she was afraid she became twice as stupid. 'Don't you know that Evadne Blair is the cousin of Redway?'

Jean blinked and shook her head.

'What exactly did you say to her?'

'Nothing much, just small talk. We met when we were both powdering our noses.'

'Going for a piss, do you mean?'

She flushed and began to shake. 'Please don't be so crude, Cyril.'

He scowled at her. 'What . . . did you . . . say to her?'

'All we talked about was how good the food was and then *she* said I must go round to her house next time. I th-thought you'd be pleased about that. You *want* me to get to know the right sort of ladies.'

'The right sort, yes. But there are certain people who are *not* useful to me. She's one.'

'Perhaps if you wrote me a list, I could avoid the people you don't want me to know?'

If he gave her a list, Jean would only betray herself with those people. 'I'm glad you're trying to mix more, but don't go to the Blair woman's house. Accept her invitation but send word that you're ill at the last minute. Right? That way she can't take offence.'

'Yes, Cyril.'

He looked at her with disfavour. What was the point of earning a lot of money on black-market ventures if you had a wife like this one? No matter what sort of clothes he bought Jean, she always looked what she was: a plain, plump and rather stupid woman.

'I'll . . . um . . . go and check how Cook is doing.'

'You do that.' It was all she was good for, running his house. Indeed, she got on better with their cook than she did with the well-off ladies she should be associating with. She was of no help to him socially in his new role as one of the richest men in town.

Nor was Fleming, who seemed to be behaving very strangely lately, as if he thought himself above the law. Not wise, that. Of course, Fleming was somewhat concerned about his gambling debts. He wasn't as good a card player as he thought, and when the gambling fever gripped him, didn't bother to keep count of how deep he was getting.

Most men were fools, even the so-called clever ones.

As they got the shop ready for opening on Tuesday, which was Christmas Eve, Aubrey told Ted he had a friend staying with him, a friend who didn't want to be seen by Fleming or his men.

Ted shot him a quick glance. 'There seem to be a lot of people at odds with your father lately.'

'He does seem to have been setting a few backs up – but then he always did.' More memories slipped into place. 'I can remember as a lad being beaten up by some other boys. He was furious that I hadn't hurt any of them in return, but I never was any good at fighting. So he had them beaten up and they didn't come near me again – nor did anyone else, even those who'd been friendly before.'

'Must have been lonely.'

Aubrey nodded. 'But I did have my sister. Anyway, enough of that. My visitor is still in bed. He was very tired, hasn't fully recovered from his war injuries yet. I'll introduce him to you later.'

From then on they were too busy to chat. It seemed as if everyone who needed to buy a last-minute Christmas gift had decided on a book and wanted advice about choosing just the right one. Which sent coins clinking into the till and had Ted looking very pleased.

Jim stayed upstairs for most of the day and took a nap in the afternoon, so, what with the busy shop, there never seemed to be a convenient time to introduce him to Ted.

As they were closing up, a group of three scruffy-looking carol singers appeared and sang 'Good King Wenceslas' with more vigour than skill. Ted gave them sixpence and let them each choose a book from what was left on the penny tray. After that, he looked at the clock and said, 'I reckon we can close now. I want to go home and you said you needed to nip along to the market for some more food.' He pressed a small envelope into Aubrey's hand. 'Your wages. Have a good Christmas.'

When he'd gone, Aubrey ran upstairs to tell Jim he was going out to the market, then did a rapid round of shopping. He was invited out to the Hall the following day for Christmas lunch and was going to risk taking Jim with him – if his friend could be persuaded to show his face in the daylight. He was quite sure Serena and Marcus would welcome any friend of his and he'd buy a cake or some biscuits to take along as an extra present. People at the markets were relaxing the food regulations a little, unofficially of course, but no one was reporting the infringements.

While he was out, he nipped over to the Weaver's Arms to wish Mrs Beamish a merry Christmas and give her the small present he'd bought – a book, of course.

'And here was me thinking you'd forgotten me,' she teased. 'Wait there.' She nipped into the back and came out with a plate covered in layers of greaseproof paper. 'I've got a cake for you. Keep it in a tin and it'll last for days. Why don't you come back for a drink later?'

'Not tonight. I'm exhausted after being on my feet all day and I'm going to have an early night. After Christmas, maybe.'

She pulled a face. 'Come tomorrow night, then. We'll be closed, but you'll be here as my guest, not a customer.'

'Well, maybe just for a quick drink.'

'If you don't turn up, I'll come and fetch you.'

He smiled as he walked home. She was a lovely woman. It was good to make new friends. She, Jim and Ted weren't the sort of people his father would approve of, but he didn't care about that. He liked people who were warm and friendly, decent people without any pretensions.

After Christmas he'd go and see his father, face up to his past. But for now he just wanted to enjoy his first peacetime Christmas for several years.

On Christmas Eve, Ernest made arrangements which would show certain people that he was not a man to be trifled with.

After that, he went to the club, because he had nowhere else to go, and to his annoyance, had found he wanted company on this night of supposed celebration. Though what there was to celebrate with a son like his, he didn't know.

To his surprise, the house seemed very empty without his daughter and he actually missed her. And Serena *was* his daughter, because he'd housed her and reared her, hadn't he? Not James Lang. She'd been quite a nice little child and he'd enjoyed people commenting on how pretty she was or how clever.

She might not have done him credit as she grew older, the cunning bitch, but she had still been there, someone to talk to. Or she had been until she took it into her head to run off to marry that fellow. There had to be a way to force her to come home again, a way to get the marriage annulled. He'd get Tolson to swear she was still a virgin. The man would do anything to have some of his gambling debts cancelled.

Ernest looked round, scowling. A house was so much more comfortable with a mistress in it, and Serena had been good at running things, very good. He could see that, now that the little touches were missing, the flowers, arrangements of leaves, small items of comfort. If he could get Frank back and see him married to a suitable young woman from a good family, there would be no need to re-marry, something Ernest didn't really want to do. He could have Serena here again and that would be enough.

There were Christmas Eve parties being held by some of the town's leading citizens, he knew, but this year he'd not received any invitations, which was another thing that had surprised him. He'd have to look into that in the new year, make sure one or two men who were under obligations to him started inviting him round to dinner again. Only, he needed a woman to be his hostess when he invited them back, dammit.

He'd treat Serena more carefully when he got her back, show her he valued her. That was where he'd gone wrong with her, he could see that now.

He met Hammerton at the club, but no one else was there whom he knew or wanted to know, just a couple of old fogies who had no family and almost lived here. 'Where is everyone?'

'They're all at home with their families,' Cyril said. 'Or at the Pulvertons' party. They didn't invite me this year. I'll make sure they regret that. Fancy a glass of claret?'

'Lovely.' Ernest sat down, feeling better already for having some company. But after they'd dined, conversation flagged a little.

'Fancy a few hands of cards?' Cyril asked.

''Fraid I can't afford it at the moment. You've been too damned lucky lately.'

'I'll take your IOUs. I know you always pay in the end.'

'You've got too many of those already. No, I think I'll have an early night. And you've got a wife at home. Won't she be missing you?'

'She's fussing over the grandchildren's presents. I came out to escape that sort of thing. You sure you won't play?'

'Certain.' Ernest stood up. 'I'll see you after Christmas.'

'Mmm. Want a ride back?'

'No, thanks. It's not far. A walk will do me good.'

But his way led past his offices and he scowled at the blackened ruins. The fire had held off inquiries for a time, but what the hell was he going to do now about paying Hammerton back? He couldn't hold on to Serena's annuity for much longer and the annual payment that he needed so much wasn't due until April.

He entered his house feeling aggrieved, and when Ruby came to take his coat, so far forget himself as to snap at her.

She looked at him in shock.

'Sorry.' He studied her. Not a bad-looking woman. 'Bring a tea tray to the sitting room, will you?'

'Yes, sir.'

When she came in with it, he stood up and took it from her, seizing the opportunity to press her breast.

She jumped back like a scalded cat.

'Why don't you join me in a cup, Ruby? You must have been on your feet all day.'

She edged back to the door. 'No, thank you, sir. It wouldn't be right.'

Clearly she wasn't free with her favours. He scowled then shrugged. Better that way, really. He'd send a message tomorrow to a man who was sometimes of use to him and who could always provide a woman to see to his needs. You had to celebrate Christmas one way or the other.

Scowling at the tea tray he went across to the decanter that always stood ready nowadays, pouring himself a big glass of brandy. A man needed something to make him sleep.

Sixteen

Christmas morning dawned with lowering skies and a threat of rain. Aubrey got up later than usual and since there was no sound of Jim stirring in the attic bedroom, he made his way downstairs, shivering in his dressing gown. He opened the damper on the kitchen stove in case there was any residual glow that could make it easier to get the fire blazing, then he went out to the lavatory.

When he came out of it, he found his way barred by two men, one of them Sam Hudd, and was so shocked by this unexpected sight that he couldn't for a moment move a muscle. As they advanced on him, he let out a yell, but they grabbed him and, although he struggled, they were far stronger than he was and it didn't take them long to subdue and gag him.

'Stick him on the cart,' said Hudd. 'I'll go inside and get some clothes for him.'

The other man nodded and slung the bound man over his shoulder, carrying him out of the back gate and rolling him up in some old carpet that was lying ready on the handcart.

Aubrey found himself lying in stifling darkness, breathing air so filled with dust and stale smells that he felt he was being smothered. He had to tell himself sternly not to panic. He knew who was behind this, of course he did, had done from the minute he'd seen Hudd. He could even guess why he'd been taken – the same old nagging to follow his father into the business of charging high rents for ill-maintained and crumbling properties – which included making sure rents were paid, even if the tenants starved, something Aubrey had never been able to stomach.

He wriggled but the ropes round his wrists didn't give at all, so he lay waiting, angry and ashamed that it'd been so easy for them to catch him. But if his father thought he could coerce him into working and living with him, he would soon discover that his son had changed. Even Serena had rebelled in the end, once their mother was dead.

Then it suddenly occurred to Aubrey that Jim was still in the house, and he began to worry about his friend, who was not yet fully recovered from months of surgery and might be permanently harmed if treated roughly. But although he strained his ears, he could hear nothing.

It seemed a very long time before he heard voices close by and the cart started moving, bumping him to and fro, helpless in his dusty straitjacket.

Jim half-woke when he heard Aubrey go downstairs, and came fully awake as he heard Aubrey yell out suddenly a few minutes later. He rolled out of bed and ran to stare out of the window, watching in horror as two brutal-looking men subdued his young friend, tied him up and carried him out through the back gate.

When one of them walked purposefully towards the house Jim hurriedly straightened the bedcovers, shoved his clothes into his suitcase and pushed it under the bed. Then he went to peer down the stairs. He knew better than to tangle with men like that in his present physical condition, and besides, he'd be of more use to Aubrey if he stayed free. He heard footsteps coming upstairs and drew back, but not before he'd seen the man reach the landing below and check all three rooms before going into the one where Aubrey slept.

There came sounds of drawers being opened, occasional grunts of effort or annoyance, then the intruder came out on to the landing carrying a suitcase. He stopped there and set it down. Jim wondered what he was doing and, to his surprise, the man started up the stairs towards the attics, presumably to check that no one had witnessed what had happened.

Jim tiptoed across to the bed, glad he was still barefoot. As he slid under it, he hoped desperately that he hadn't left anything out to show that the room was occupied.

Footsteps went towards the next room, then came into Jim's. From underneath the bed, he could see only the man's heavy boots and the lower few inches of his trousers. For a few nerve-racking moments he tried to keep his breathing quiet while the other turned from side to side as if studying the bedroom.

With another grunt the man went out again and Jim buried his head in his hands, so relieved he felt sick. He heard those footsteps clump down the stairs, stop for a moment then go quickly down the lower flight of stairs. A minute later, there was the sound of the back door banging shut and Jim wriggled from under the bed and peeped out of the window. The man was walking down the back garden with a suitcase in his hand. Jim could see a handcart in the back alley, with a couple of rolls of carpet on it, in one of which poor Aubrey was hidden. The suitcase was slung on the cart as well.

One man started pushing and the other walked beside it. They vanished round the corner and Jim stood for a moment or two wondering what the hell was going on, then flung on his clothes. At the back door he listened but could hear nothing, so ran down the garden and into the alley. He could see the tracks of the handcart on the damp ground and followed them quickly to the end, just in time to see the two men cross Yorkshire Road and vanish from sight.

He moved to look cautiously down Yorkshire Road. The men were walking along it, going away from the town centre. They were making no attempt to hide and one was laughing at something the other had said. They turned off into one of the downhill side streets, an area where the more affluent folk lived, with views down to the river. After hesitating a moment, Jim risked following them again.

The first narrow street provided the rear access to the big houses on Cavendish Terrace. He saw one of the men closing a gateway behind the third house along. Of the cart there was no sign, so presumably they'd taken their captive inside. Jim decided discretion was the better part of valour and hurried back to the bookshop. The place seemed horribly empty without Aubrey.

It was the work of a few moments only to complete his morning toilet and gobble down a piece of bread and jam. There was only one person to whom he could go for help now.

When the jolting stopped, Aubrey could not help groaning in relief, and once the old carpet was unwound, he sniffed in the fresh air as deeply as he could with his mouth gagged.

'Sorry about that,' Hudd said.

Aubrey could see from his smirk that Hudd wasn't in the least sorry. The other man came towards him and he couldn't help flinching away, which made the smirk broaden into a smile. But all the man did was untie his legs and pull him roughly to his feet. He stumbled and thought they were going to let him fall, but at the last minute Hudd reached out to grab the back of his dressing gown and steady him.

'Your father's waiting for you, but I reckon you'd better get dressed first,' he said. 'I can release you if you'll promise not to call out.'

Aubrey nodded and when the gag was removed, he said nothing.

'Here. Put these on.' Hudd opened a suitcase.

Aubrey dragged his clothes on anyhow and followed his captors, relieved not to be facing his father dressed only in pyjamas.

They walked towards the house but cut across the back garden rather than entering through the scullery and kitchen. The French doors of the small sitting room the family used every day were slightly ajar, and Hudd nodded dismissal to the man who'd been helping him, before indicating with a mocking wave of his hand that his prisoner should go in first.

Inside the room, Aubrey's father was waiting for him. For a moment he froze then pulled himself together and stared back steadily at the man who had made his childhood so unhappy. But the encounter immediately set images cascading through his brain and, with a gasp, he fumbled for a chair. Someone guided him to it and helped him sit, then he put his head in his hands, rocking to and fro as the pain ebbed and flowed.

'He gets like this when he starts remembering something, sir,' Hudd said.

It was the room as much as the sight of his father that had set him off this time, Aubrey decided. He could remember now being beaten in here, harangued, mocked, scolded.

When his head cleared a little he turned towards the man standing in front of the fireplace, hogging the warmth as he always did. Aubrey didn't speak, didn't ask why he'd been brought here, because he knew that was what his father wanted him to do.

Just then the door opened and Ruby started to come in.

'Get out!' Ernest snapped.

Aubrey seized the moment. 'Help! Fetch the police. They're holding me against my will. Hel—' Hudd's hand covered his mouth and his father stalked across to the door to yell, 'Don't come in here again. My son is ill, doesn't know what he's saying.'

But Aubrey could still see Ruby across the hand that was holding him, and he put every ounce of silent pleading into his eyes that he could.

She backed out, muttering, 'Sorry, sir.'

'You'll say nothing of this or you'll lose your place,' Ernest snapped.

'No, sir. Of course not, sir.'

When the door had closed on her, Hudd let go of Aubrey, who leaned his head back with a sigh.

'Do that again and I'll have you permanently gagged.'

'Will you? And how long do you think you can keep me a prisoner here, Father?'

Ernest gave one of his icy smiles. 'As long as I need to, with Dr Tolson caring for you. We can simply drug you if you prove too troublesome.'

Aubrey shuddered as another memory slotted into place. They'd done that before when he was much younger and had tried his hand at rebellion. He'd been vilely ill as a result, because the drug they'd used to sedate him hadn't agreed with him, and he had taken so long to recover, Tolson had been worried about him.

'I see you're beginning to remember, Frank.'

'Why did you have me brought here by force?' Aubrey

didn't waste time telling his father to call him by his new name.

'Because you didn't come willingly. You should be living at home where you belong, not working in a damned bookshop. I don't want people gossiping when they realize who you are. You're *my* son and, one way or the other, you'll behave like it, or I'll have you locked away.'

Aubrey didn't reply. He only hoped Jim could get help for him.

'How did you come to lose your memory and where have you been all these months?'

Aubrey leaned back in his chair. 'It's a long story. Any chance of my getting a cup of tea first? My throat's dry as dust after that carpet they rolled me in.'

'Fetch him some tea,' Ernest said impatiently.

Hudd hesitated. 'Will you be all right with him?'

'Of course I will. He's a runt as well as a coward.'

Though burning with the old indignation at his father's casual use of the same old insult, Aubrey said nothing, more in control of himself than he had ever been when he lived here. At his father's prompting, he began his tale, making it last for as long as he could. He stopped at intervals to sip the strong black tea gratefully, and when Hudd refilled his cup, nodded thanks before continuing his story.

'How did you come to be working for Bailey, then? You should have come straight home.'

'Sheer chance. I didn't know who I really was when I arrived in Tinsley and it seemed like a good opportunity. I've always liked books, as you know.' He explained about his job, going on at length about the convenience of the flat above the shop until told to shut up.

His father wasn't pleased, was tapping his fingers on his chair arm, but this time Aubrey welcomed the pause in questioning and rested his head against the back of the chair, closing his eyes as he waited for his father to get to the point, which was: what was going to happen to him now?

The front doorbell rang and footsteps crossed the entrance hall to answer it.

'See if that's Tolson,' Ernest said irritably.

Hudd came back a moment or two later, followed by the

family doctor, who stared from the older man standing by the fire to the younger man sitting in an armchair.

'He didn't want to come back home and I believe he's behaving irrationally,' Ernest announced. 'Examine him, if you please. And don't take too long about it.'

'If he's been ill, I should do that properly. You don't want to harm him, I'm sure.'

Ernest scowled. 'Take him up to his bedroom, then. Hudd, you go with them. I'll give orders to the staff that they're to say nothing about his presence here.'

Aubrey heaved himself to his feet when ordered to and didn't have to feign the dizziness.

Tolson came across to him. 'What's the matter?'

'I'm remembering things. It always makes me dizzy and gives me severe headaches. The doctors told me to rest if I could when it happened.' He rubbed his temple.

'Is he making that up?' his father asked.

'Probably not. Resting is standard treatment in cases like this.'

'Then you'd better give him something to keep him quiet till he recovers.'

'That'll only make it worse,' Aubrey said quickly. 'It's sleep I need, not drugs.'

'Do as you're told, Tolson!' Ernest snapped. 'I'll be very angry if he causes trouble. He's got to learn to toe the line. Surely being in the Army has toughened up even a softie like him?'

Accompanied by Hudd, the doctor went up with Aubrey to the bedroom that had always been his. There Tolson gave him a thorough examination, after which he produced a hypodermic filled with colourless liquid. At the sight of it Aubrey began to struggle, but Hudd held him down while the doctor injected him. To his astonishment Tolson winked at him and rolled his eyes quickly in the direction of Hudd, unseen by the other man, shaking his head as if to say be quiet.

'I used this drug because others disagree with him,' the doctor said, and looked meaningfully at Aubrey. 'He'll start to feel sleepy in about ten minutes, and he'll be sound asleep in half an hour.'

Hudd grinned. 'That'll make my life easier. How long does this stuff last?'

'About four hours. I'll come back when it starts to wear off and if necessary give him another injection.'

'If you go down and tell Mr Fleming, doctor, I'll stay here until he falls asleep.'

'Very well.' Without a backwards glance, Tolson left the room.

Downstairs, Fleming stopped pacing up and down the library to ask curtly, 'Well, how is he?'

'You can see the scars from the explosion which injured him, but there's nothing wrong with him mentally.'

Ernest gave him a long, level stare. 'If necessary, you'll find that he's mentally incompetent and admit him to that asylum of yours as a private patient.' When the other man didn't respond, he added, 'You will unless you want your gambling debts to become public knowledge.'

'And if I do this thing for you?'

'We'll knock another fifty pounds off your debts.'

Tolson sighed but nodded. 'Your son will be sound asleep in half an hour, and will stay asleep for about four hours. We have to be careful about injecting him, though. You know how ill he was as a boy.'

'I'll risk it. Make sure you're back by the time he wakes. I've told the staff Frank's not himself and needs medical treatment.'

Tolson nodded. 'I'll get off home, then. It *is* Christmas Day, you know.'

'Not when people are sick and need you!'

When he'd left, Ernest resumed his pacing, then went upstairs to look at his son, who did indeed seem sleepy. He beckoned Hudd over to the door and whispered, 'Come down when he's asleep. I have an errand for you.'

'Should we leave him alone?' Hudd queried.

'I'll look in on him every now and then. Tolson says he'll be unconscious for four hours once he's fully asleep, but you'll be back within a couple of hours, so I doubt we have anything to worry about.'

'I'll tie him up just to be sure,' Hudd said. 'You can't be too careful. If he woke early and escaped, we could be in trouble.'

'Not with Tolson on our side.' Ernest gave one of his tight smiles. 'Trust me. The doctor is rather anxious to please me.'

He went back downstairs to write a note to his daughter for Hudd to deliver.

When Hudd finally left him alone, Aubrey waited a few moments then risked half-opening his eyes to peer out through his lashes. As he'd thought, the bedroom was empty, but he was tightly trussed so couldn't escape. Cursing under his breath, he began to struggle with the bonds, working desperately to loosen them, but Hudd knew his work and had tied both hands and feet tightly, so there was no slackness in the ropes.

Was there any chance of a rescue? And even if someone did rescue him, would people believe his side of things when a respected doctor like Tolson said he was mentally incompetent? That thought made him frown. Why had Tolson not drugged him? Why had he made it plain to Aubrey how to behave to simulate the drug's effects? Perhaps he remembered how ill Aubrey had been last time they drugged him and didn't want to take any risks. It seemed too much to hope that Tolson was trying to help him escape.

The door opened and Ruby peeped in, gasping at the sight of him and casting a terrified look over her shoulder.

'Please!' Aubrey whispered. 'Go and fetch help. My father is keeping me a prisoner.'

She shook her head, looking near to tears. 'I daren't.'

'Then can you loosen these ropes, so that I can try to escape? *Please*, Ruby.'

With another terrified look down the corridor she came inside.

'Shut the door or he might guess someone's here,' Aubrey told her. 'That's it. Now, see if you can untie my hands and feet.'

She pulled the covers back but as she started trying to undo the knots, footsteps came up the stairs, heavy footsteps which could belong to only one person in this house. With a muffled yelp of terror, she covered Aubrey up again and looked round in panic for somewhere to hide.

'Get under the bed,' he whispered, closing his eyes.

Whatever happened to her, he intended to play the drugged patient.

The door opened, footsteps came towards the bed and stopped.

The silence dragged on, then Ernest muttered, 'I know you're my get, unlike *her*, but how the hell did a son of mine turn out so stupid?' With a growl of annoyance he left the room, closing the door quietly behind him.

Aubrey waited until the footsteps had faded into the distance, then called in a low voice, 'It's safe to come out now.'

Ruby emerged from under the bed, her face white with terror, and backed towards the door. 'I'm sorry, sir, I daren't do it. I just . . . daren't.'

Before he could speak, she had left the room.

Jim slipped out of the rear of the shop and made his way along back alleys to the main road leading out to Horton. He hurried along it, wishing he had some form of transport and fretting about how long it would take him to get help for Aubrey. But he didn't want to go to the police without some support, because, from what he'd learned since he came back, Fleming was now a man of some importance in the town, even if he wasn't liked.

By the time he reached the front door of the Hall, Jim was glowing with exertion. It seemed a long time before anyone answered.

'Yes?'

'Are you Marcus Graye, Serena's husband?'

'Yes.'

'I'm a close friend of Aubrey's. I'm staying with him, only he's in danger and needs help.'

Marcus gestured him inside and took him through to a sitting room, where a young woman was sitting talking to another man.

The sight of her made Jim stop dead and clutch the door frame. Dear heaven, it could have been Grace when she was younger! Only it wasn't, he could see that now. This woman had a more determined expression and her eyes were different, less gentle, more watchful.

'This is a friend of your brother's, Serena.' Marcus turned to his companion and asked, 'Are you all right?'

'Just a bit out of breath. Sorry. My name's Jim and I got to know Aubrey at the convalescent home. We became really good friends and I'm staying with him for a few days. But this morning two men attacked him when he was down the back and carried him off. I couldn't help him.' He looked down at himself ruefully. 'They were very large fellows and I'm still recovering from major wounds. So I followed them and they took him to the rear of a house on Cavendish Terrace.'

He could see he had their full attention now. 'Aubrey had told me about meeting his sister again, Mrs Graye, so I came straight to you for help. I'm not sure what's going on, but I presume it's his father who's got hold of him.'

'Damn Fleming!' Marcus said bitterly. 'Can't we even have Christmas in peace? How come they didn't capture you too, Jim?'

'I hid under the bed when one of them came into the house for some of Aubrey's clothes. Not courageous of me, I know, but it seemed better to stay free so that I could fetch help.'

'Very much better,' Marcus agreed.

'Why on earth would the man kidnap his own son?' Den asked. 'What good would that do if your brother doesn't want to live with him, Serena?'

'Fleming is fond of using force. I suppose he did it because Aubrey hadn't gone back to see him and was living elsewhere. That would infuriate him. And I should think he intends to force Aubrey to go and live with him. He used to be able to coerce my brother into doing what he wanted, one way or another. I think he'll find it more difficult now.'

'He wanted to force *you* to go back to him, too,' Marcus commented. 'Would have declared you mentally incompetent rather than let you go. And . . .'

They looked at one another in horror.

'Do you think he'll do that to Aubrey if my brother won't do as he says?' she asked in a horrified whisper. 'He was so used to me and my mother doing as he told us, to servants jumping at his command and tenants of his horrible houses living in fear of him, that I think he's grown to feel he can force anyone to do what he wants. Look at how he stole my money and had his office burned down to cover his tracks. He enjoys bullying people, has a warped view of the world. I could tell you a lot about nasty tricks he's played on people, things I've had to stand by and watch for years, not to mention the schemes I've heard him hatching with Sam Hudd and—' Serena's voice broke, and when Marcus put his arm round her shoulders, she leaned against him with a sob.

'Maybe he's the one who's mentally unstable? He certainly sounds to be suffering from delusions,' Den suggested.

She sighed. 'Maybe. I think he's just wicked.'

There was silence as each of them thought about the situation.

It was Marcus who spoke first. 'I should think he'll definitely try again to get you back, Serena, because he wants your money. If he's been unlucky in his gambling he could be desperate.'

'He probably wants me to run his house and act as his hostess, too, but I'm *not* going back, whatever he threatens.' She looked at Marcus. 'The trouble is, the thing that really worries me, he always gets his revenge for imagined insults, even if he has to wait for years. We'll never be safe from him unless we go and live somewhere else, never.' For the first time, her certainty that she wouldn't return to Fleming's house was shaken. What if Fleming threatened her husband's life? In even this short time, she'd grown to love Marcus and would do almost anything to keep him safe.

He took her hand and patted it gently. 'I don't want to leave here, so we'll have to expose him for what he is and make sure he's locked away for a very long time.'

'How can we do that? He's been clever enough to stay on the right side of the law – just – for years.' She shook her head, feeling there was little hope of catching Fleming, then became aware that Marcus was biting his lip, looking at her differently. 'What's the matter? Have you thought of something?'

He nodded.

'Well? Tell me.'

'I think we can only expose Fleming through you, my darling, much as I hate to say that. But only if you're willing. You'd need to be very brave and let him take you back for a short time . . . I promise it wouldn't be for long. Then we'll bring in Den and show that you and your brother are perfectly normal. Could you bear to do that, go back to him for a few hours? If we crack him on one thing, I think we'll find a way to crack him on others, at least that's been my experience with men who were fiddling the system in the Army.' He looked at her. 'I'll understand if you don't want to do it, find another way.'

She shuddered. 'If it's the only way.'

'I expect we'll be hearing from him soon, now that he has your brother.'

Sam Hudd grinned as he leaned back in the car and let himself be driven to the Hall. He was looking forward to seeing Miss Serena's face when she read the note from her father. Stupid bitch! Did she really think she could go against Mr Fleming? Hudd had seen a long time ago on which side his bread was buttered, and had worked hard to make himself indispensable to his employer. If she'd any sense, she'd have done the same with her father, because Fleming rewarded quite generously those who helped him.

Hudd enjoyed his work, liked having power over people. He was sorry, really, that the war had ended, because it had offered a lot of opportunities for a man like Mr Fleming to make money, and thus for Hudd to do the same.

When the car stopped outside the Hall, he got out quickly and went to hammer on the front door.

It was opened by Graye and for a moment the fool stood there staring, as if shocked to see who had arrived. 'What do *you* want?'

'To speak to Miss Fleming.'

'There's nobody of that name here.'

Hudd sighed. The man was proving a nuisance, as he'd expected. 'To speak to my employer's daughter, then.'

'What about?'

Serena's voice came from inside the hallway. 'Let him in, Marcus. We may as well see what he wants.'

Hudd sauntered in, letting them show him into the sitting room, where he took a seat without being asked.

'Well?' she asked. 'What does Fleming want?'

He handed over the note. 'Your *father* wants you to go and see him.'

'I won't do it.'

'Not even to help your poor little brother?' Hudd could have laughed out loud to see the dismay creep over her face.

'My brother? What do you mean?'

'Mr Frank is presently in your father's house and he's in a bad way, under Dr Tolson's care.'

'I don't believe you. I saw Aubrey only a day or two ago and he was perfectly well.'

'He may be well physically, but he's not well mentally. We picked him up at the back of the bookshop this morning, acting irrationally. Rather than send him to the asylum, your father took him home, where he can be cared for properly. And he wants *you* to come home and care for Mr Frank, because you'll make all the difference to how well he recovers, he's sure.'

Hudd watched her put her hands to her face. He could see tears running down her cheeks. Aha! He had her now. Well, it had always been obvious how fond she was of her brother. People usually had a weakness you could exploit, Mr Fleming had taught him that. He waited another minute. 'It's that or send him to the asylum.' He didn't make any other threats but leaned back and watched her.

She turned to Marcus. 'I can't leave Aubrey in their hands, can't risk them ill-treating him. He's only just starting to get his memory back.'

'I'm not having you go back there, Serena,' Marcus said. Scowling, he turned to Hudd. 'Tell your master she'll nurse her brother here if he needs looking after.'

'Mr Fleming wants to keep an eye on Mr Frank himself – and he wants to heal the breach with his daughter,' Hudd said. He watched with delight as she turned towards her husband with a pleading expression on her face.

'Marcus, perhaps I'd better . . .'

'No, Serena! I'm not having it.'

She jerked to her feet and went to the window, standing looking out of it, her hands clasping the sides of her bent head as if she was in pain. Hudd grinned at Marcus. He reckoned Mr Fleming had been absolutely right. Her brother was her weak spot.

She turned round and straightened her shoulders. 'I'm going, Marcus. He's my little brother and I *can't* leave him alone in their hands.'

'I'm sorry, but I forbid you to do it, Serena.'

'How will you stop me?' she asked.

'By force, if necessary.'

Hudd stood up, pulled his revolver out of his pocket and smiled at Serena. 'If you'll get your coat, miss, I'll take you to your brother.'

'I'm sorry, Marcus.' She ran out of the room.

'I'm not sorry.' Hudd was enjoying himself. 'You're not good enough to marry a Fleming.' He backed carefully out of the room and found her waiting in the hallway. 'Go and get in the car, miss.'

In silence she went outside, and Hudd followed her, keeping a careful watch on Graye. The fellow came to stand in the doorway of the sitting room, then followed Hudd to the front door, looking furious. But he did nothing. Well, what could he do against a gun? Guns had been really easy to buy during the war. They made difficult things simple sometimes. Hudd enjoyed using them.

As the car drove off, he leaned his head back, smiling. 'Your father will be very pleased to see you. He's missed you. And your brother really needs you.'

She said nothing, just stared down at her clasped hands.

Hudd left her alone. Didn't want her creating a fuss until he had her inside the house. Then she could fuss all she liked. She'd be where Mr Fleming wanted her and she'd not find it possible to get away again.

The minute the car had driven away, Marcus fetched Jim and they hurried out to the stables with Den. Vic had the horse and cab ready, as they'd planned. It was galling to have to go into Tinsley by this slower means of transport, but it was all they had and there were few trains running today. Marcus kept worrying about Serena and whether their plan had exposed her to too much danger the whole of the way into town. He was relieved when Jim didn't try to make conversation.

A glance at his new acquaintance showed a man looking so unhappy that Marcus wondered what had caused such a depth of sadness. If he was just a friend of Aubrey's, then Jim should be worried, but not sad like this, surely?

But then his own anxiety about Serena took over and he forgot the other man. He hoped to heavens this ploy would work. He shouldn't have put her at risk. Only – could he have stopped her once Hudd turned up and made his threats about her brother? As she'd said when they were discussing this and he'd worried about her safety, she'd make up her own mind and do as she saw fit. Marcus knew she had grown fond of him, but now he had to wonder if her love for her brother wasn't much stronger, and he couldn't help feeling jealous of their closeness.

Oh, hell, why was he worrying about such things now? Just let her stay safe, that was the main thing, whether they tricked Fleming into giving evidence of his criminal activities or not. Marcus couldn't bear it if any harm came to her.

'She's an intelligent woman,' Den said quietly. 'If anyone can pull this off, she can.'

Marcus shrugged. 'I wish we hadn't put her in this position, but it's done now, so we'd better make sure we get her out safely.'

By the time they got into town, rain had set in, a heavy downpour that darkened the day and kept people off the streets. Vic left the horse and cab with a friend, who was surprised to be roused from his family celebrations on Christmas Day but who cheered up when offered double the usual payment.

Marcus pulled his collar up towards his hat to protect his neck, but it was impossible to keep dry whatever you did, with the driving wind and rain slashing sideways. 'We need to see Redway first. None of this will work unless we have unimpeachable witnesses and the law on our side.' He turned to Jim and found that the man had gone.

'Jim said he wanted to fetch someone,' Den said, as Vic rejoined them.

'Did he say who?'

'No, not a word. Just slipped away.'

'You don't think . . . he was sent by Fleming to spy on us?'

Vic shook his head. 'No. I liked him, and anyway, he seemed genuine enough, knew too much about Aubrey's convalescence to be a fake.'

'Let's go and find Redway, then.'

They wasted time by going to the lawyer's residence, where no one answered the door and there were no lights showing, as there were everywhere else on such a dark, stormy day. Marcus went to bang on a neighbour's door and found that Redway was staying with his cousin Evadne, but the neighbour didn't know exactly where she lived. Somewhere on East Street, or was it Upper East?

Door-knocking on East Street led them at last to Miss Blair's house, where they were admitted by Evadne herself. By this time all three men were soaked and Marcus was in a fever of impatience to go and rescue his wife.

Back at the Hall, Pamela managed to eavesdrop from the upper landing as Serena left with Hudd. Ada found her there after the men had left. She was leaning against the wall, looking dizzy.

'You shouldn't be out of bed, ma'am.'

'I have to be. They're going to confront Fleming. You know what happened when Lawrence did that. He had him beaten up and my poor boy lost heart, went downhill rapidly.'

The maid looked at her mistress aghast. '*You* can't do anything. You're not well.'

'And we both know I'll get no better. So why not spend what little strength I have in defeating that horrible man? Ada, you will help me, surely? After all, look at the way he treated your family too till we found them somewhere else to live.'

After a short pause, the maid nodded and helped her mistress into the bedroom, where she began to pull out warm clothes, her expression grim.

'Before you help me dress, go and tell Hill to harness a horse to my old carriage. I don't care how dusty it is. I just need to get into town.'

The maid nodded. She knew Mr Lawrence hadn't been as blameless as his mother liked to think, but he still hadn't deserved to be milked of so much money in what, Ada and her mistress were both sure, were games of chance where some folk were cheating.

When she got back from the stables, she found her mistress half-dressed and helped her finish, then went for her own coat and hat. As the two of them walked slowly down the stairs, with Pamela leaning heavily on her maid, Pearl came out of the servants' quarters.

She looked from one to the other. 'Where are you going? You're not fit to go out, Mrs Lonnerden.'

'I must. But first I need to find my son's old revolver.' She held up one hand. 'Don't try to stop me, Pearl. Your own young man is at risk, too, as well as my nephew. You know what can happen when Fleming takes against someone.'

For a moment Pearl hesitated, then she nodded. 'I know where the revolver is and I know how to load it too. There are some advantages to working in a munitions factory.'

The two maids exchanged worried glances, then sat the old lady down while they got everything ready.

'Should we let her do this?' Pearl whispered.

'If it's what she wants, ill as she is, why not? You've surely guessed that she . . . ?' Ada hesitated.

'That she's dying? Yes. My granny's friend had that same look to her. There was nothing the doctors could do. And to tell you the truth, I *am* worried about my Vic, so, if she knows a way to stop that man, I'll help her in any way I can.'

As the wind howled around the house and rain beat a tattoo against the panes of glass, Ada shivered. 'It's a terrible day. Look at that rain.'

'We've been wet before and survived it.'

'But will she?'

Seventeen

Serena sat in the back of the big car, lost in thought. When Hudd said something, she ignored him. When he touched her arm to get her attention, she jerked away from him. 'Leave me alone! I don't even want to speak to you. It's my brother I'm going for and only him.'

He let her be. He'd heard enough by judicious eavesdropping to know that Fleming wasn't her father, which was a real turn-up for the books, because the mistress hadn't seemed the sort to say boo to a goose. Well, Miss Serena would soon be brought into line by his employer. Mr Fleming had had her under his thumb before and he'd put her back and keep her there this time. As for that snotty-nosed fellow she'd married, he was in for a few shocks and Hudd would be happy to help administer them. He didn't know when he'd taken such a dislike to a man. The car stopped, jerking him out of his reverie. 'Here we are, miss. Let me help you out.'

'I can get out on my own.' She shook off his hand, glaring at him, and she looked so pretty he blinked in amazement, because he'd never thought that of her before.

They went in the rear way and she swept through the kitchens with a nod to Cook and a smile for Ruby, who both looked surprised to see her. She didn't need to be told where to go, but just to be on the safe side, Hudd followed her.

When Serena reached the sitting-room door, the reality of what she was doing hit her so hard she stopped for a moment, feeling as if prison walls were closing round her. She'd hoped never to come back here, never to be in *his* power again, but if she didn't carry this through, didn't succeed, she'd never feel safe again, either for herself or for the two men she loved. Fleming had to be stopped, exposed for the villain he was.

She took a long, slow breath and felt her face settling into its old mask, hoped it would stay like that, was terrified of betraying her feelings or the real reason she was here.

Hudd pushed open the door. 'Allow me, Miss Fleming. It's your daughter, sir.'

Ernest looked up, but didn't stand. 'You'll need to remove your coat and hat.'

'I want to see my brother before I do anything.' As he smiled at her, he looked so cool and confident that a pang of the old fear shot through her belly.

'Help my daughter off with her coat, Hudd.'

She did it herself, because he was a very strong man.

'And the hat.'

She removed it, noticing the way Hudd was studying her body, and wished she was wearing her old bulky clothes, which had made her feel protected. That was silly, she knew, but you couldn't help how you felt.

'Now come and sit down, Serena.'

'When I've seen my brother.'

Another jerk of his employer's head had Hudd force-marching her to the fireplace and pushing her down in a chair.

'You are not in a position to dictate what happens, Serena, and I'd be obliged if you would remember that from now on.'

What she remembered most was the old feeling of helplessness, and she had to cling to the belief that Marcus wouldn't let her down, that he would get both her and her brother out of here.

'Now that you're back, you will forget that silly nonsense of your mother's. I *am* your father and I intend to remain so. And you will *not* be going back to that man, who only married you for your money.'

'And you don't want my money?'

'Of course I do. But I've earned it. I gave you a home, brought you up – and in the lap of luxury too.' He leaned forward. 'Let's put it this way, in case you're in any doubt of the consequences of rebellion against my wishes: if you care at all about Graye, if you want to see him remain . . . unhurt . . . you will stay with me and do exactly as I tell you from now on.'

A sick feeling settled in Serena's stomach as she looked at him and knew he meant it, knew she'd been right to come. He'd have her Marcus killed without a second thought, but she would prevent that if she had to give up her freedom to do so.

'I see you're beginning to remember the power I wield in this town.' He smiled. 'And I see you do care for him. How very foolish of you! It'll make it easier to persuade you to heed me.'

She didn't speak and he didn't seem to need any reply from her.

'You'll find that Frank is in a very confused state, doesn't even acknowledge his own name. Once we let him wake, I'll trust you to persuade him to co-operate with me from now on. If not, he'll find himself locked away and kept docile by drugs until he does come to his senses.'

'And if I don't co-operate?'

Fleming rolled his eyes at the ceiling. 'Why do I need to keep repeating this? If you don't co-operate, your husband will meet with an accident. But I'm sure that when you've had time to reflect, you'll see the sense of doing what I require – and so will Frank.'

Fleming had an exalted air to him today, she thought in surprise, a certain wild look to his eyes that she'd never seen before. What had happened to make him like this? Had the power he wielded gone to his head? How could he possibly think he would continue to get away with this?

She bent her head and said nothing, feeling something inside her shrivel.

'I'll take you up to see your brother now, just to show you what awaits you if you disobey me.' He stood up. 'Come, Serena.'

She followed him upstairs, keeping her face expressionless until she saw Frank lying bound and drugged in bed. Then she couldn't hide her fear from Fleming, just as he couldn't hide from her the pleasure he was taking in this.

'Well?' he asked at last as the silence dragged on.

'I'll do as you say.'

'You will address me as Father.'

'Sorry . . . Father.'

Fleming nodded and moved towards the door.

Only as she was turning to follow him did she see Frank open his eyes and wink at her. That put heart into her as nothing had since she entered this house. Her brother wasn't drugged! How had he managed that? But he was tied up.

Ernest led the way back down the stairs. 'As soon as the shops open again, we'll buy you some more flattering clothes. This time you'll do credit to me. You won't be marrying anyone, though, because I need you here to run my house, but eventually we'll find a wife for Frank so that the family name can be carried on.'

When they got to the sitting room, Fleming sat down and carried on talking, explaining his plans for her in great detail. He seemed to be enjoying himself.

She nodded, said yes and no in the way she had always done, but avoided meeting his eyes, so that he wouldn't see the anger simmering inside her. She kept wondering how long it would take Marcus to get here and how Frank had avoided being drugged, but she didn't let herself glance at the clock, as that might make Fleming suspicious.

The minutes ticked by very slowly.

She was afraid, more deeply afraid than ever before in her life.

Justin Redway listened in horror as Marcus told him what had happened. 'The man's run mad.'

'I think he ran mad years ago but he's not hiding it as well now. Perhaps he's grown to feel he's invulnerable. The war has certainly given him a lot of opportunities to go his own way.'

'I'll have to consult Marley about how best to do this,' Justin said.

'There isn't time.'

'Then we'll have to make time. I could be held to be a biased witness, because I'm Serena's lawyer. We *must* have someone present who is above suspicion.'

'Won't I do?' Den asked. 'I'm a doctor, Mrs Graye's doctor, actually.'

'You're a friend of Graye's as well. Look, I'll get my hat and coat on, then we'll go and see Marley.'

As they went out of the front door, Marcus stopped. 'This is all taking longer than I'd expected. Look, Redway, you and Vic go and fetch Marley. Vic, make sure no one hurts Redway. Den and I will go to Fleming's house to keep watch from outside. I don't want him hurting my wife. If he tries to do that, I'll get her out of there whatever it takes.'

'He won't hurt her, I'm sure of that. Everyone thinks she's his daughter.'

'Won't he? I'm not so certain. Especially if he feels threatened.'

With a shrug, Justin strode off through the streets, accompanied by Vic, not even noticing the occasional person who called 'Merry Christmas'. But when they got to Marley's house, they found that his old friend was out of town, spending Christmas with his daughter in Bury.

The only other magistrate in Tinsley was Crandall, who had more than once acted for Fleming. Worried sick, Justin hesitated, wondering what to do. Then he turned back towards the town centre, explaining the situation to Vic as they walked. He'd have to bring Crandall into it, but that worried him. He'd never got on with the fellow, who was famous for fussing about details and missing the point.

Marcus slipped through the gate at the rear of Fleming's house, looking round for somewhere to hide. He left Den outside to watch his back as he moved forward to the corner of what had been the stables and now housed a shiny new car. No safe vantage point here. He risked being seen if any of the servants came outside. Taking a chance, he ran across the garden to crouch behind some bushes.

After a minute or two, Den joined him there. 'What now?'

'I don't know. That room on the very left is the dining room, so it's probably our best way of getting in. Between it and the kitchen block is the family's sitting room. Fleming's in there with Serena, so I daren't get too close. I wonder if the French windows to the dining room are locked?'

'Too risky, old fellow, with servants around.'

'I've got to take the chance. I'm worried about Serena. Look how stiffly she's sitting. I've a feeling something's gone wrong, so if necessary I'll go in openly and bring her out of there, then we'll think of some other way to trap Fleming later. Stay there and I'll have a reccy.' On that word, he ran across to the French window, tried it and found it open, so slipped inside.

Den followed, but hesitated outside, waiting to see if the way was clear. He shivered as rain began to fall again, not as heavy this time, but steady and very cold.

Marcus crept across to the inner door of the dining room, listening carefully and trying not to make a noise. But when he had nearly reached it, a man stood up from behind a big armchair and smiled at him. 'I saw you cross the garden from upstairs, Mr Graye. Come to see Mr Fleming, have you? Let me show you through to the sitting room.'

Marcus stood still, then admitted to himself that he'd messed this up. If love didn't make you blind, it certainly made you careless of your own safety. He hoped Den would get out of the garden before they discovered him as well, and wondered what Fleming would do about this. If he showed any sign of getting violent, Marcus would inform him that several other people knew he'd come here and why – and they knew that he was unarmed as well.

'This way, sir.'

As Marcus walked through the door, something hit him over the head from behind and he fell, pain shooting through him. He tried to roll out of the way of another blow, but was too slow to avoid the next one, which knocked him half senseless.

Hudd smiled to see the snooty fellow brought low, then ran to get the fancy cord that held back the curtains in the dining room, locking the French windows as he did so, in case there was anyone else out there, though he hadn't seen anyone. Graye was groaning, so Hudd quickly bound his hands, and as his prisoner began to regain consciousness, hauled him to his feet and marched him out into the hall.

Opening the door of the sitting room, he thrust his captive forward. 'Look what I found, sir.'

With a cry of dismay, Serena jumped to her feet.

Fleming grabbed her shoulder and pushed her back down on the chair and whispered, 'If you know what's good for you – and for him – you'll stay there and make no attempt to help him! The slightest attempt and we'll shoot him dead before your eyes. I have a gun in my pocket.' He patted it and she could see the shape. She knew he would do what he threatened, so she did as she was told.

None of them saw Ruby, who had been just about to enter the hallway and had therefore seen what was going on. She clapped one hand to her mouth to keep back a cry, and after a moment's hesitation, ran for the back stairs.

Serena closed her eyes for a moment, knowing Fleming was watching her as much as Marcus, and when she opened them, gave her husband a long, level look which offered no clue as to her feelings. She waited, motionless.

'Bring him forward,' Fleming ordered. 'I'm pleased that you're doing your job so well, Hudd, very pleased. You won't find me ungrateful. Now do me the favour of staying here while I talk to Mr Graye. We wouldn't want him to get too excited, would we?' He looked Marcus up and down scornfully. 'Strange way to come calling. You should have used the front door. It'd have looked better. As it is, you've played into my hands.'

He looked at Serena again and it was to her he spoke. 'I've sent for Crandall, who's on duty as magistrate, and you'll tell him you want Graye prevented from coming near you, that you made a mistake in marrying him, that the marriage was never consummated and you're so afraid of him offering you violence that you've sought refuge with me here.'

Serena looked at him without saying a word.

'She'll not do it,' Marcus said. 'The mistake was ours in letting her come to see you, but I'm here to take her away again.'

'Oh, she won't be leaving. She's eager to stay and look after her brother, aren't you, my dear? And as I said, she now wants the marriage annulled because she's afraid of you. That *is* what you want, isn't it, Serena?'

'Yes, Father.'

Marcus stared at her in alarm. Her voice and whole demeanour were different. She didn't even look like the same woman, so subdued and colourless did she seem. 'I don't believe that. Serena darling, you can stop pretending now and I'll take you home. Tell Fleming he's wrong about our marriage.'

She bowed her head and stared down at her lap. Marcus's safety depended on her compliance with what her father dictated, because Fleming would be happy to use the gun. She longed to run to her husband and feel his arms around her, but didn't dare. Fleming laughed out loud, Marcus called her name again, but she kept herself very still, summoning up the old ways that had served her before in this unhappy house.

'You see,' Fleming said. 'My daughter is a sensible woman, not one of your modern independent types. She knows how to obey.'

As the doorbell rang, Marcus struggled to get free of Hudd and found himself pushed against the wall, with his head twisted so that he couldn't breathe properly.

As the doorbell sounded again and there was no sound of Ruby going to answer it, Fleming went out and himself opened the front door. 'Thank heavens you're here, Crandall. We've had to restrain an intruder.' He gestured towards the sitting room, where Marcus was still struggling with Hudd.

Crandall marched into the room, his voice booming out. 'Stop this at once, man! What the hell do you think you're doing?'

The grip on his head and neck loosened suddenly and Marcus could breathe again, but he knew they'd tricked him nicely. He seemed able to do nothing right today. And why was Serena not even looking at him? Surely she hadn't really caved in to Fleming's threats?

While this was happening, Justin had also rung the doorbell. When no one answered it and he heard shouting from inside, he tried the front door and found it unlocked. Crandall's wife had said he was coming here and Justin could only pray that the magistrate had already arrived. 'You stay here, Vic. No good all of us putting ourselves in his clutches.'

He closed his umbrella and pushed the door open. There was a great deal of noise coming from the room at the rear, so he moved quietly forward to see what was going on. What he saw made him march inside the room, where Hudd was holding his client in what was clearly a painful position.

'Let go of him!' Justin shouted, and only then did the people in the room seem to notice him.

Hudd didn't remove his hands from Marcus's neck. 'I daren't, sir. He's too dangerous.'

Justin smashed his umbrella down to break Hudd's hold. That move made the man curse, but he let go of Marcus's neck at least. 'My client couldn't breathe, Crandall. Wouldn't you struggle for breath?'

Marcus was wheezing and gasping, unable to loosen his collar because his hands were still bound behind him.

'Who let *you* into my house, Redway?' Fleming demanded. 'Get out at once.'

'The door was open. I knocked and called out, and when I saw my client being so violently restrained, I felt I'd better come in.' He felt for his pocket knife, and before anyone could stop him, pulled it out and cut the cord binding Marcus's hands behind him.

With a groan, Marcus brought his hands forward and said in a voice that rasped still from the pressure on his throat. 'Hudd hit me on the head then tied me up. When he started trying to strangle me, of course I struggled against him.'

Crandall stared at him as if he'd suddenly grown horns. 'That's not what it looked like to me.'

Fleming said smoothly, 'He's lying, of course. I'm delighted you're here, Crandall. I'm sorry to call you out, today of all days, but I want Graye forbidden to come near my poor daughter, who's had to flee from his violent behaviour.'

Marcus looked at Serena, expecting her to deny this, but she sent him a quick glance, shook her head slightly and bowed it again. He could only guess that some threat was being held over her head, perhaps a threat to her brother. Why else would she be doing as Fleming ordered? 'Don't do this, love,' he begged, speaking to her only. 'Think of yourself. We'll find another way to help Aubrey.'

She didn't answer and Fleming moved quickly to her side, one hand on her shoulder, fingers digging in cruelly.

'I think you'd better leave, Mr Graye,' Crandall said. 'And I wouldn't advise you to come here again or I'll be forced to lock you up for the sake of this young woman's safety.'

At that moment a voice said from the doorway, 'You're doing too much locking people up, Father.'

Aubrey came into the room, having taken a minute or two to straighten his clothes and give the terrified Ruby time to leave the house. She'd sworn she'd not return, whatever anyone said, and that she was leaving Tinsley on the first train she could catch, but he'd persuaded her to go to the Weaver's Arms and wait there.

He was surprised to see so many people, but wasn't surprised by the anger on his father's face, anger that was quickly banished.

'My poor son, how are you feeling now?'

'I'm feeling fine, just as I was until your men kidnapped me this morning.'

Fleming turned to Crandall. 'You see. He's delusional, needs protecting because he can't tell what's real and what isn't.'

The magistrate stared at the slight young man.

Aubrey looked back steadily. 'I've been under the supervision of several doctors for the past few months, first as I was recovering from my injuries and then when I worked as an orderly in a convalescent home. I think they would have known if I was mentally unstable, don't you? I'll be happy to give you their names and the address of the convalescent home.'

'And *I* think that Tolson, who's been your doctor for years, would know you better than any of them could,' Fleming said.

Crandall nodded. 'Good fellow, Tolson, very sound.'

Marcus seized the opportunity to go and stand by his wife. 'You all right?'

She whispered, 'Marcus, keep away, save yourself!' then, as Fleming swivelled round to stare icily at her, she bowed her head again and pressed her lips together.

Fleming took a couple of steps back, to stand between her and her husband. 'You shouldn't encourage your brother, Serena. He could harm himself. And you've been in a very fragile state yourself since your mother's death, or you wouldn't have married a near stranger who only wants your money.'

Crandall stared at Marcus distastefully. 'He's Lonnerden's cousin and that's no recommendation. The fellow was a loose fish if ever I met one, and his father wasn't much better.'

'I'm prepared to forget what Graye has done this time,' Fleming said, 'if you'll just get him and Redway to leave. My family and I need to talk. We've a lot of time to make up with Frank.'

'I'm not staying here,' Aubrey said at once, 'nor is Serena. We'll leave as well.'

Fleming smiled at him. 'Your sister is definitely staying here. You might think about joining her.'

Aubrey stared at her. 'Serena, surely not?'

'I can't leave,' she said in a toneless voice.

Justin put out one hand to restrain Marcus from going to her. 'I don't think you can do anything at the moment.'

'I'm not leaving without her,' Marcus said, folding his arms.

'You'll leave now or I'll call in the police,' Crandall snapped.

Serena looked at her husband. 'Go. Now. Please, Marcus.'

'Why?'

'Because I want you to.'

He let Justin pull him into the hall, and after a moment's hesitation, Aubrey turned to join them.

'You'd better stay here until Tolson arrives, young man,' the magistrate called.

'I'd rather be in a police cell than here,' Aubrey said. 'My father's a liar and my sister doesn't really want to stay, you know.'

Fleming made a soft tutting sound. 'You see, Crandall? And he's just heard her say she does.'

'Poor fellow. We'd better keep him here, for his own sake.'

Hudd moved between Aubrey and the door to the hall.

Justin said to Marcus in an urgent undertone, 'We can do more if we're free – for both of them. Come *on*!'

So Marcus, after one last glance backwards at Serena, walked towards the front door.

Hudd shoved Aubrey back into the sitting room, so that he tumbled to the floor, and followed Marcus, grinning. As Justin opened the door, however, four men pushed their way in and two of them grabbed Hudd, quickly muffling his cries. The man who was clearly their leader looked at Justin and Marcus. 'What's been happening?'

'This is Aubrey's friend Jim,' Marcus explained, and then told him quickly what had occurred.

'I think we need to go back. I have a few things to say to Fleming, and for that I need witnesses. And perhaps when your wife hears what I have to say, she'll think differently about staying.'

'I'm more than happy to return,' Marcus said grimly. 'What about him?' He gestured to Hudd.

'He can come too, but my brothers will keep an eye on him.'

Jim led the way into the sitting room again, where Fleming and Crandall were now sitting down, looking very cosy together, while Aubrey stood beside Serena, who was shaking her head to something he was whispering. Everyone turned to see who had come in.

Fleming jumped to his feet. 'I don't know where you found reinforcements, Graye, but you can just take your men and leave. She's *not* coming back to you and I have a magistrate here to witness what's going on.'

Crandall nodded vigorously.

'I'm not connected to Mr Graye,' Jim said mildly. 'And if you don't mind, I'll sit down too. I've been a long time recovering from war injuries and I'm still not myself.'

'Whoever you are, I wish you to *leave*!' Fleming snapped. 'I'm too busy to see anyone.'

Jim looked across at Aubrey and Serena, smiling. 'What I have to say is going to shock you, Serena, and I'm sorry I have to do it so publicly. When I tell you that my name is James Lang, would it mean anything to you?'

She stared at him open-mouthed, then nodded. 'Yes. Mother told me about you. But if you weren't dead, you ran away and left her, so I'm not sure I care whether you've come back or not.'

Jim looked across at the magistrate, who was frowning in an attempt to follow this. 'I'm Serena's real father.'

Crandall blinked in shock.

'She looks like him,' Justin pointed out.

Reluctantly, Crandall nodded.

'And she also looks like her mother,' Jim said in a low voice, smiling at Serena, but with sadness clear beneath that smile.

'I don't know why he's trying to cause trouble, but it's a pack of lies and I want him out of this house,' Fleming said. 'Of course he's not her father. I am. Everyone knows that.'

Crandall shifted uncomfortably, staring from one man to the other. 'They do look very alike, and I remember the talk at the time. She was born only six months after the marriage.'

'They don't look alike. And he's *not* her father, probably not even James Lang!' Fleming shouted, but when he tried to move towards Jim, one of the other men stepped forward.

'I'm Jim's brother and no one knows better than me who he is.'

Jim turned back to the magistrate. 'I have papers back where I'm staying which prove who I am, but it's more important now that I tell my daughter what happened, why I left, and I'd like you to be a witness to that.' When the other man nodded, he went on, 'Over thirty years ago, I was going to run away with Grace Illingham and marry her, because I loved her dearly and because she was carrying my child. I didn't care about her money, only about her.'

Fleming made a loud scoffing noise.

'Let him continue,' Crandall snapped.

'Ernest Fleming paid some men to capture me and prevent me from meeting Grace. They were to take me to Liverpool and put me on a ship bound for Australia. I had to work my passage and it took several weeks, but when I got there, I sent an urgent telegram to my brother, so that he could tell Grace what had happened. 'I tried to find a job on a ship going back, but my brother's reply showed me it was useless. Grace had married Fleming and was expecting a child. He said they seemed happy enough together. Later he told me she had a baby girl and that the child was well looked after. I knew if I came back, I'd upset everyone's life to no avail. As far as the world was concerned, the baby was Fleming's. And Grace was legally his too.'

Fleming glared at him. 'The baby *was* mine and you can't prove differently. I was married to the baby's mother. You weren't even in England, from what you say.'

Jim looked at Serena. 'What I'm saying is true. Come away now, love.'

But she stayed where she was.

'Serena, you can't stay here with him,' he pleaded.

Fleming looked at them all triumphantly. 'You see. She *wants* to stay with me. She knows I'm her real father.'

Everyone turned to stare at Serena but she was looking at Marcus, her love showing clearly in her eyes. 'I can't leave him,' she said, anguish in her face.

'Why not?'

'Because she doesn't want to,' Fleming interjected, putting one hand in his pocket and staring at her.

Serena could have wept but if she once started she'd not stop crying, so she didn't allow herself that luxury. She knew that if she tried to leave the house with Marcus, it was tantamount to signing his death warrant. Better he stay alive without her than be a target for Fleming's hatred.

There was silence in the room, then Aubrey went across to Jim. 'I wish you were *my* father.'

Serena swallowed hard, feeling Fleming's hard gaze on her and holding fast to her determination to save Marcus's life.

In the hall, the woman who'd been half-carried inside the house pushed her two companions aside. 'He has to be stopped and I'm the only one who can do it. Wait for me outside. It'll be better for you if you pretend to know nothing of what I intend to do.'

'But you can't walk without help,' Ada protested.

'I think I can walk far enough with my stick.' Pamela fumbled in her pocket. 'Go.'

As her companions left the house, she somehow found the strength to walk towards the door of the room from which voices were coming, pausing in the doorway to regain her breath as they all stared at her. 'I need to sit down,' she announced.

No one who saw her could doubt that, but she waved away offers of help. 'Near the fire.' She moved across the room leaning heavily on her stick. Only when she got close to Fleming did she stop again, raise the hand that had been hidden beneath the dangling ends of the fox fur round her neck and look at him. 'I'm doing this for Lawrence and for all the other people you've hurt.'

As Crandall opened his mouth to order her to stop, she fired at point-blank range, giving Fleming no time to move away.

As he crumpled slowly to the ground, she stood there, swaying slightly, her face a yellowish white but her expression one of satisfaction.

The room rang with shouts and exclamations of shock.

'Secure her!' Crandall ordered.

She smiled and held out the revolver, butt first. 'I shan't try to escape.'

Jim took the weapon from her, while Crandall went to peer down at Fleming's body and the bloody mess of his chest.

'Fellow looks dead,' he muttered.

There was a hammering on the French windows. 'Let me in! I'm a doctor,' Den called. Justin went to unlock the door and Den came into the room, soaking wet and shivering. 'I was watching what happened.' He knelt beside Fleming, examined him quickly, then shook his head. 'He's quite dead. Why did you shoot him, Mrs Lonnerden?'

'Because he was both evil and insane,' Pamela announced in a steady voice, her expression calm. 'He made my son's last weeks unhappy and when I heard what he was doing to my nephew and his wife, I realized that only I could really help them. Even if they'd escaped today, he would have got his revenge on them later.'

'He had a gun in his pocket and had threatened to kill Marcus if I tried to leave,' Serena said suddenly.

'You see.' Pamela smiled round radiantly. 'I'm dying, Mr Crandall, have only a few weeks to live at most, so it doesn't matter what they do to me now. But these young people have all their lives ahead of them.' She fumbled for a seat and subsided into it.

There was a buzz of low-voiced conversation and Hudd tried to leave the room, but one of Jim's companions barred his way.

Crandall scowled round. 'No one is to leave without my permission. Someone fetch the police. Redway, will you do it?'

Justin nodded and left.

Marcus saw his aunt swaying and helped her to a chair.

'Go to your wife,' she said when she was seated, flapping one hand in dismissal.

'You'll be all right?'

'Of course I will.'

Marcus drew Serena to one side. 'Could you not have trusted me to look after myself?'

'No. You're an honest man. And even if we went away from here, he'd have traced us. I knew him too well, Marcus. When I ran away, I was risking my own life, but that was my choice, though I'd intended to use my inheritance to get as far away as I could. I didn't know then that he'd stolen my money, or I'd probably not have dared leave.'

As she looked at him, love glowing in her eyes, he crushed her to him, kissing her and hugging her close. She raised her face and kissed him passionately, putting her arms round his neck, needing to feel the living warmth of him.

'Have a bit of decency, you two!' Crandall's voice thundered out.

With a smile, Marcus moved his head back, put his arm round her shoulders, and they turned to face the room.

'Mrs Lonnerden, you may consider yourself under arrest for murder,' the magistrate went on.

'Yes, of course.' Pamela smiled at Marcus. 'Dear boy, could you please send Ada to wherever they take me. Ask her to bring some clothes. And don't worry about me. I shall die happy now.'

Crandall shook his head, as if unable to believe what he saw and heard.

Serena kept a tight hold of Marcus's hand but looked across at her real father, standing next to her brother, and smiled.

Epilogue

The funeral of Pamela Lonnerden was held two months after the burial of Ernest Fleming. It was attended by a strange mixture of people. Those who considered themselves 'county' gentry and had only come out of pity for the poor woman stared in amazement when they saw that her family and servants were standing together, making no pretence of weeping, but were smiling at one another as if this was a happy occasion. When her nephew delivered a eulogy praising her as a brave woman, not even pretending to hide the fact that she'd committed a murder, eyebrows were raised.

After a brief reception at the Hall, Pamela's county acquaintances left, but Marcus had already invited those he considered real friends, whether old or new, to stay behind.

Gladys hovered near the door, still wearing her apron, uncertain whether to join them as invited. Serena winked at her husband and went across to their maid. 'Come and sit over here, Gladys.'

'Are you sure it's all right for me to be here, ma'am?'

'Very sure. You're mentioned in the will, so you have to be here for the reading. And why don't you take off that apron? It doesn't seem right just now, because you're not here as a maid.'

Looking relieved, Gladys took a seat next to Ada and Pearl, while Vic, Den and Jim sat behind them.

Marcus looked round, then nodded to Justin, who picked up the will and the letter he'd kept with it. He began to read Pamela's last words:

> I want to thank my nephew for his help during the last difficult months of my life. I may not have expressed my appreciation adequately, but it was sincere, believe me, Marcus.
>
> I have some money of my own, left to me by an aunt, and this I'd like to share among you. I kept this money secret from both my husband and Lawrence, or they'd have spent it. Whatever is left after the other bequests have been paid is to go to my nephew, Marcus, and I will trust him and Mr Redway to see the following bequests paid:
>
> To Ada, who has been with me a long time, two hundred pounds, with my thanks for her loyalty in troubled times.
>
> To Gladys, who has also been loyal and hard-working, one hundred pounds.

Ada smiled and nodded as if this was no surprise to her, but Gladys let out a squeak of shocked delight, then clapped one hand to her mouth.

> To Pearl and Vic, to pay for a really good wedding, twenty pounds.

They beamed at one another and reached out to hold hands.

> To Jim and Aubrey, who don't need any money, I leave my very best wishes and hope that they have a happy life.

I've left instructions for two bottles of champagne to be opened for everyone to drink to the future. When the reading is finished, Ada will show Marcus where we hid the wine so that Lawrence couldn't drink the cellar dry. I think you'll find some pleasant surprises there, Marcus.

And finally, I wish it understood that I have no regrets for what I did. That man did not deserve to live and, if he had, would have hurt many more people. Even if I'd had to pay the full penalty of the law, I'd have done so gladly.

Pamela Lonnerden

When Justin folded up the papers and sat down, Ada stood up. 'Gladys and I will go and get the champagne now.'

Marcus went to open the door for them. 'As long as it's understood that you come back to drink a glass with us.'

She nodded and the two women left.

Jim turned to Aubrey, with whom he was still staying. 'What are you going to do with yourself now?'

'Go to university and study to be a doctor. I can't think of any more worthwhile career. I'm hoping Marcus will take over Father's business and make sure all the houses are properly repaired and maintained and the tenants treated fairly.'

His brother-in-law nodded.

'And I'm hoping that you'll buy the bookshop from Ted and settle down in Tinsley. After all, you've no one waiting for you in Australia.'

'How did you know I was staying on in Tinsley? I haven't said anything.'

Aubrey grinned. 'Think I don't know that you've been seeing Mrs Beamish at the Weaver's Arms?'

'Can't keep anything secret from you, can I, lad?'

The two men smiled at one another.

'I'm glad you're staying,' Aubrey said softly. 'One day I'll find a girl and marry, then you can be granddad to our children.'

Jim nodded and blew his nose vigorously.

As people began to discuss the will, Marcus went across to thank Justin for his help during the past few weeks. 'You must send me a bill.'

Justin grinned. 'Sorry, but it was a labour of love to help Pamela. She saved me from trouble, too, don't forget.' He smiled as Serena came to join them. 'Perhaps you two can now start to make a proper life for yourselves.

The smile they gave one another was answer enough.

Den came over with a brimming glass of champagne in one hand and a half-glass in the other. 'There you are, you two.' He smiled at Serena. 'I don't think mothers-to-be should drink much.'

She blushed furiously and Justin grinned at her. Then he called out, 'Has everyone got a glass? Good. Then I'd like to propose a toast. To Pamela Lonnerden, who has made happiness possible for all of us here.'

Everyone raised their glasses and sipped. Gladys sneezed and looked embarrassed, then took another more cautious sip.

Marcus raised his voice again. 'I'd like to propose a second toast, if you don't mind, because there were two women who made all this possible. If Serena hadn't so courageously run away from her father, I'd never have met her and we wouldn't all have had such a happy outcome. To Serena – a very independent woman, and may she remain so.'

As he blew her a kiss and raised his glass, Serena felt tears of joy fill her eyes. She had more than she'd ever hoped for, far more. It had been worth all the trouble. She caught her brother's eye and he raised a glass to her in a private toast, patting his stomach suggestively.